DARK NIGHT
OF THE
MOUNTAIN MAN

DARK NIGHT
OF THE
MOUNTAIN MAN

WILLIAM W.
JOHNSTONE
AND J.A. JOHNSTONE

PINNACLE BOOKS
Kensington Publishing Corp.
www.kensingtonbooks.com

PINNACLE BOOKS are published by

Kensington Publishing Corp.
119 West 40th Street
New York, NY 10018

PUBLISHER'S NOTE: Following the death of William W. Johnstone, the Johnstone family is working with a carefully selected writer to organize and complete Mr. Johnstone's outlines and many unfinished manuscripts to create additional novels in all of his series, like The Last Gunfighter, Mountain Man, and Eagles, among others. This novel was inspired by Mr. Johnstone's superb storytelling.

First Printing: December 2023
ISBN-13: 978-0-7860-4356-9
ISBN-13: 978-0-7860-4357-6 (eBook)

10 9 8 7 6 5 4 3 2 1

Printed in the United States of America

CHAPTER 1

It was safe to say that Nelse Andersen had been drinking when he encountered the bear. Every time Nelse drove his ranch wagon into Big Rock to pick up supplies, he always stopped at the Brown Dirt Cowboy Saloon to have a snort or two—or three—before heading back to his greasy sack outfit northwest of town.

Smoke Jensen happened to be in the settlement that same day, having come in to send some telegrams related to business concerning his ranch, the Sugarloaf.

A ruggedly handsome man of average height, with unusually broad shoulders and ash blond hair, Smoke stood on the porch of Sheriff Monte Carson's office, propping one of those shoulders against a post holding up the awning over the porch.

The lawman was sitting in a chair, leaning back with his booted feet resting on the railing along the front of the porch. His fingers were laced together on his stomach, which was starting to thicken a little with age.

At first glance, neither man looked like what he really was.

Smoke was, quite probably, the fastest and deadliest shot of any man who had ever packed iron west of the Mississippi. Or east of there, for that matter.

As a young man, he'd had a reputation as a gunfighter and outlaw, although all the criminal charges ever levied against him were bogus. Scurrilous lies spread by his enemies.

These days, he was happily married and the owner of the largest, most successful ranch in the valley. In fact, the Sugarloaf was one of the finest ranches in all of Colorado. Smoke was more than content to spend his days running the spread and loving Sally, his beautiful wife.

Despite that intention, trouble still had a habit of seeking him out more often than he liked.

At one time, Monte Carson had been a hired gun, a member of a wolf pack of Coltmen brought in by one of Smoke's mortal enemies to wipe out him and his friends.

It hadn't taken Monte long to figure out who was really in the right and switch sides. He had been a staunch friend to Smoke ever since, even before Big Rock had been founded and he'd been asked to pin on the sheriff's star.

Pearlie Fontaine, another member of that gang of gunwolves, had also changed his ways and was now the foreman of the Sugarloaf. Smoke couldn't have hoped for two finer, more loyal friends than Monte and Pearlie.

Or a finer day than this, with its blue sky, puffy white clouds, and warm breeze. Evidently, Monte felt the same way, because he said, "Sure is a pretty day. Almost too pretty to work. What do you reckon the chances are that all the troublemakers in these parts will feel the same way, Smoke?"

"They just might," Smoke began with a smile, but then he straightened from his casual pose and muttered, "or not."

Monte saw Smoke's reaction and brought his feet down from the railing. As he sat up, he said, "What is it?"

"Hoofbeats. Sounds like a team coming in a hurry."

Monte stood up. He heard the horses now, too, although

Smoke's keen ears had picked up the swift rataplan a couple of seconds earlier.

"Somebody moving fast like that nearly always means trouble."

"Yeah," Smoke said, pointing, "and here it comes."

A wagon pulled by four galloping horses careened around a corner up the street. The vehicle turned so sharply as the driver hauled on the team's reins that the wheels on the left side came off the ground for a second. Smoke thought the wagon was going to tip over.

But then the wheels came back down with a hard bounce and the wagon righted itself. The driver was yelling something as he whipped the horses.

Monte had joined Smoke at the edge of the porch. "What in blazes is he saying?"

"It sounds like . . . *bear*," Smoke said. "Is that Nelse Andersen?"

The wagon flashed past them. Monte said, "Yeah, I saw him drive by a little while ago, not long before you showed up. Looked like he was on his way back to his ranch."

They watched as the wagon swerved down the street and then came to a sliding, jarring stop in front of the Brown Dirt Cowboy Saloon. Nelse Andersen practically dived off the seat and ran inside, leaving the slapped-aside batwings swinging to and fro behind him.

"Well, I have to find out what this is about," Monte said. "He can't be driving so fast and reckless in town. He's lucky he didn't run over anybody."

"I'll come with you. I'm a mite curious myself."

By the time they reached the saloon and pushed through the batwings, Andersen was standing at the bar with a group of men gathered around him. A rangy, fair-haired man, he had a drink in his hand, which was shaking so badly that a little of the whiskey sloshed out as he lifted the glass to his mouth.

The liquor seemed to steady him. He thumped the empty glass on the bar and said, "It was ten feet tall, I tell you! Maybe even taller!"

One of the bystanders said, "I never saw a grizzly bear that tall. Close to it, maybe, but not that big."

"This wasn't a regular bear," Andersen insisted. "It was a monster! I never saw anything like it. It had to weigh twelve hundred pounds if it was an ounce!"

He shoved the empty glass across the hardwood toward the bartender and raised expectant eyebrows. The bartender looked at Emmett Brown, the owner of the place, who stood nearby with his thumbs hooked in his vest pockets. Brown frowned.

A man tossed a coin on the bar and said, "Shoot, I'll buy him another drink. I want to hear the rest of this story."

Brown nodded, and the bartender poured more whiskey in the glass, filling it almost to the top. Andersen picked it up and took a healthy swallow.

"Start from the first," the man who had bought the drink urged.

"Well, I was on my way back to my ranch," Andersen said. "I was out there goin' past Hogback Hill, where the brush grows up close to the road, and all of a sudden this . . . this *thing* rears up outta the bushes and waves its paws in the air and roars so loud it was like thunder crashin' all around me! Scared the bejabbers out of my horses."

"I think it scared you, too," a man said.

Andersen ignored that and went on, "I thought the team was gonna bolt. It was all I could do to hold 'em in. The bear kept bellerin' at me and actin' like it was gonna charge. I knew I needed to get outta there, so I turned the team around and lit a shuck for town."

Emmett Brown had come closer along the bar. "You had a gun, didn't you? Why didn't you shoot it?"

Andersen tossed back the rest of the drink and once again set the empty firmly on the bar.

"I didn't figure that rifle of mine has enough stopping power to put him down. I could'a emptied the blamed thing in him and it might've killed him eventually, but not in time to keep him from gettin' those paws on me and tearin' me apart." Andersen shuddered. "I wouldn't'a been nothin' but a snack for a beast that big!"

"I still say you're exaggeratin'," claimed the man who had said he'd never seen a grizzly bear ten feet tall. "You just got scared and panicked. Maybe it seemed that big to you, but it really wasn't. It couldn't have been."

Andersen glared at him and said, "Then why don't you go out there to Hogback Hill and see for yourself? I hope that grizzly gets you and knocks your head off with one swipe o' his paw!"

"I don't cotton to bein' talked to like that—" the man began as he clenched his fists.

"That's enough," Monte Carson said, his voice sharp and commanding. "You're not going to bust up this saloon because of some brawl over how big a bear is."

Enthralled by Andersen's story, the men hadn't realized that Smoke and Monte were standing at the back of the crowd, listening.

Now they split apart so that the sheriff and Smoke could step forward. Nelse Andersen turned from the bar to greet them.

"Sheriff, you better put together a posse and ride out there as fast as you can."

"Why would I do that?" Monte asked. "I can't arrest a bear. Assuming there really is one and that he's still there."

"You don't believe me, Sheriff?" Andersen pressed a hand to his chest and looked mortally offended.

"Those do sound like some pretty wild claims you're making."

Smoke said, "I've seen some pretty big grizzlies, but never one that was more than ten feet tall and weighed twelve hunderd pounds. I think you'd have to go up to Alaska or Canada to find bears that big."

"Well, Smoke, no offense to you or the sheriff, but I'll tell you the same thing I told Hodges there. Why don't you ride out there and have a look for yourself? A critter as big as the one I saw is bound to have left some tracks!"

Smoke exchanged a glance with Monte and then said, "You know, I think I just might do that. Especially if you come along and show me where you saw him, Nelse."

Andersen swallowed hard, opened and closed his mouth a couple of times, then he nodded and said, "I'll do it. I got to go home sometime, and I'll admit, I'll feel a mite better about travelin' on that stretch of road if you're with me."

"I'm ready to go if you are." Smoke looked at Monte again. "Are you coming?"

"No, I'd better stay here in town," the sheriff said, adding dryly, "since I don't really have any jurisdiction over bears. But you'll tell me what you find, won't you, Smoke?"

"Sure," Smoke replied with a chuckle.

One of the bystanders said, "How about the rest of us comin' along, too?"

"Might be better not to," Smoke said. "A big bunch might spook that bear and make him attack, if he's still out there."

The real reason Smoke didn't want them coming along was because he knew how easy it was for a group of men to work themselves up into a nervous state where they might start shooting at anything that moved. That could lead to trouble.

A few men muttered at the decision, but Smoke was so well respected in Big Rock that no one wanted to argue with him. He and Andersen left the Brown Dirt Cowboy, but not until Andersen cast one more longing glance at the empty glass on the bar and sighed in resignation.

Smoke's horse was tied at the hitch rail in front of the sheriff's office. He swung into the saddle and fell in alongside the wagon as Andersen drove out of Big Rock. The Sugarloaf was located off the main trail that ran due west out of the settlement, but Andersen followed a smaller trail that angled off northwest toward the small spreads located in the foothills on that side of the valley.

As they moved along the trail, Smoke chatted amiably with the rancher, who was a bachelor, well-liked but not particularly close to anybody in these parts. Andersen asked after Sally, as well as Pearlie and Cal Woods, another of Smoke's ranch hands. He didn't seem to be affected much by the whiskey he had consumed. Smoke had heard that Andersen had a hollow leg when it came to booze, and now he was seeing evidence of that.

They covered several miles before Andersen pointed to a rugged ridge up ahead on the right and said, "That's Hogback Hill."

"I know," Smoke said. "Good name for it. It looks like a hog's back, sort of rough and spiny."

Andersen was starting to look apprehensive now. "That brush on the right is where I saw the bear. He must've been down on all fours in it. When I came along, he just reared up bigger'n life. I really thought he was gonna eat me."

Smoke's sharp eyes scanned the thick vegetation they were approaching. "I don't see anything moving around in there," he said. "Or hear any rustling in the brush, either."

"I didn't see or hear anything out of the ordinary until suddenly he was right there, no more than twenty feet from me. He's a sneaky one, that bear is. He was layin' up, waitin' to ambush me."

Smoke tried not to grin as Andersen said that with a straight face. The rancher appeared to believe it. Smoke supposed he ought to give the man the benefit of the doubt. As far as he could recall, Andersen didn't have a reputation for going around spreading big windies.

"We'll be ready, just in case," Smoke said as he pulled his Winchester from its saddle scabbard under his right leg. He laid the rifle across the saddle in front of him.

A moment later, Andersen pulled back on the reins and brought his team to a stop. "This is it," he said. "This is the place." He pointed into the brush. "Right there. I'll never forget it."

Smoke studied the bushes and listened intently. There was no sign of a bear or any other wildlife, other than a few birds singing in some trees about fifty yards away.

"I'm going to take a closer look," he said.

"Are you sure that's a good idea?"

"I don't think there's anything in there." Smoke swung a leg over the saddle and dropped to the ground, holding the Winchester ready in case he needed it. He had spotted something that interested him, and as he moved into the brush, using the rifle barrel to push branches aside, he got a better look at what he had noticed.

Quite a few of the branches were snapped around the spot where Andersen said the bear had been, as if they'd been broken when something large and heavy pushed through the brush. A frown creased Smoke's forehead as he spotted something else. He reached forward and plucked a tuft of grayish brown hair from a branch's sharply broken end.

That sure looked like it could have come from a bear's coat.

Smoke moved closer, pushed more of the brush aside, and looked down at the ground. Some rain had fallen about a week earlier, so the soil was still fairly soft, not dried out yet.

After a long moment, he turned his head and called, "Come here, Nelse."

"I ain't sure I want to," the man replied. "What did you find?"

"Better you come take a look for yourself. There's nothing around here that's going to hurt you."

With obvious reluctance, Andersen set the brake on the wagon, wrapped the reins around it, and climbed down from the seat. He edged into the brush and followed the path Smoke had made.

When Andersen reached Smoke's side, Smoke pointed at the ground and said, "Take a look."

Andersen's eyes widened. He breathed a curse as he peered at what he saw etched in the dirt.

It was the unmistakable paw print of a gigantic bear.

CHAPTER 2

"So he was telling the truth? There really is a monster bear roaming around out there?"

Monte Carson sounded as if he were having trouble believing what he had just said.

Smoke, straddling a turned-around chair in the sheriff's office, said, "We only found three tracks, and they were scattered some. I couldn't tell from them exactly how tall the varmint is, but they were deep enough that I can say he's pretty heavy. Might go a thousand pounds."

"So not as big as what Nelse claimed, but still a mighty big bear."

"Yeah," Smoke agreed. "I don't recall ever seeing one that big around here."

"What did you do with Nelse?"

"Rode with him back to his ranch." Smoke smiled. "He didn't much want to travel alone. He kept looking back over his shoulder like he was afraid that bear had climbed into the wagon with him."

"Then you came back here instead of heading home?'

Smoke nodded. "Sally's not expecting me back at any particular time. I thought it would be a good idea to let you know there was some truth to what Nelse said. There was a good-sized bear within a few miles of town earlier today. The tracks prove that."

The broad shoulders rose and fell in a shrug as Smoke continued. "Of course, that doesn't mean it's still anywhere around these parts. When you watch bears moving around, they look like they're just lumbering along, but they can move pretty quickly when they want to."

"Yeah. Kind of like runaway freight trains."

"Anyway, this one has had enough time to cover some ground. He could be a long way off by now."

"Or he could be wandering around the edge of town." Monte sighed. "I'm going to have to warn folks, Smoke. They need to be on the lookout and especially keep an eye on their kids."

"I agree, but I wish there was some way to avoid a panic."

"It was too late for that once Nelse Andersen started guzzling down whiskey and spewing his tale," Monte said. "You know some of the fellas who were in the Brown Dirt Cowboy have already started spreading the story by now."

"More than likely." Smoke rested his hands on the chair's back and pushed himself to his feet. "Let folks know that first thing tomorrow morning, Pearlie and I are going to try to pick up that bear's trail and find out where it went from Hogback Hill. If it left this part of the country, then people can stop worrying about it."

"And if it's still around here somewhere?"

"Pearlie and I will find it and drive it on out of the valley if we can."

"What if it won't leave?"

"Then we'll deal with it," Smoke said with a note of finality in his voice.

* * *

For such an apparently huge creature, the bear proved to be surprisingly elusive. Smoke and Pearlie found its tracks leading north from Hogback Hill the next morning and followed them for a while, but the trail disappeared when it entered the rocky, mostly barren foothills at the base of the mountains in that direction.

When they finally reined in and admitted defeat after casting back and forth among the hills for several hours, Pearlie shook his head disgustedly and said, "We need Preacher with us. That old boy can follow a trail better'n anybody who ever drew breath."

"I can't argue with that," Smoke said. The old mountain man had been his mentor and like a second father to him for many years. It was said he could track a single snowflake through a blizzard. "There's no telling where Preacher is, though. He could be anywhere from Canada to old Mexico."

Pearlie rubbed his beard-stubbled chin and said, "We're liable to have folks from town roamin' around out here on the range lookin' for the critter, figurin' they'll shoot it and be acclaimed as heroes, but more than likely they'll accidentally shoot each other."

"I know," Smoke said, nodding, "but I'm hoping the bear actually has moved on and that as time goes by without it being spotted again, people will forget about it. It may take a while, but things ought to go back to normal eventually."

"Maybe." Pearlie didn't sound convinced. "Problem is, when folks get worked up about somethin', all their common sense goes right out the window."

Smoke couldn't argue with that statement.

Three days later, a middle-aged cowboy named Dean McKinley was following one of his boss's steers that had strayed up a draw. Water ran through there any time it rained very much, but that dried up quickly, sucked down by the sand underneath the rocky streambed.

The iron shoes on the hooves of McKinley's horse clinked on those rocks as he rode slowly, swinging his gaze back and forth between the draw's brushy banks.

McKinley had heard about the bear. Another cowboy who rode for the same spread had been in the Brown Dirt Cowboy that day and had brought back the tale of Nelse Andersen's run-in with the giant beast.

As far as McKinley was concerned, Andersen was a loco Scandihoovian who drank too much, but the story had had the ring of truth to it.

The last thing McKinley wanted to do was run into a grizzly bear while he was out there alone on the range.

Maybe the smart thing to do would be to turn around and hope the steer found its way back home, he told himself.

Then the blasted critter had to go and bawl piteously, somewhere up ahead of him. To McKinley's experienced ears, it sounded like the steer was scared of something.

He hesitated for a couple of heartbeats, then muttered a curse under his breath and dug his bootheels into his horse's flanks, sending it loping forward.

He had just rounded a bend in the draw when something loomed in front of him, moving his way fast. McKinley couldn't hold back a startled yell as he tugged hard on the reins and brought his horse to an abrupt stop. His other hand dropped to the butt of the revolver holstered on his hip.

Then he realized it was the steer charging toward him, wild-eyed with fear. McKinley jerked his mount to the side to get out of the way. The steer's run was an ungainly thing, but it was moving pretty fast anyway as it charged past him.

"What the devil?" McKinley muttered as he twisted in

the saddle to look behind him. The frantic steer disappeared around the bend, heading back the way McKinley had come.

The cowboy was still looking back when his horse let out a shrill, sudden, terrified whinny and tried to rear up. McKinley hauled hard on the reins to keep the horse under control as he looked in front of him again.

Twenty yards away, from around another bend, came the bear.

The creature was enormous, even on all fours. To McKinley's eyes, it seemed like the bear was as big as the horse he was on, maybe even bigger.

And it was coming fast toward him, panting and growling.

"*Yowww!*" McKinley cried as he realized what was happening. The steer had fled in blind panic from the bear. Now it was his turn. The massive beast had already covered half the distance between them by the time McKinley got his mount wheeled around and kicked it into a run.

The horse took off like a jackrabbit, so fast that McKinley had to reach up and grab his hat to keep it from flying off. He didn't really care about the hat. Grabbing it was just instinct.

The bear was so close that McKinley could hear its breath rasping. He thought he could feel the heat of it on the back of his neck, but that was probably just his imagination. The cow pony, once it got its hooves under it, was running fast and smooth now.

Unfortunately, a bear could run just about as fast as a horse. That was what McKinley had heard. It appeared to be true, but as he glanced back over his shoulder, he saw that the bear wasn't gaining on him, either.

It might come down to which animal tired first or whether the horse tripped.

If they went down, McKinley knew, it would be all over.

He suddenly remembered that he had a gun on his hip.

He knew better than to think a Colt would stop a huge grizzly bear, but he clawed the iron out of leather anyway and triggered it behind him without looking. Maybe the racket would make the bear stop, if nothing else. He pulled the trigger until the hammer clicked on an empty chamber.

A bellowing roar sounded. McKinley looked back and saw that his desperate ploy might have worked. The bear had stopped and reared up on its hind legs. It swatted at the air with its massive paws and continued to roar.

At the same time, the racing horse was putting more distance between it and the bear. McKinley clung to the saddle. They swept around another bend, and he could no longer see the bear.

Of course, it could resume the chase, if it wanted to, but with each stride, the horse put the huge, hairy menace that much farther behind.

Even so, McKinley didn't heave a relieved sigh until the draw petered out and he emerged onto open range again. He reined in, turned his mount, and looked back.

No sign of the bear.

The monster had gone back to wherever it had come from, McKinley thought.

The steer he had followed up the draw stood about fifty yards away, cropping calmly on grass as if nothing had happened. McKinley glared at the steer for a moment and then shook a fist at it as he called, "Next time you go wanderin' off and find yourself on the menu for a bear, I'm gonna let the dang thing have you, you blasted cow critter!"

The next day, Smoke and Pearlie were leaning on one of the corral fences, watching as Calvin Woods cautiously approached a big gray horse.

"He's givin' you the skunk eye, Cal," Pearlie called to his young friend. "Don't trust him."

"I wasn't planning on it," Cal replied. "But I'm not gonna let some jugheaded horse think he's gettin' the best of me."

"Now, I don't know why he'd think that," Pearlie drawled, "just 'cause he's already throwed you half a dozen times today."

Cal scowled over his shoulder, then turned his attention back to the gray. He spoke softly to the horse as he reached out with one hand. The gray blew a breath out, making his nostrils flare, but he didn't shy away as the young cowboy stroked his neck.

"All right now," Cal said. "You and me are gonna be friends, horse. You just take it easy." He lifted his left foot, fitted it into the stirrup. "No need to get spooked. I'm not gonna hurt you."

He grasped the reins and the horn and lifted himself into the saddle. His eyes were wide with anticipation as he settled down in the leather.

The gray didn't budge, just stood there calmly.

"Well, son of a gun," Pearlie breathed. "Maybe the boy's done it."

Equally quietly, Smoke said, "Look at the way that horse's tail is flicking."

From atop the gray, Cal said, "See, I told you I'd—"

The horse exploded underneath him.

The gray was a sunfishing, crow-hopping, end-swapping dynamo as Cal yelled in alarm and clung to the saddle for dear life. It was an effort that was doomed to fail. Only a handful of seconds elapsed before Cal sailed into the air and came crashing down on the ground inside the corral.

The horse bucked a few more times as it danced across the corral, seemingly celebrating its triumph.

"Are you all right, Cal?" Pearlie called.

Cal groaned, sat up, and shook his head groggily. He had lost his hat when he flew out of the saddle. He looked around for it, spotted it, and started to crawl toward it on his hands and knees.

"You'll get him next time," Pearlie said, then added under his breath to Smoke, "or not."

Smoke smiled. He was glad that Cal wasn't hurt and admired the young cowboy's determination, but something else had caught his attention.

"Rider coming," he said with a nod toward the trail that led to the Sugarloaf from the road.

Pearlie squinted in that direction and then said, "That's Monte, ain't it?"

"Yep," Smoke replied. He turned away from the corral and started toward the ranch house, intent on finding out what had brought the lawman out there.

Sally must have sensed somehow that company was coming because she came out the front door onto the porch as Smoke walked toward the house. She wore an apron over a blue dress, and her thick dark hair was pulled back and tied behind her head. She'd been cooking, and she dusted flour off her hands as Smoke approached.

She was the prettiest woman he'd ever seen. The smartest, bravest woman he'd ever known. The former Sally Reynolds had been a schoolteacher when he first met her up in Idaho. It was her students' loss and his gain when she'd agreed to become his wife.

"Did you know Monte was coming out here today?" she asked.

"Nope," Smoke replied. "He must have news of some sort."

It probably wasn't good news, he mused. Otherwise, he

would have waited until the next time Smoke came into Big Rock to talk to him.

Monte loped up and reined in. Sally smiled and said, "I hope you're in the mood for some nice cool lemonade."

"That sounds like the next best thing to heaven," he replied. "I'm much obliged to you."

Pearlie had followed Smoke from the corral. He took the horse's reins from Monte when the sheriff dismounted.

"I'll take care of this ol' boy for you, Monte."

"Thanks, Pearlie."

Smoke said, "Come on up onto the porch and sit down."

Sally had gone back into the house. She returned a few moments later carrying a tray with a pitcher and three glasses on it. She poured lemonade for all of them, then joined Smoke and Monte in the wicker-bottomed rocking chairs on the porch.

"What brings you out here, Monte?" Smoke asked after taking a sip of the cool, sweet beverage.

"That bear again," Monte said.

"The giant bear Nelse Andersen saw?" Sally said. "Smoke told me about it."

"It's been spotted again?" Smoke asked.

"More than spotted. It chased Dean McKinley and nearly got him."

"McKinley . . ." Smoke repeated as he tried to put a face with the name. "Puncher who rides for Bart Oliver's Boxed O brand?"

"That's right," Monte said. "He followed a steer up a draw, and that bear nearly got both of them."

The Boxed O was a small outfit bordering the foothills to the northwest, five or six miles from the Sugarloaf. Bart Oliver, who owned the spread, worked it with his two teenaged sons and a couple of hired hands, one of whom was Dean McKinley.

"McKinley wasn't hurt?"

Monte shook his head. "No, he was able to get away on horseback."

"He was lucky, then. Bears are mighty fast when they want to be."

"Yeah. McKinley said he emptied his six-gun at the beast. He probably missed with all his shots, and even if he didn't, a .45 slug wouldn't do more than annoy a grizzly unless you hit it just perfectly."

"Not likely from the hurricane deck of a running horse, especially when the fella pulling the trigger was probably scared to death."

"No probably about it," Monte said. "McKinley still looked pretty shook up when he came into town and talked about it this morning."

"So now folks are all worked up about the bear again," Smoke said. "I sure was hoping it had moved on."

Almost a week had passed since Nelse Andersen's encounter with the bear. Phil Clinton, editor and publisher of the *Big Rock Journal*, had printed a story about it on the paper's front page that was picked up and reprinted by one of the Denver newspapers, so it was doubtful that anybody in this whole part of Colorado hadn't heard about the giant bruin.

But after a few days of hunting parties going out to search for the creature with no success, most of the interest had died down.

This latest development would change all that.

"I'm hoping you'll agree to try to track it again," Monte said. "I'm going to issue an order for everybody in the valley to stick close to home and stay out of the way so you can find the bear and deal with it."

"Kill it, you mean?" Sally said, with a slight frown of disapproval.

Monte shrugged. "I'd be fine if the varmint just wasn't around these parts anymore, but I don't know how you'd guarantee that. Even if you drove it off a long way, it could come back. They can range for hundreds of miles."

"First thing is to find it," Smoke said. "I'm certainly willing to try again. I'm not sure you'll be able to get people to stay home, though."

"It'll be easier if I can tell them that you're on the trail. They'll want to give you a chance to succeed. I appreciate you taking on the chore, Smoke."

"I'll do my best."

Monte drank some of his lemonade and then sighed. "I hope you can get him. Andersen and McKinley were lucky. That luck probably won't hold up. Sooner or later . . ."

"Sooner or later, somebody who runs into that bear is going to wind up dead," Smoke said.

CHAPTER 3

Chuck Haskell was a fierce little banty rooster of a man with graying brown hair and a bristling mustache of the same shade. Tough as whang leather, he had been a top hand cowboy until the horse he was riding spooked at a rattlesnake, threw him, then fell on him, twisting his right knee badly enough that it never quite recovered.

That was the only time a horse had ever gotten the best of Haskell.

The injury left him with a limp and meant he couldn't spend fourteen hours a day in the saddle anymore, but he still knew more about horseflesh than just about anybody, and the animals responded to him. His boss, the ranch manager of the Eastern syndicate–owned Rafter M, kept him on as the head wrangler, in charge of the ranch's string of horses.

Haskell also served as a mentor to the younger members of the crew. He had been a tough sergeant in a Union infantry unit during the Civil War, so he knew how to chew out men when they needed it and praise them on the rare occasions when that was appropriate.

On that day, he was on his way far up the valley to pick up a dozen mustangs that the Rafter M was buying to add to its string. It was a long enough ride that he wouldn't get there by nightfall. He planned to camp and reach his destination by the middle of the next morning.

The ranch manager had offered to send a couple of the hands with him to help. Haskell had scoffed at that idea.

"The day I can't handle a dozen broomtails by myself is the day you can put me in a rockin' chair on the porch, Brodie Wilkes," he told his boss. "Better yet, put me in the ground, 'cause I'll be dead!"

"Take it easy, Chuck," Brodie said. "I just thought you might like a little company. Ain't none of us as young as we used to be." The ranch manager paused, then added ominously, "Besides, there's that bear roamin' around. You don't want to run into him by yourself."

Haskell snorted dismissively once again. "That bear's just a figment of somebody's overactive imagination. Nelse Andersen's got too much of a thirst to be relied on, and young cowboys like Dean McKinley are always given to flights of fancy."

"Smoke Jensen found bear tracks," Brodie pointed out. "Smoke's as level-headed as can be."

"Oh, there are bears around here, no doubt about that," Haskell said with a shrug, "but not giant ones like folks are talkin' about. And Smoke's just goin' by paw prints. He's never actually laid eyes on the critter, from what I've heard."

"No, I reckon not," Brodie conceded.

"Smoke's been huntin' the critter for what, two weeks now? He would've found it if it was still around, or one of the other bunches out lookin' would have." Haskell shook his head. "No, if some giant bear was in these parts, it would've showed up again by now."

"The thing could still be dangerous, even if it's a normal-sized grizzly. They killed plenty of trappers in the old days!"

"Maybe so, but I've run into bears before. If you stand your ground, yell at 'em, and shoot a gun in the air, they'll run away, more often than not."

"You're a stubborn old coot, you know that?"

Haskell had just grinned, pleased by the assessment.

He still wasn't worried about all the stories he'd heard concerning the rogue bear as he made camp in a clearing with some large boulders around it. He picketed his horse on good graze, gathered wood for a campfire, and cooked some biscuits and bacon as night fell. A coffeepot sat at the edge of the fire.

Haskell sat cross-legged as he ate. There was a time he would have hunkered on his heels because that was what cowboys did. His bad knee wouldn't stand that anymore. He hated making concessions to age and injury, but sometimes a man didn't have any choice.

He had just taken a sip of the strong, black brew from his tin cup when he heard something behind him. He was sitting with his back to one of the boulders. Moving deliberately, he set the cup on the ground. He didn't want to act like he was spooked.

Still sitting on the ground, he half-turned and put his hand on the butt of his holstered gun.

"Howdy," he said to the darkness. "Anybody there? You're welcome to come on in. Got enough coffee and grub to share, if you're of a mind to have some supper."

There was no answer except for a faint scraping sound. Then, suddenly, a shadowy figure loomed up and rushed toward Haskell, who yelled in alarm and tried to leap to his feet as he fumbled with his Colt.

With his bad knee, though, he wasn't as nimble as he once was, and he was in a bad position to start with.

He hadn't even cleared leather when death fell on him, rending and tearing.

"Are you going bear hunting again today?" Sally asked Smoke as she faced him from the other end of the breakfast table.

Smoke leaned back in his chair, pushed away the empty plate that had been filled with flapjacks and bacon, and reached for his coffee cup.

"I can't keep on just wandering around the valley," he said. "I've got a ranch to run. Anyway, I haven't seen hide nor hair of a giant grizzly or any other bear in the week I've been looking. I know quite a few of them used to be around these parts, but I think most of them have moved higher up in the mountains to get away from all the people who have come in."

Sally smiled and said, "I remember you shot one the first year we lived here, when we just had the little log cabin. Preacher skinned it and made a rug out of the hide."

"Seems longer ago than it actually was, doesn't it?"

"A lot has happened since then." Sally shook her head. "We've led eventful lives. Especially you, Smoke."

"Better than being bored, I reckon."

"I'd agree with you most of the time . . . when there's not too much powder smoke in the air."

Smoke chuckled. He knew Sally was just joshing with him, at least to a certain extent. She was well aware that life had its trials, and she had burned some of that powder she spoke of, too. She'd never been one to back down from trouble, although she didn't go out of her way to look for it, either. Now and then she accused him of that, and he couldn't exactly deny it . . .

Smoke heard a footstep on the porch, then a knock at the front door, which opened to admit Pearlie.

"Hate to bother you this early, Smoke," he began as he came into the kitchen and took off his hat.

"Sun's up, isn't it?"

"Well, yeah."

"Then I'd say it's late, not early. What brings you here, Pearlie?"

"Monte's ridin' in. Spotted him a minute ago, comin' along the trail."

Smoke glanced at Sally and frowned slightly. Considering that it would have taken Monte a while to ride out there from town, it actually was a little early in the day for the sheriff to be paying a visit.

After downing the rest of his coffee, Smoke pushed his chair back and stood up.

"Do you think Monte would like some breakfast?" Sally asked. "There's still a little left."

"I don't know, but you can go ahead and pour him a cup of coffee. He's likely to want that after riding out here."

Smoke followed Pearlie out of the house, snagging his hat and his gun belt from the hooks beside the front door where they were hung.

Monte rode up a minute later. Cal was there to take his horse from him when he dismounted.

"Thanks, Cal." Monte nodded to the other men as he greeted them, "Smoke. Pearlie."

"Morning, Monte," Smoke said. "I'd ask what brings you out here, but I know you'll tell me . . . and I have a hunch it's not anything good."

"That dang bear show up again?" Pearlie asked.

"I don't know, but we've got a missing man," Monte responded. "You know Chuck Haskell."

"Sure," Smoke said.

"Feisty little fella," Pearlie said. "Wrangles horses for the Rafter M, don't he?"

"That's right. Brodie Wilkes, the manager out there, sent a rider in last night so he was at my office early this morning. Day before yesterday, Haskell rode up north to bring back a jag of mustangs, and he didn't show up yesterday evening like he should have."

"You mean he ain't even a whole day late yet?" Pearlie said. "Shoot, that's nothin'. Drivin' horses like that, a man can get delayed for all sorts of reasons."

"I know, but Haskell's getting older and he's sort of crippled up, too. Wilkes is worried about him."

"Did he have anybody with him to help handle those mustangs?" Smoke asked.

Monte shook his head. "No, he's the prideful sort and a mite cantankerous, to boot. I know he'll probably turn up today and be just fine, but I thought I'd ride up the same trail he would have used and take a look around."

"It won't hurt anything," Smoke allowed. "I'll come with you."

"That's what I was hoping you'd say."

From the porch, Sally asked, "You have time for a cup of coffee first, though, don't you, Monte? And maybe a plate of flapjacks?"

The lawman grinned. "I reckon it'd take a giant grizzly bear to keep me from accepting that kind offer, Sally."

Smoke and Monte rode out a short time later, after Monte finished his second breakfast for the day. Pearlie and Cal offered to come along, too, but Smoke pointed out that quite a bit of work needed to be done around the ranch. He didn't think he and Monte were liable to run into anything that the two of them couldn't handle.

Instead of going back to Big Rock, they cut across the valley. The Sugarloaf had been the first ranch in those parts.

Smoke had explored the valley thoroughly and knew every foot of it, although there were sections he hadn't visited in quite some time, such as the area where they were headed on that day.

In late morning, they reached the trail Chuck Haskell would have used and turned to follow it. More miles fell behind them without any sign of anything out of the ordinary, before Smoke suddenly reined in and pointed at some black specks wheeling around in the sky.

"Blast it, I see 'em," Monte said with a scowl as he looked at the birds circling high above them. From the size of their wingspans, their black coloring, and the way they glided gracefully on the air currents with only an occasional flap of those wings, both men recognized them as buzzards.

"Could be a lot of reasons they'd be circling," Smoke said. "Maybe a dead cow or some other critter. This doesn't have to mean something happened to Chuck Haskell."

"Maybe," allowed Monte, "but it's not a good sign, either."

They rode on, watching the swooping birds of prey in the clear blue sky. Something about the beauty of the day made the sight even more ominous. Buzzards ought to be circling under a gray, threatening sky, Smoke thought, not the sort of day where he'd like to take Sally out for a picnic and maybe some sparking on a blanket spread out on a soft carpet of grass.

They came to a line of trees and brush that ran alongside the trail for several hundred yards. A cluster of boulders lay behind the growth. Smoke slowed his horse and then stopped. Monte followed suit.

"I seem to recall there's a clearing back there by those rocks that would make a good place for a man to camp," Smoke said. "There's room for a fire and some decent graze for horses."

Monte tilted his head back to look up. "Those scavengers are almost right overhead. I reckon we'd better take a look, Smoke." He drew his rifle from the saddle boot. "But not without being ready for trouble."

"Never hurts anything to be ready," Smoke said. He withdrew his Winchester from its scabbard, too. They nudged their mounts into motion again and rode into the trees with the butts of their rifles resting against their thighs and the barrels pointing into the air.

The trees and brush were spread out enough that it wasn't difficult to weave through the line of vegetation. As they came into clear sight of the boulders, Smoke spotted a dark, irregular circle on the ground and pointed it out to Monte as they reined in.

"Somebody built a campfire there and then let it burn down and go out."

"The coffeepot's still sitting there at the edge," Monte said with a grim note in his voice. "Looks like there's a frying pan in the ashes, too. Something interrupted Haskell's supper."

The two men dismounted and moved closer on foot. Smoke stopped short at the sight of another dark, ragged stain where something had splashed on the ground and dried.

Monte saw it, too, and breathed a curse. "That's blood, isn't it?"

Smoke went to a knee beside the stain, tested it with a finger, and nodded as he rubbed that finger with his thumb.

"Yeah, I'd say it is. Somebody lost quite a bit of it, too."

"More than a man could lose and expect to live." Monte looked around. "But where is he?"

"If it was Haskell, and if that bear got him . . ."

Monte groaned. "Oh, hell. The bear dragged the body

off, didn't it? We'll never find poor Chuck, because he's inside that blasted bear's belly by now."

"Let's keep looking," Smoke suggested. "Maybe we'll find something that'll tell us for sure what happened."

Holding the rifles ready, the two men split up and began searching warily around the boulders.

Smoke saw several more dark splotches on the ground that he thought were probably blood. When Monte called from the other side of the boulders, saying, "I've got more blood over here," Smoke grimaced. That much blood, splattered over so large an area, was bleak evidence of the carnage that had happened there.

Moments later, Smoke heard an obscene oath rip out of Monte's mouth. His old friend was generally a fairly mild-spoken man. For Monte to exclaim like that, something must have really shaken him. Smoke hurried around the boulders.

By the time he reached Monte, the sheriff was bent over, leaning against a boulder with one hand while he threw up the breakfast he had eaten earlier at the Sugarloaf.

"Monte, what in blazes—"

Monte interrupted him with a jerky motion of his other hand, waving Smoke past him.

Smoke stepped farther around the boulder and frowned as he saw a smaller rock lying on the ground. It was about the size of a man's head, he thought.

Then he stiffened as he realized that rocks didn't have mustaches.

Etched in permanent lines of agony, the face of Chuck Haskell stared up unseeingly at Smoke.

What was left of the neck was bloody and ragged, almost as if the head had been ripped right off the body.

CHAPTER 4

It took a nip from the flask that Monte carried in his saddlebags for medicinal purposes—and this certainly qualified—to settle his stomach and his nerves.

"You know the kind of life I led when I was a younger man, Smoke," he said ruefully as he tucked the flask away. "I've seen plenty of bad things in my life. Mighty bad. But I'm not sure I ever saw anything like old Chuck Haskell staring up at me like that . . . *with just his head laying there on the ground!*"

Smoke had seen bad things, too. Worse than Chuck Haskell's decapitated head, in fact. But he never let himself think about those things for very long because that way lay madness, as Shakespeare put it.

With a tight grip on his emotions, Smoke said, "We'd better look around some more and see what else we can find."

Eventually, they found more of Haskell's remains, but not enough that a complete body could have been pieced together from them. Quite a bit of it was missing, in fact.

Even so, Smoke was a little surprised that they located as much as they did. He would have expected the bear to consume the entire corpse. If indeed it *was* a bear.

More searching turned up the horse Haskell had ridden. The picket rope and pin were still attached to the animal. It had pulled loose from where it was picketed and fled, which was to be expected. Horses were naturally terrified of bears.

The only reason the saddle mount hadn't returned home to the Rafter M was because the picket pin had gotten caught in a low fork in a tree. The horse tugging on it had just wedged it in tighter. Eventually, the horse might have broken the rope, but for now it was stuck where it was as effectively as if it had been tethered there deliberately.

They wrapped the remains they found in Haskell's blankets, then bundled up everything inside the wrangler's slicker. Smoke tied the gruesome package securely and lashed it in place over Haskell's saddle. The smell of blood made the horse skittish, but it settled down after a few minutes.

Before they left, Smoke took a good look around. Monte watched him and asked, "See any bear tracks?"

"No, but as rocky as the ground is around these boulders, I'm not surprised," Smoke said. "This varmint is good at not leaving much of a trail, too. I'd say he's pretty smart."

They rode back toward the Rafter M, leaving the site of Chuck Haskell's death behind them, but the memories of what they had seen there would stay with them for a long time.

Dusk was settling over the valley when Smoke and Monte rode up to the Rafter M headquarters. The ranch dogs heard them coming and ran out barking to greet them. That canine commotion brought the crew from the manager's house, where they had been eating supper.

Brodie Wilkes stepped out in front of the other men,

wiping grease from his hands on his shirt. He stopped short as he realized that the two visitors had brought another horse with them . . . and that horse carried an ominous-looking burden.

"Aw, hell!" Brodie let out in a furious exclamation as Smoke and Monte reined in. "That's Chuck, ain't it?"

"I'm afraid so, Brodie," Monte said. "What's left of him, anyway."

"What does that mean?" asked one of the young cow-boys who had followed Brodie out of the house.

"It means the bear got him and there ain't much left of him!" another puncher guessed.

Monte sighed and nodded. "I'm afraid that's right. He was, uh, torn up pretty bad. Smoke and I brought back—" the next words choked Monte for a second—"all we could find of him."

Brodie gestured curtly to his men and said, "Get him off'a there and into the bunkhouse."

"You might want to take him to the barn," Smoke suggested. "There's nothing you can do for him now."

"We can get him ready to give him a proper burial."

Monte shook his head. "There's not really enough left to get him ready. If I was you, I'd leave him wrapped up and just lay him to rest that way in the morning."

Brodie sighed and scrubbed a hand over his rugged features. Like Smoke and Monte, he was a veteran frontiersman and had seen plenty in his time, good and bad, but this development was enough to leave him shaken.

"All right," he said. "Take him in the barn." To Smoke and Monte, he went on, "You boys light down from those horses and come inside. We've got plenty of grub and coffee."

"I'm obliged to you for the offer, Brodie," Monte said, "but I need to get back to Big Rock."

"And I should head for the Sugarloaf," Smoke added.

"You're gonna ride at night with the critter that . . . that did *that* roamin' around loose?"

Brodie nodded toward the men who had untied the bundle containing Haskell's remains and were carrying it carefully into the barn.

Smoke and Monte looked at each other. Monte said, "He's got a point."

Smoke wasn't afraid to head back to the Sugarloaf that night. However, he didn't see any point in tempting fate. With Pearlie, Cal, and the rest of the crew at the ranch, Sally would be fine. She might wonder why he hadn't returned, but she had known when he rode out that there was no telling what he might run into. She wouldn't worry about him being gone for one night.

"All right," Smoke said. "We're obliged to you for the hospitality, Brodie."

"Not as obliged as we are to you fellas for findin' Chuck." Brodie shook his head. "The poor devil."

Smoke and Monte spent the night in the bunkhouse with the Rafter M crew, then the next morning they lingered long enough after breakfast to attend Chuck Haskell's burial.

As Smoke had suggested, the remains were left in the slicker, which was then wrapped carefully in another blanket and placed in a pine coffin that had been hastily knocked together the previous evening from boards kept in a shed for whatever purposes might arise—including grim ones such as this.

The ranch had a small private cemetery inside a wrought-iron fence on top of a little rise overlooking the headquarters. The enclosure contained half a dozen graves, and now another one was added to it.

Brodie Wilkes read from the Bible and said a prayer over the grave. That was the extent of the service. Afterward, while a couple of the hands were filling in the grave, Monte asked the ranch manager, "Did Chuck have any relatives I need to get in touch with?"

Brodie shook his head. "Not that I know of. He was married once, I remember him sayin', but she left him and took up with another fella while he was off fightin' in the war."

Monte made a face and said, "That's mighty tough luck. They have any kids?"

"If they did, Chuck never spoke of 'em. He got along well with the rest of the crew, and he had a few friends here in the valley that he knew from back in the army days, but I don't reckon he was really close to anybody."

"You mind if I go through his gear in the bunkhouse, just in case there's a letter or something from somebody who should be notified?"

Brodie waved a hand. "Help yourself, Sheriff. We want to do things proper-like."

However, Monte's search didn't turn up anything to point him in the direction of Chuck Haskell's possible relatives. Maybe the old wrangler really was alone in the world.

A short time later, Smoke and Monte headed out, riding together for a while before their trails parted. Monte followed the trail back to Big Rock, while Smoke rode across the valley toward the Sugarloaf.

He arrived late in the morning. At first glance, the ranch appeared to be deserted. No one came out of the barn as he rode up.

Sally opened the front door and stepped out onto the porch, though, causing a feeling of relief to go through Smoke. Her smile made his heart leap, as usual.

He swung down from the saddle, went up the steps quickly, and pulled her into his arms. His mouth came down on hers in a long, passionate kiss. When their lips parted, she laughed and smiled up into his face.

"My goodness, what was that for?" she asked. Then, before he could answer, she went on, "Never mind. If that's the sort of greeting I'm going to get when you come home, you should leave more often."

"You don't really want me to go away any more often than I have to, do you?"

"Well, no, not really," Sally admitted. Her arms were around Smoke's waist. She tightened them and rested her head on his broad chest for a moment, saying without looking up, "Honestly, if you never left again, it would be all right with me." She raised her head. "But you can still give me kisses like that any time you want to."

"Sounds like a good idea," Smoke murmured. He proceeded to do so.

A few minutes later, she was sitting in one of the rocking chairs while he propped a hip against the porch railing and thumbed his hat back.

"Where is everybody?" Smoke asked.

"Out on the range where they should be," Sally answered. "Pearlie let the men know in no uncertain terms that just because you weren't around this morning, that didn't mean it was a holiday."

Smoke chuckled. Pearlie was a stern taskmaster with the crew, but he did it in such a way that all of the Sugarloaf cowboys loved him and would have charged hell with a bucket of water if he'd asked them to. They felt the same way about Smoke and Sally.

He was concerned about one thing, though, and grew more serious as he said, "I'd have thought somebody would stay around here, in case you needed anything."

"Pearlie said he'd leave someone if I wanted him to, but they're moving stock up into the higher pastures for the summer, and I figured it would be better to have the full crew for a big job like that."

"That's probably true," Smoke admitted with a shrug, "but having one or two men fewer wouldn't have made that much difference in the job."

A slight frown creased Sally's forehead. "You've never worried much about me being alone here, Smoke. You know I can take care of myself." She drew in a sharp breath as something occurred to her. "Oh, wait. Is this about Nicole?"

Smoke's jaw tightened. Years earlier, he had left his first wife, Nicole, and their infant son, Arthur, alone to tend to ranch business, and when he returned both were dead, brutally murdered by gunmen working for Smoke's enemies.

That horrible tragedy had prompted the bitter memories that passed fleetingly through his mind the day before, when he and Monte discovered Chuck Haskell's gory remains.

But now he shook his head and said, "No. That was a different time and a different place. I was more worried about that blasted bear."

"You found something?" Sally's eyebrows rose. "Oh, no! Did it attack someone?"

"It killed Chuck Haskell," Smoke said.

Sally put a hand to her mouth in horror and sat there for a moment before saying, "I'm so sorry. I . . . I didn't actually know Mr. Haskell, just saw him a few times in town, but that's still terrible. You're sure the bear was responsible?"

"Well, it sure looked like *a* bear attack. Since I wasn't there when it happened, I suppose I can't say for sure that it was the same bear."

"That's certainly the most likely explanation, isn't it?"

"Yeah," Smoke said. "It would be a mighty big coincidence if there were two critters like that roaming around, but I guess you can't rule out the possibility."

"You weren't able to track it?"

Smoke shook his head. "That varmint really knows how to throw folks off the trail."

"Were . . . were you able to recover Mr. Haskell's body?"

Smoke knew she was asking if the bear had eaten the wrangler. He wasn't going to go into details with her about what he and Monte had found, so he just said, "Yes, we did. We took him back to the Rafter M, and Brodie Wilkes and the rest of the crew gave him a decent burial in the ranch's graveyard. We spent the night there last night, and Haskell was laid to rest this morning."

Sally sighed. "Well, there's that to be thankful for, anyway, I suppose. What happens now?"

"I don't know," Smoke replied honestly. "We can hope the bear will move on and this trouble will be over."

"But that's not actually what you're expecting, is it?"

"No, not really," Smoke said.

Five days later

Roy Ford was a tall, wiry man with a long face, a prominent jaw, and graying fair hair. A few years earlier, he had bought one of the established ranches in the valley and settled in to run it with his family. An old friend had written to him and praised the country around there, and Ford, who had owned a freight line in Kansas, had long wanted to get out of that business and find a spread of his own. So he'd sold the freight line and moved to Colorado.

The RF Connected was the brand he used and the ranch's new name. Ford's wife, Marie, loved it there, as did their four children, two boys and two girls, ranging from fourteen to nineteen. Normally, Ford was mighty happy about settling there, too.

But not that day.

That day was downright miserable.

The weather had turned threatening suddenly. The air was still warm, but it was heavy with impending rain. Black clouds filled the formerly blue sky. Thunder rumbled in the distance, and jagged fingers of lightning clawed through the dark, overcast sky. Gusts of wind whipped the pine branches as Ford rode along the crest of a ridge.

A short time earlier, he had ridden into the higher reaches of his spread to check on some horses he had in a fenced pasture. When he'd arrived there, he'd been disgusted to see that some of the fence rails had been knocked down and the pasture was empty.

It looked like something had spooked the horses, causing them to lunge against the fence over and over until they broke through it. Ford had checked the rails on the ground, made from saplings he had cut and peeled, and had seen horse hair stuck on rough spots here and there.

The first thing Ford had thought of was that blasted bear he had heard so much about. The whole valley was buzzing about it, like a swarm of angry hornets. Horses hated bears. If one of them had come prowling around the pasture, the horses might have been frightened enough to bust out like that.

Roy Ford had thought long and hard about turning around and riding back to his ranch house. A little less than a week earlier, Chuck Haskell had met a grisly end at the claws and fangs of the monster that had invaded the valley.

Ford had hardly been able to believe that when he heard the news. Chuck had survived so much, back there in the war, and then to be ripped apart by a bear . . .

So it made good sense to light a shuck for home. Nobody had ever accused Ford of having good sense, though, especially when it came to saving a dollar. He had quite a bit invested in those horses. With a storm coming on, there was no telling how far or fast they would run. Storms spooked horses as much as bears did.

He could try to follow them for a little while, at least, he decided.

The trail led even higher. As thunder rolled again, he began to worry about lightning. As if he didn't already have enough to concern him, he thought with a disgusted snort. *Runaway horses, giant bears, and now the chance that I might get fried by a lightning bolt . . .*

One such bolt chose that moment to sizzle down and strike a pine tree about a hundred yards away. The ear-splitting crack and the sharp tang of ozone in the air made Ford's horse dance skittishly and then rear up.

Ford yelled as he lost his grip on the saddle and toppled backward off the horse.

He never had been as good a rider as some.

Suddenly terrified of being set afoot out there if his mount bolted, Ford tried to scramble up. The fall had stunned him and knocked the breath out of him, though. His movements were slow and awkward.

Another lightning flash split the dark afternoon air. Still on his knees, Ford looked up.

What he saw silhouetted against that glare made him almost cry out in sudden terror.

CHAPTER 5

Rain in the summer was always welcome, since the lack of it brought the danger of drought, but the problem with a heavy rain at this time of year was that when the sun came out the next day, it made the air so steamy a man almost felt like he was walking around underwater.

Monte Carson was mulling that over in his head as he walked toward Lambert's Restaurant, figuring to get himself an early lunch on the day after a line of strong summer thunderstorms had rolled through the area.

His route took him past Longmont's, the business that was both a high-class drinking establishment and a fine eatery. Louis Longmont, the gambler and gunman who owned the place, was another old friend. Briefly, Monte considered stopping there instead of going on to Lambert's.

He spotted Louis himself headed toward him along the boardwalk, likely returning to the saloon and restaurant following some errand. Slim and always dapper, on that day Louis was dressed in a black suit and matching Stetson. A nickel-plated, pearl-handled revolver rode holstered on his hip.

Because of his elegant garb and the fancy gun, sometimes men had taken Louis for a harmless dude and decided to have some fun with him. When the hooraw-ing went too far, however, they quickly realized their mistake. Unfortunately for them, sometimes the mistake proved to be a fatal one.

Louis's smile and voice were mild and friendly as he said, "Good morning, Monte. A bit uncomfortable, isn't it? I believe *sultry* is the appropriate word."

Monte paused, took off his hat, and used the red-and-white, polka-dotted bandanna he pulled from his pocket to mop sweat off his forehead. He said, "Big Rock's high enough in elevation that it never stays this hot and sticky for long. We'll get a nice cool breeze by evening, I'll wager."

"Would you like to bet a hat on it?"

Monte laughed. "Make a wager with Louis Longmont? What kind of plumb idjit do you take me for? Have you *ever* lost a bet, Louis?"

"Of course I have," Louis answered with a faint smile, "but not many." He leaned his head toward the door. "Would you like to come in and have some coffee?"

Longmont's had the best coffee in all of Big Rock. Maybe the best in Colorado. Monte knew that, but he said, "I appreciate the invitation, but my stomach's set on the rolls over at Lambert's—"

Pounding hoofbeats and the rattle of rapidly turning wagon wheels made Monte break off in midsentence. He turned to look along the street and felt his guts clench and his heart sink as he spotted the wagon speeding toward him.

"Do you recognize the lady at the reins?" Louis asked.

"I think it's Marie Ford," Monte replied. The woman handling the running team wasn't wearing a bonnet. Her long brown hair, streaked with silver, blew out behind her head. The faces of several half-grown kids peered anxiously over her shoulder.

Monte stepped out into the street and raised a hand.

"Mrs. Ford!" he called, not knowing whether she could

hear him over the racket of the wagon and team. "Mrs. Ford, slow down!"

At first, he thought she was going to barrel right on past him, but then she suddenly seemed to notice him and hauled back on the reins. She had to put quite a bit of effort into it to slow and then stop the charging horses.

The vehicle rocked and bounced to a halt, though not before going several yards past Monte. He trotted after it and felt another surge of foreboding as he saw a long, blanket-wrapped shape in the back of the wagon.

All four of Roy and Marie Ford's teenaged children were in the back of the wagon, their faces pale and strained. The eyes of both girls were red and swollen, as if they had been crying.

At least none of the kids were wrapped up in that blanket, Monte thought. As terrible as the situation likely was, at least he was grateful for that.

Of course, that really left only one person it could be . . .

"Mrs. Ford, let me help you—" Monte began as he reached the wagon.

"Help me?" she interrupted him with a shrill, hysterical edge in her voice. "You can't help me. Not unless you can bring Roy back to life!"

Monte looked at the oldest boy, who was sixteen or seventeen, and tried to remember his name. He'd never been good at dealing with upset females, so he thought it might be better if he approached the youngster on a man-to-man basis.

The name came to him. Monte said, "Edgar, can you tell me what happened?"

Before the boy had a chance to answer, his mother cried, "I'll tell you what happened! That monster killed him! Ripped him to shreds!"

Louis stepped up alongside the wagon seat and reached

out to grasp the woman's hand in both of his. In a soft, soothing voice, he said, "Please, Mrs. Ford, come inside with me. You can have a cup of coffee and sit down and rest while the sheriff deals with this terrible tragedy."

Monte didn't expect that to do any good, but Mrs. Ford responded to Louis's gentle tone and touch and allowed him to help her down from the wagon. Louis put an arm around her shoulders and steered her toward the door of Longmont's.

Looking back, he said, "You children come along, too. No matter what you've seen until now, you don't need to see any more."

They clambered down from the back of the wagon and followed Louis and their mother. Mrs. Ford's shoulders shook as she began to sob. The girls were crying, too, while the two boys made visible efforts to remain stoic . . . but tears shone in their eyes, as well.

Monte was relieved when the family was inside Longmont's and off the street. He could find out the details of what had happened later, after Marie Ford had a chance to calm down some. He turned back to the wagon but then swept a hostile glare across the crowd that was gathering around the vehicle.

"You folks just go on about your business," he snapped.

"This *is* our business, Sheriff," Phil Clinton said as he pushed his way to the front of the crowd. The newspaperman went on, "If this is another bear attack, then all of us have a right to know about it. Especially the press."

Monte couldn't really argue with that stance. Because of that blasted bear, an aura of fear hung over the entire valley that was as oppressive as the humidity in the air.

"You can stay, Phil," he said. "The rest of you, clear out. Whatever happened out at the Ford spread, I reckon you'll hear about it soon enough."

A great deal of grumbling came from the citizens, but as Monte continued to glower at them, they began drifting off.

By the time the crowd of townspeople around the wagon had cleared away, two more men had joined Monte and Clinton. Monte didn't feel like he could turn them away, since they were Dr. Colton Spaulding, Big Rock's leading physician, and Tom Nunnley, who, in addition to owning a hardware store, served as the settlement's undertaker.

"You're going to have to take a look under that blanket, Sheriff," Dr. Spaulding said when Monte hesitated. "We can't be of any help until we know what the situation is."

"I've got a hunch it's well past the time when you could've been any help, Doctor," Monte said. He had seen how something dark had soaked through the blanket in numerous places. "But I reckon your services are gonna be required, Tom."

With that, Monte grimaced, leaned over the wagon's open tailgate, and reached into the bed to grasp a corner of the blanket. He pulled it back, working it loose where it had been tucked in. He wasn't sure which end of the corpse he was about to uncover, but at least, judging by the shape, it was still in one piece, unlike Chuck Haskell.

If Roy Ford's head rolled out when he pulled that blanket loose, that would be the last straw, Monte thought. He would resign, head for Mexico, find himself a peaceful cantina somewhere, and sit in the shade sipping tequila for the rest of his days while he listened to some *viejo* strum a guitar . . .

Ford's head didn't roll out. It was still attached to the man's body, but Monte's stomach rebelled anyway, and he was glad he hadn't gotten around to that early lunch yet.

"Good Lord," Tom Nunnley muttered. Spaulding pursed his lips and leaned forward to study the grisly sight more carefully, but despite the natural detachment of a medical man, horror and revulsion lurked in his eyes.

Roy Ford's face wasn't recognizable. It barely looked human. Something had shredded it, ripping through the features until the whiteness of bone from the skull was visible in several places.

The torso below that, what Monte could see of it, looked almost like a side of beef. The flesh had been torn and pulled back until the skeleton was visible.

Monte turned away. So did Nunnley and Clinton. The editor looked like he might be sick at any moment. Monte knew the feeling.

"What do you think, Doc?" he asked.

"The wounds resemble those of a wild animal attack," Spaulding said. "They're consistent with wounds that would be left by claws. Sharp claws.

Monte heard rustling as Spaulding lifted the blanket to examine the corpse further.

"The body is largely intact but extensively mauled," the doctor went on. "The throat is slashed, so there would have been a great deal of rapid blood loss. Mr. Ford probably died relatively quickly." Spaulding paused, then added in a musing tone, "I'd say that quite a few of these injuries occurred postmortem."

"You mean after he was dead?"

"That's right, Sheriff."

Monte scraped a thumbnail along his jaw and frowned in thought. "So Ford was dead, but the bear kept tearing into him, anyway."

"I didn't say it was a bear that did this. I said the injuries are consistent with those a wild animal would inflict in an attack."

"Well, what else could it have been?"

"A mountain lion, perhaps?" Spaulding pulled the bloody

blanket back up over the body and tucked it in again. "But your basic point is correct, Sheriff. Whatever did this wasn't simply killing prey for food. It was . . . maddened, is the only word I can think of."

"Like a hydrophobia skunk," Tom Nunnley said. "Can bears get hydrophobia?"

"I don't know," Monte said, then he pointed a finger at Clinton and added quickly, "Don't you print that about the hydrophobia, Phil. It's bad enough that everybody around here is in a lather about that bear without having them think it's mad, to boot."

"But isn't that news?" Clinton asked. "Don't the people have a right to know?"

"Not just yet," Monte insisted. "Maybe I can't order you not to print it, but I'm asking it as a favor."

Clinton hesitated but then nodded with obvious reluctance. "Fine," he said. "I'll wait a while, but it's liable to come out anyway, Sheriff. It's hard to keep things quiet when everybody in the valley is scared and talking."

"Maybe so, but I want to keep a full-blown panic from breaking out as long as I can."

A short time later, Monte sat at a table in Longmont's with Edgar Ford. They had cups of coffee in front of them. With the mood Monte was in, he couldn't really appreciate the brew, but he welcomed its bracing effect.

Especially since he'd caught Louis's eye and nodded. The bartender had inconspicuously added a dollop of brandy to the sheriff's cup before one of the serving girls brought the coffee over to the table.

Louis had taken Marie Ford and her three younger children

into his private living quarters so they would be out of the public eye and could rest a bit.

Monte needed to know what had happened, though, so he'd asked Edgar to stay behind and talk to him for a spell.

"I'm the one who found him, Sheriff," Edgar said now. He had both hands wrapped around his coffee cup but seemed to have forgotten it was there as he stared straight ahead. "Pa didn't come home last night, so this morning I went out to look for him. We . . . we were afraid his horse might've spooked in the storm, thrown him, and run away."

"Where did you find him?" Monte asked. He hated having to question the kid.

"Up beyond our high pasture where we kept some horses. I knew he was headed up there to check on them when he rode out from our home place. When I got there, the fence was down and the horses were gone."

Monte leaned forward. "Did it look like the bear knocked the fence down to get at the stock?"

Edgar shook his head and said, "No, I think the horses knocked some of the rails loose. That's the way it looked, but they might have done it because they were scared of the bear. Something spooked them, that's for sure."

"You didn't see any sign of the horses themselves?"

"No. I reckon they're up in that high country somewhere. There are plenty of places for them to hide. My little brother and I will have to root them out when . . . when we get a chance."

The youngster swallowed hard, no doubt thinking about how he and his brother would have to be responsible for running the RF Connected from now on.

Another thought occurred to Monte. He asked, "Did you see any hoofprints around that could have come from other riders?"

Edgar frowned as he looked across the table at the lawman. "Why, I don't know, Sheriff. With that many horses, it would have been pretty much impossible to tell a difference."

"I suppose so."

"You think somebody *stole* our horses?"

"It's not likely, but I have to consider every possibility."

"Maybe so, but horse thieves didn't do that to my father. Nothing human did."

Monte nodded and said, "What did you do after you found that the horses were gone?"

"The tracks that I did see were headed higher, so I followed them. I knew that's what my pa would have done. I wound up on the ridge that leads up to Rockford Pass. That . . . that's where I found him, about half a mile along."

Edgar's hands tightened around the cup. He swallowed again, blew out a breath, controlled his emotions with a visible effort, and lifted the cup to take a sip of the strong black brew. His hands shook, but only a little.

The kid had sand, Monte thought.

"I hate to have to ask, Edgar, but what did you do then?"

"I . . . I knew right away there was nothing I could do for my pa. So I looked around for his horse, found it not too far off, and wrapped him up and put him over the saddle to take him home. That was the only thing I could do."

"That was a man-sized job," Monte said, "in more ways than one. I reckon you did good at it, too."

"Thanks, Sheriff. My ma carried on for a while . . . we all did . . . and then she said we had to bring him to town." Edgar's shoulders rose and fell slightly. "So here we are."

"We'll take care of everything else," Monte told him. "Your family went to the Baptist church, isn't that right?"

"Yes, sir."

"I'm sure Pastor Owen has heard about what happened by

now. He'll be by to see you and your family. Why don't you get your mother and your brother and sisters and go over to the hotel for now? You can stay there for a few days until . . ."

"Until after the funeral? What about our spread? Somebody will have to look after it."

"I'll talk to Smoke Jensen. I'm sure he won't mind sending a couple of the Sugarloaf crew over there to take care of things for a few days. Maybe they can look for those missing horses, too."

Edgar said, "I heard Mr. Jensen was going to hunt down that bear. I wish he'd found it before now."

Monte nodded slowly. "I expect Smoke feels the same way."

CHAPTER 6

"You know good and well this isn't your fault, Smoke," Sally said the next day as she sat on the divan in the parlor of their ranch house. She watched as Smoke paced angrily back and forth on the rug, almost like a caged animal.

Monte sat in an armchair near the fireplace. "Sally's right, Smoke," he added. "We all know you've spent a lot of time hunting for that varmint."

"Wasted a lot of time is more like it," Smoke said as he paused. "If I'd found that bear when I first went looking for it, Chuck Haskell and Roy Ford would still be alive now."

"You can't know that. I told you, Doc Spaulding said he couldn't be sure it was a bear that attacked Ford. It might have been a mountain lion. We get some pretty big ones around here from time to time."

"Mountain lions won't hardly attack humans unless they're starving. It's the middle of summer. Plenty of game around. Attacks usually happen in the winter."

Sally said, "But I thought Dr. Spaulding said it wasn't like the animal was after food. More like it was—"

"Mad," Smoke finished. "I don't know if that makes things better or worse. Worse, I'd say, because it means whatever did this is even more unpredictable than we thought."

Monte had ridden out to the Sugarloaf earlier in the morning to deliver the latest bad news. Just as Monte had predicted, as soon as Smoke heard what had happened, he'd called Pearlie into the house and told the foreman to send two of the hands across the valley to the RF Connected to hold down the fort there for the time being.

"I'll tell 'em to take Winchesters with plenty of ammunition and keep their eyes open," Pearlie had said with a grim nod.

Now, Monte said, "I persuaded Phil Clinton not to say anything in his newspaper about the chance of hydrophobia, at least for now, but he's right, folks are going to gossip and rumors will start to fly. I'd like for him to write a story about how you're going to track down the bear and kill it. Running it out of the country won't be enough to satisfy folks anymore. Not after what the blamed thing's done."

"I've already said I'd try to find the bear," Smoke said. "I feel like I've already ridden from one end of the valley to the other looking for it." He smacked his right fist into his left palm. "Somehow, it's dodged me so far, but its luck can't hold out forever. I'll get that old Sharps of mine out. I keep it clean and ready to go in case I ever need it."

Monte nodded. "Now that sounds like a mighty good idea. If a Big Fifty will knock down a buffalo, it ought to take care of a bear, even a big grizzly like this one."

"Might take more than one shot," Smoke allowed, "but first I have to find it." He nodded. "Tell Phil Clinton I'm going on the hunt again."

"And this time you won't come back without that monster's hide," Monte said as he lifted a clenched fist.

Smoke hoped that was true. For Chuck Haskell's sake,

and Roy Ford's, and for the sake of anyone else who might get in the way of that killer.

Gridley, Wyoming

A strong man could almost throw a rock from the main street of Gridley, Wyoming, and have it land over the border in Colorado. All of the settlement was in Wyoming, but it served as the supply center for a number of ranches on both sides of the state line. There had been talk of a railroad spur coming to Gridley. If that ever happened, it would grow into a real city.

For now, though, it was a good-sized town, complete with a three-block-long business district that included a couple of mercantiles and livery stables, a hardware store, a millinery shop, a blacksmith, a saddlemaker, a couple of lawyer's offices, a doctor's practice, a domino parlor and pool hall, and half a dozen saloons.

And a bank.

That establishment was on Graham Blake's mind as he rode into Gridley. Without being too obvious about it, he took a good look at the one-story brick building as he rode past. It was the biggest building in town, taking up more than half a block. The largest of the two general stores occupied the rest of the middle block on that side of the street.

The bank was the only one in this part of the country, so all the ranchers around there kept their money in it and had payrolls shipped in to it. It would have been nice if Blake and his friends could have timed things so that payroll money was in the vault, too, but the rest of the gang didn't want to wait that long.

Besides, the bank probably put on extra guards whenever

that cash came in. Between those times, they would relax their vigilance. That was just human nature.

Graham Blake knew a lot about human nature. At one point in his life, back in Illinois when he was a young man, he had started studying to be a doctor. He might have made a good one, too, if he hadn't decided it was too much work and he'd rather be an outlaw. He had good looks and a calm voice that made people have confidence in him.

He reined toward the hitch rail in front of the general store next to the bank. Two of the horses already tied there were familiar to him. They belonged to Frank Holt and Lester Stoughton, two of his men.

Across the street, in front of the hardware store, Bob Kramer and Harry Dunning had tied their mounts. Down at the corner, Ken Bennett and Paul Deere were watering their horses at a trough, but they began leading the animals toward the hitch rail in front of the hardware store as soon as they saw Blake.

Kramer and Dunning would stay where they were to keep an eye on things along the street. They had ridden in together, while the other five had drifted into Gridley separately, with Blake showing up last.

Blake, Holt, Stoughton, Bennett, and Deere would enter the bank and carry out the actual holdup. They had done this half a dozen times before, pulling off the jobs without a hitch. They'd had to kill a couple of star packers who'd tried to stop them as they made their getaways, but that was the only blood that had been spilled.

Blake paused at the bank's front door. Bennett and Deere were tying their horses next to his. Holt and Stoughton would be inside already, standing at the counter where forms could be filled out, waiting for the others.

None of them bothered wearing masks. There was nothing very distinctive about any of them. They were all average height and build. They didn't shave for a couple of weeks before pulling a job, and as soon as they were well away, they would stop and scrape off the thick stubble. Any descriptions of them that were circulated by the law would be almost worthless.

It was better to be smart than lucky, Blake had decided early in his criminal career. He'd tried to abide by that maxim ever since.

He put his hand on the knob, twisted it, and walked into the bank.

Holt and Stoughton were right where they were supposed to be. Blake heard the footsteps of the two men following him right outside on the boardwalk. He left the door open so they could walk in unhindered.

The tellers' cages, three of them, were to the right. Only one was occupied at the moment. A couple of desks were to the left. Two young men in suits sat at those desks, working on papers spread out in front of them. Straight ahead and to the rear, behind a fencelike railing, was a larger desk where an older man sat in a swivel chair, reading a newspaper. That would be the bank president, Blake thought.

All the way at the back, on the right, was the thick door of the vault.

Blake walked past the two young clerks, one of whom looked up and said, "Excuse me, sir, can I help you?"

Blake smiled and said, "No thanks. I need to talk to your boss, there."

He nodded toward the man behind the big desk.

The older man must have heard the exchange. He lowered the newspaper and sat up straighter in the swivel chair as he looked at Blake, who was dressed like a reasonably successful rancher. There was nothing suspicious about his appearance, except maybe the two weeks' worth of beard, and that could be explained by the possibility that he had just gotten back from a cattle drive.

In which case, he might be in possession of a considerable amount of money from selling his herd, money he might want to deposit in the First Bank of Gridley.

That possibility made the bank president smile. He folded the paper and said, "Good day to you, sir. What can we do for you?"

Blake drew his gun, leveled it at the man, and said, "You can open that vault and empty it for us, so I won't have to blow a hole in you the size of my fist."

It was difficult to take in something like that immediately, so the bank president continued smiling at Blake for a heartbeat before he realized what was going on.

Then the smile vanished. A glare as dark as a looming thunderhead replaced it as the man rose to his feet and thundered, "How dare you!"

The other four bandits were in the bank by now, their guns drawn, and they were covering the two clerks and the lone teller. Blake flicked a glance at them, felt confident that everything was going smoothly so far, and opened the gate in the railing so he could step closer to the president's desk.

"Now that you got to bluster a little, get busy doing what I told you. I'm not joking, mister. I'll shoot you if you don't cooperate. I imagine one of these fine young fellows will be happy to open the vault if it means saving his own life."

The florid-faced older man opened and closed his mouth a couple of times as he stared down the barrel of Blake's gun. Then resignation appeared in his eyes. The lines of his face sagged in defeat. He dropped the folded paper on the desk and started to turn toward the vault.

Gun-thunder erupted on the street outside, clearly audible through the bank's open front door.

The racket made Blake twist around. It was an instinctive reaction, one he couldn't control. He looked across the street and saw Kramer and Dunning crouched by their horses, the guns in their hands spouting smoke and flame as they fired toward somebody Blake couldn't see.

Dunning suddenly tried to whirl around, evidently alerted by an attack from another direction. He didn't make it before a shotgun boomed. A load of buckshot struck him, shredding his midsection and lifting him off his feet to toss him backward into the street.

That was all Blake had time to see, because he heard shoe leather scuffing behind him and turned back to the desk to see the bank president charging around it at him.

Even though the man was older, he was bigger and heavier, with a longer reach. If he got hold of Blake, Blake might not be able to stop him from taking his gun.

So he pulled the trigger instead of risking that. The revolver bucked and roared against his palm. The bank president stopped like he'd run into a wall. His head jerked back, with a red-rimmed black hole now visible a couple of inches above his left eye.

His knees buckled and he went down hard, crashing to the floor in front of Blake.

More shots boomed, filling the air inside the bank with the deafening reports. Blake turned from the body of the man he'd just killed and saw his companions shooting the teller and the two clerks to doll rags. Maybe one of the bank workers had pulled a gun, or maybe the other outlaws had been too keyed up not to start pulling their triggers when the shooting started outside.

At this point, it didn't matter, Blake knew.

Hoping to come out of this disaster with something, he ran to the vault door and twisted the handle. Maybe it was unlocked.

The handle didn't budge, and all four of the men who might have known the combination were lying on the floor in bloody, unmoving heaps.

Blake bit back a curse and spun toward his men. "Go! Go! Get out of here!" he yelled at them as he charged toward the door.

As he passed the bank president's desk, he grabbed the folded newspaper. It had a few drops of crimson splattered on it. Blake couldn't have explained the impulse, even if someone had asked him about it. He didn't even think consciously about what he was doing, other than fleeing from the scene of the botched robbery.

The outlaws charged out of the bank. Across the street, Bob Kramer was mounted. He twisted back and forth in the saddle, throwing lead at the townspeople who were rushing toward the bank. Shots came back at him, forcing him to lean forward over his horse's neck.

Blake and the other four men threw themselves onto their horses as they fired wildly up and down the street. They weren't likely to hit anything, but maybe the flying bullets would make Gridley's defenders duck for cover.

The hammer of Blake's gun fell on an empty chamber as he kicked his horse into a run. He leaned forward, too, making himself as small a target as possible. The other five bank robbers followed him as he rode south out of the settlement as hard as he could.

He jammed the iron back in its holster and looked over his shoulder. The others were strung out in a ragged line. Men from town fired rifles after them. Blake saw dust kick up in several places where bullets struck, but none of the horses faltered and none of his men cried out or fell off.

The citizens of Gridley would put together a posse to come after them. Blake had no doubt about that. He and his men had gunned down at least four of the townspeople. No telling how many Kramer and Dunning had gotten during the exchange of fire outside. The other folks in the settlement wouldn't let that go.

So he continued pushing his horse as hard as he could. He would ride the beast into the ground if he had to, but a better course of action would be to watch for an isolated ranch where he and the others could steal some fresh horses.

They were in Colorado now and had been almost since they'd first galloped out of Gridley. That thought never entered Blake's mind. A posse bent on revenge wouldn't care about state lines. They would just keep coming until their horses played out or until the possemen had had enough. They might be in such a hurry to go after the outlaws that they would forget to bring along any supplies. That would force them to turn back.

Blake had seen it happen before.

The outlaws' lives depended on staying ahead of the pursuit until that happened.

That night, Blake and the others made camp in some rocky hills, in a little cup with ridges on three sides and a big boulder on the other that would block sight of the small fire they had built.

"I'm mighty sorry, Graham," Bob Kramer said as he hunkered next to the flames. He held a cup of coffee liberally laced with whiskey. "I reckon Harry just lost his head when he saw that badge-toter start to go in the bank. We would've whistled to signal you the way we have in the past, so you could've got the drop on him when he came in, but there just wasn't time. He came out of that mercantile and was almost at the bank door before we could do anything."

"So Harry shot him," Blake said. "Even though that roused the whole town against us."

Kramer shrugged. "Like I said, Harry lost his head."

"And he paid for it," Paul Deere put in.

"Yeah," Kramer agreed glumly. "We didn't know a deputy was going to charge up with a scattergun."

Even though he was seething with fury inside, Blake didn't show it. He was as calm as ever as he said, "It's a shame about Harry, but considering the circumstances, we were lucky to get off as lightly as we did. We lost just one man, and I'm pretty sure we've given that posse the slip."

"But we didn't get any loot," Frank Holt said, "and we need money, Graham. We're just about broke."

"I know," Blake said, nodding. "I'll think of something, boys. Don't worry."

There were bound to be other cow country banks in Colorado, he thought as he sat with his back propped against the boulder and nursed a cup of coffee.

The seven of them—six, now—had gotten together up in Montana and worked their way south through Wyoming, hitting banks and holding up a few stagecoaches along the way.

Blake had it in mind to wind up eventually in Mexico, so continuing south made sense. They would avoid Denver and the other large settlements and find a bank in another small town.

Paper crackled as he shifted his position. That reminded him of the newspaper he had crammed into his pocket after snatching it off the dead bank president's desk. He pulled it out now and unfolded it, smoothing the wrinkled, bloodsplattered newsprint.

"What's that?" Lester Stoughton asked.

"A newspaper."

"I can see that." Stoughton frowned. "Is that the paper that bank president was readin' when we went in there?"

"That's right."

"So *that's* the haul we made from the bank?"

"The vault was locked," Blake snapped, "and with all those guns going off, there wasn't time to try for any cash in the tellers' cages. I like to stay informed about what's going on in the world, so I grabbed the paper on the way out."

"You're not like most bank robbers, Graham, you know that?" Deere observed.

Blake ignored the comment and looked at the newspaper in the flickering firelight. It came from Denver, and nothing on the front page really caught his attention until he noticed a story below the fold that appeared to have been reprinted from another Colorado paper, the *Big Rock Journal*.

As Blake read, his heart began to slug harder in his chest. This story was interesting, very interesting . . .

And it might be just what they needed to recover from the disaster in Gridley.

CHAPTER 7

Edgar Ford had described the spot where he found his father's body well enough to Monte that Smoke had no trouble locating it, as well, once the sheriff had passed along the information to him.

Pearlie and Cal had both lobbied heavily to be allowed to come along on the hunt. Smoke didn't need to go out looking for that killer bear on his own, they argued. Some unforeseen disaster might befall him. Even Smoke Jensen could run afoul of bad luck, and then there wouldn't be anybody around to help him.

Despite all the strong friendships he'd made in his life, Smoke knew he could be something of a loner at times. He supposed he'd developed that solitary streak during the months-long spell when he'd been a wanted outlaw, on the run from the spurious charges against him, friendless and alone with enemies on every hand.

But things were different now, he reminded himself. He had friends and family and was a well-liked, thoroughly respected citizen. There was no reason for him to turn away help.

With that in mind, and also to soothe any worries Sally might have about him, he agreed to let Pearlie and Cal accompany him, but only one at a time.

"You can take turns," Smoke told them. "Figure out between you who gets to come along first."

With Pearlie being the foreman, Cal knew he would pull rank, so to speak, so he got in a gibe first.

"Age before beauty, isn't that the old saying? That means I reckon you get first crack at that bear, Pearlie."

"Reckon I'd go first either way," Pearlie shot back. "Too bad for you, Cal. I figure Smoke and I will bring back that dang bear's hide mighty quick-like."

"Not unless we do a better job of finding it than I have so far," Smoke pointed out.

On that day, it didn't seem like his luck was going to change. He and Pearlie were both good trackers, but even though they found the spot where Roy Ford had been killed, they weren't able to turn up any bear tracks.

"How does a critter that size manage to move around without leavin' any sign?" Pearlie wanted to know.

"Sometimes he does leave sign. Broken branches, bits of hair stuck on things, a paw print here and there . . . He's no phantom, but he *is* clever."

"Or she."

"Or she," Smoke agreed. "We don't really know."

Pearlie rubbed his chin. "I wonder if it could be a mama bear with a den somewhere around here. They can go plumb loco sometimes if they think somethin' is threatenin' their cubs."

That was an angle Smoke hadn't considered. It might have some validity, he decided. His gut told him that probably wasn't the case, but they couldn't rule it out.

"We'll look for smaller tracks, too," he told Pearlie. "Just in case there are cubs around."

They followed the ridge all the way to Rockford Pass and on to the other side without finding bear tracks of any size. The only sign they came across was hoofprints, and there was nothing unusual about that. Not a lot of people used this pass when leaving the valley to the north, but it was a route known to many.

Those horses that had busted out of Roy Ford's pasture were still missing, too. They could have left the tracks.

As the days passed, Smoke continued searching for the bear, making wide circles out into the valley from the site of Ford's killing, since that was the last place the beast was known to have been. Sometimes Cal was with him, sometimes Pearlie, and their frustration grew just like Smoke's did.

"I swear," Cal said one day as they rode next to a small creek, "I figured Pearlie would find that critter if anybody could. He can sniff out bear sign a mile away!"

Smoke laughed. "There's a big difference between real bear sign and those treats that Sally fries up," he said, referring to the doughnuts she made, often called bear sign by cowboys because their circular shape resembled the tracks left by the big, shaggy creatures.

"Oh, I know that," Cal said. "I was just joshin'. Something to pass the time, I reckon."

The creek reached a spot where it tumbled down a slope for about twenty feet, forming a miniature waterfall. The two riders reined in for a moment.

They were high enough there that they could see out across a fairly wide, level vista. Smoke made out a trail that followed the far side of the flats, a mile or more away, before the ground started rising again.

He spotted something moving along that trail and leaned forward in his saddle. Cal noticed the reaction and said quickly, "What is it, Smoke? You see something?"

"Yeah, but it's not what I thought at first." Smoke pointed. "There's a wagon over yonder, heading toward Big Rock. At first, all I saw was movement, but then I realized it was too big even to be a rogue grizzly bear."

Cal shaded his eyes with his hand as he peered toward the distant trail. "Who do you reckon it is? Looks like the back of it's boxed in, not open or with a canvas cover like a ranch wagon would be. Whoever it is must live in it."

A smile tugged at Smoke's lips as he said, "I've got a hunch it might be old Doc Endicott."

"A traveling sawbones?"

Smoke shook his head. "I don't know if he's a real doctor or not, but that's what he always called himself. He's a peddler and a tinker. Sells all sorts of goods out of his wagon, and he can repair lots of different kinds of machinery. He used to come through these parts pretty often, but it's been several years since I've seen him. Didn't know if he was even still alive, to tell you the truth, but from what I can tell at this distance, that looks like his wagon."

"Maybe we'd better try to catch up to him and warn him to be on the lookout for that bear."

"Might not be a bad idea," Smoke said, nodding slowly. "Besides, if it is Doc, I wouldn't mind saying howdy to him. Come on."

Smoke heeled his horse into motion, and they set off beside the waterfall, down the slope to cross the flats toward the distant trail.

Dr. Cleveland J. Endicott clucked at the horses pulling his wagon and lightly slapped the reins against their backs. He was eager to reach Big Rock and talk to some old friends there.

It was a warm day, but that wasn't the only reason sweat ran down Endicott's round, flushed face.

He was nervous, too. He had heard about what had happened in these parts. His pale blue eyes, set deep in pits of gristle under bushy white eyebrows, darted back and forth between both sides of the trail as they searched for any potential threats.

So far, Endicott hadn't seen anything out of the ordinary on this hasty journey, but that didn't mean trouble couldn't be waiting right around the next bend in the trail.

He wasn't accustomed to being this afraid. He didn't like it.

For most of the past fifteen years, he would have said that all the fear had been knocked out of him by the war. After you'd worked in a field hospital during a battle, with the fetid air in the tent reeking from the smells of powder smoke, blood, and rotting flesh, with the ground shaking almost constantly under your feet from the cannon fire bombarding the area, with men screaming and mangled arms and legs you'd just sawed off of unlucky young soldiers piling up around your feet . . .

After you'd lived through that sort of experience, it seemed reasonable that nothing would ever be bad enough to bother you again.

But that was wrong, Endicott realized now.

Having his own mortality brought home to him was enough to rattle any man's nerves, no matter what he'd been through in the past.

If you stuck high-topped boots, woolen trousers, a once-white shirt, a fraying cravat, a long gray duster, and a black derby on a water barrel, that would look sort of like Dr. Cleveland J. Endicott. His name, complete with the title, was painted on both sides of the wagon he drove, although he hadn't practiced medicine since the end of the war and had sworn never to do so again. He'd had enough of battling futilely against the frailties and limitations of the human body.

He much preferred selling pots and pans, doodads and

foofaraws, sharpening knives, and working on windmills. Nobody died because of any of those things.

The four big draft horses that pulled Endicott's wagon were strong and sturdy, but they didn't possess much speed. They tended to plod along. He kept trying to urge them to a faster pace because he was eager to reach his destination, but there was only so much he could do to hurry them.

Then he drove past some rocks and around a bend, and what was waiting in the trail made the horses come to a rearing, sliding halt as Endicott reflexively hauled back on the reins.

He might have tried to pull the team around and flee, but the rocks crowded in too close on both sides. He dropped the reins, twisted on the seat, and attempted to scramble onto the top of the wagon.

The effort was doomed to failure. Even if he'd made it, that wouldn't have saved him. He was halfway onto the roof when he was grabbed, and thrown to the ground. His derby flew off, landed in the trail, and rolled a couple of feet before curving to the side and wobbling to an upside-down stop.

Endicott tried frantically to get up but was slammed back down. The impact stunned him so that he couldn't get out of the way of the blow that smashed into the side of his head.

That didn't quite knock him unconscious. He was barely aware of being dragged along the trail and then off of it.

Then came pain, enough of it to make him scream, but only once before he spiraled down into never-ending blackness.

The same way so many of those boys on his operating table had done, all those years ago.

* * *

Smoke and Cal made good time as they traveled across the flats. They were mounted on good horses, and the terrain was accommodating. They reached the trail on the far side and turned to follow it southeast, the same direction the wagon they had seen a short time earlier had been traveling.

That wagon had been rolling at a pretty good clip, Smoke recalled, which was a little puzzling if it belonged to the old peddler Doc Endicott. Smoke couldn't remember ever seeing the old-timer in a hurry. He was always easygoing and slow-moving.

Even so, Smoke expected to catch up to the wagon in a relatively short period of time. Two men on horseback could move faster than a good-sized vehicle could.

"Does this Doc fella live in his wagon?" Cal asked.

"As far as I know, he does. He might have a regular home somewhere else. I wouldn't have any idea about that, but when he's traveling around the country he stays in the wagon. At least, he did on all his other visits to Big Rock." Smoke paused, then added, "But like I said, it's been a while."

"Must've been before I was around these parts," Cal commented, "because I don't remember the hombre at all. Does he put on, like, a medicine show?"

Smoke shook his head. "No, he doesn't sell any kind of snake oil. Just regular household goods. Pots and pans, dishes, cutlery, sewing supplies for the ladies, dress material, curtains, hand mirrors, shaving razors . . . I don't reckon I could tell you all the things he sells. He has one of those wheels you operate with your foot to sharpen knives and ax blades, things like that. Always does quite a bit of business along those lines. Any machine that has gears in it, he can make it work, no matter how bad it's messed up."

"Sounds like a—what do you call it—jack of all trades."

"That's a pretty good description of him," Smoke agreed. "He's a friendly cuss, too, always with a laugh or a joke." Again, Smoke fell silent for a moment before continuing. "I always got the feeling he wasn't really as jolly as he made out to be, though. Like he was covering up for some sort of pain in the past."

Cal looked over at him. "Something he did that weighs on his conscience, you mean?"

"No, not exactly. It wasn't guilt I saw in his eyes. I reckon . . . horror would be more like it."

Cal shuddered a little as he rode. "The fella's come to the right place, then," he said. "With that rogue grizzly on the loose and nobody knowing where it's gonna turn up next, folks around here are pretty horrified, all right."

They were approaching an area where scattered rocks crowded close to the trail on both sides. Smoke frowned as he looked past the rocks and spotted something in the shade of some trees a couple of hundred yards farther on.

"Isn't that the wagon we've been following?" he said.

Cal squinted and said, "Sure looks like it. Painted bright red and yellow like it is, it'd be hard to mistake it for anything else. Maybe this Doc Endicott fella stopped to rest his team."

"Maybe," Smoke agreed, but he pressed his bootheels a little harder against his horse's flanks and sent the animal trotting forward at a faster pace. Cal followed suit without asking.

As they came up to the wagon, Smoke read the lettering on the side that confirmed the vehicle belonged to Dr. Cleveland J. Endicott. The words TRAVELING EMPORIUM, KNIFE SHARPENING, AND MECHANICAL REPAIR were painted underneath the name in fancy script.

Smoke reined in and lifted his voice to call, "Doc! Doc Endicott!"

"Reckon he's in the back?" Cal asked. He pointed to a door in the rear wall of the enclosure, much like the door of a Gypsy caravan.

Smoke moved his horse over so he could lean from the saddle and rap on the door. "Doc! Are you in there? Are you all right?"

"Doesn't look like he's anywhere around, Smoke," Cal said with a frown. He stood up in the stirrups and looked around. "I don't see him anywhere. Where do you reckon he went?"

A sense of unease stirred inside Smoke. "We weren't all that far behind him. The wagon couldn't have been stopped here for very long. Which means that if he's on foot, he couldn't have gotten very far." Smoke drew his Winchester from the saddle boot. "Let's split up and take a look around. Be careful."

Cal nodded and pulled his rifle from its saddle sheath. Smoke told him to take the area to the right of the trail, while Smoke searched on the left. They moved out, riding slowly and warily, the Winchesters held ready.

Smoke rode out about fifty yards from the trail and then began riding in increasingly larger circles as he studied the ground for tracks or anything else that might point him toward the man he was looking for. He called, "Doc! Doc Endicott!" and heard Cal doing the same thing on the other side of the trail.

After several minutes of futile searching, Cal shouted, "Smoke! Hey, Smoke, over here!"

The young cowboy sounded excited but not particularly alarmed. Whatever he had found wasn't an urgent threat, but it was something he thought Smoke needed to take a look at.

Smoke rode to join him. Cal pointed to something on the ground and said, "Those are drag marks, aren't they?"

Smoke studied the marks, which were long and narrow and relatively straight. After a moment, he said, "Looks like what a man's bootheels might leave if he were being dragged, all right, but something had to be dragging him. Do you see any paw prints?"

Cal studied the ground intently, then let out an excited yelp and pointed again.

"There!"

Smoke moved his horse over next to Cal's and peered down. His heart hammered harder as he saw the same print Cal had spotted.

"It's the grizzly, Smoke! No doubt about it."

Smoke swung down from the saddle and hunkered next to the track for a long moment before saying, "Bear sign, all right, and not the good kind."

"That killer grizzly got Doc Endicott," Cal said.

"We don't know that for a fact yet," Smoke cautioned as he straightened. "Let's see if we can follow those marks."

Smoke mounted again. He and Cal rode slowly, keeping their eyes on what they had taken to be drag marks. Sometimes the sign vanished for a short stretch, then reappeared, depending on what kind of ground they were covering. Some of it was too rocky to take a print.

They found several more bear tracks, as well. Beyond a doubt, the trail they were following led toward a thick clump of trees and brush that backed up against a bluff.

As they came closer to it, Cal looked askance at the vegetation and said, "Uh, Smoke . . . I really don't want you to think poorly of me, but I'm not sure I want to go poking around in there. Not if there might be a monster grizzly with a taste for human flesh hiding in that brush."

"Yeah, but an innocent man might be in there, too," Smoke reminded him.

"Dadgum it. I guess we don't really have any choice, do we?"

"Not really," Smoke agreed, "but I want you to wait out here while I go in and take a look."

"Not hardly! I mean, I don't want to go against what you say to do. You're the boss, after all, but it doesn't seem fair for you to run all the risk."

Smoke said, "You don't understand. I want you to wait out here so there'll be somebody to come and rescue me if that bear is in there. It'll be up to you, Cal."

"Well . . . I reckon you're just trying to make me feel better." Cal swallowed. "But I won't argue with you. Just be careful, all right?"

Smoke slid his Winchester back in the saddle boot and pulled the Sharps from the scabbard on the horse's other side. He checked to make sure the heavy-caliber rifle was loaded and then dismounted in front of the thicket.

"That Sharps is a single-shot," Cal said. "What if one round's not enough?"

"I have my Colt," Smoke reminded him, "and it's better for close work, anyway. Things come right down to it, I've got a knife, too."

"Lord have mercy," Cal muttered. "Only Smoke Jensen would be talking about fighting a giant grizzly with a knife."

"Preacher did it one time," Smoke said. "He won, too. Surely you've heard him tell that story."

"Well, yeah, but that's Preacher."

Smoke would have laughed if the situation hadn't been potentially so serious. He knew what Cal meant about Preacher. The old mountain man was so legendary that it was hard to believe any feat might be beyond him, even slaying a grizzly bear with nothing but a knife.

As Preacher's friend Audie, the diminutive professor

turned fur trapper, had once said of him, he was like a hero out of mythology, capable of things beyond the ken of mortal men.

But in Preacher's case, it was true: he really had killed a bear in a hand-to-paw fight, armed only with a knife.

As Smoke looked at the thicket, he thought, not for the first time, that it would have been nice to have Preacher there with him . . .

He paused only for a heartbeat, then pressed forward into the dense growth.

CHAPTER 8

Smoke used the barrel of the Sharps to push aside some of the brush. He looked for broken branches and bits of hair like he had seen at the spot where Chuck Haskell's body had been found.

After a few moments, he stiffened and then reached out to pluck a tuft of hair from the rough bark of a pine tree trunk. Whatever had scraped by there had knocked some of the bark off, as well. Smoke saw the small pieces lying on the ground at the base of the tree.

"Doc?" he called softly, not expecting any answer.

When he didn't get one, he moved deeper into the thicket. Smoke's sense of smell was as keen as his other senses. He sniffed the air, testing it for the rank odor of bear.

He didn't smell that, but he did detect something else in the air, a sharp, coppery tang that put his teeth on edge.

That was the scent of freshly spilled blood.

Smoke forced his way past more of the clinging branches, maneuvered around some trees, then stopped short as he caught sight of something red through tiny gaps in the brush.

After waiting a few seconds to make sure it wasn't moving, he reached out with the Sharps and moved some branches aside with the barrel.

A blood-covered ruin of a face peered back at him, unseeingly.

Smoke, who seldom cursed, caught his breath and then bit back the oath that the gory sight almost startled out of him.

The dead man's features were so damaged that it was difficult to recognize him, but Smoke was confident it was Doc Endicott. As he moved closer and pushed more branches aside, he got a better look at the body. The stocky shape and the distinctive garb, right down to the familiar derby hat lying on the ground next to the corpse, confirmed what he'd expected to find.

"Hey, Cal!"

"Yeah, Smoke?"

"Endicott's in here, all right. Dead. And it looks like the bear's gone."

"I never met the man, but I'm sure sorry he didn't make it." The young cowboy paused, then asked, "Is he . . . uh, is he torn up pretty bad?"

"That's right," Smoke said. Deep gashes that had bled freely covered not only Endicott's face but also his chest and arms and legs. The damage wasn't quite as extensive as it had been on the other bodies, but almost.

Maybe that killer grizzly was getting jaded, Smoke thought. *Maybe killing humans wasn't as much of a thrill as it had been starting out.*

"You need some help getting him out of there?"

"Yeah, bring a blanket and come take this rifle from me."

Cal forced his way into the thicket, grunting with effort as he struggled through the brush. He reached Smoke's side and traded the rolled-up blanket he'd brought with him for the rifle.

"You sure the bear's gone?"

"I don't see or smell it, so I assume it is. Keep your eyes open, anyway," Smoke added.

"Oh, believe me, I intend to."

Cal looked around nervously, his head on a swivel as he kept his thumb looped over the Sharps' hammer, ready to draw it back and fire if he needed to.

Getting the body bundled up in the blanket was awkward, but Smoke managed. Then with the great strength in those broad shoulders, he lifted Endicott and carried him out of the thicket as he would have a baby.

Cal followed, still watchful.

They went to the peddler's wagon, where Cal opened the door at the back, and Smoke leaned in to place the body carefully on the floor, in a narrow aisle between a bunk and some storage cabinets. Sections of the wagon's sides lifted on the outside and locked open to reveal display shelves, Smoke recalled from Endicott's previous visits to Big Rock.

Cal said, "Looks like you got some blood on your shirt anyway, even with him wrapped up in that blanket."

"I'm not surprised. Sally's pretty good about being able to get blood out of a shirt."

"Somehow I'm not surprised by that," Cal said. "I'm sure she's had plenty of practice."

"Why don't you tie your horse to the back of the wagon? You can drive it to town, unless you'd rather I do it."

"No, I don't mind driving. Might be a good idea for you to ride a little ahead and make sure that bear's not still lurking around somewhere."

That seemed like a pretty good idea to Smoke, too. He waited until Cal climbed onto the driver's seat and took up the reins before he nudged his mount into motion.

He held the animal to a slow walk as he looked at something in the trail that caught his eye. It was a slightly weaving mark in the dust, a sinuous shape that reminded him of a snake's path. But it only ran for about a dozen feet before disappearing next to a very faint, circular depression in the dust some six inches in diameter.

The wagon was already rolling. The team's hooves obliterated that serpentlike mark before Smoke thought to tell Cal to hold up a minute.

It probably wasn't important anyway, he thought as he heeled his horse to a faster gait.

Their route took them past the road to the Sugarloaf, but they bypassed the ranch and headed directly to town. The wagon's arrival in Big Rock generated an immediate uproar, as Smoke had known it would.

Many of the citizens had lived there long enough to recognize Doc Endicott's vehicle, even though he hadn't paid a visit to the settlement in several years. The name written in gaudy letters on both sides confirmed that.

The fact that Calvin Woods was on the driver's seat, handling the team, instead of the rotund peddler, alerted people that something was wrong. Some of them gathered around the wagon and walked alongside it as they called questions to Smoke and Cal.

Monte Carson must have heard the commotion. Smoke was headed for the sheriff's office, but before he got there, Monte had emerged from the building and was waiting on the porch with a worried frown on his face.

"Howdy, Smoke," Monte called. "Isn't that old Doc Endicott's wagon? Never mind, that's a dumb question. I see his name on it, but where's Doc?"

Smoke reined in, and Cal brought the wagon to a stop in front of the office. Smoke leaned forward in the saddle, inclined his head toward the wagon, and said, "He's in there."

"Sick? Or . . ."

The grim look on Smoke's face answered the question.

On the way into town, he had considered trying to keep the peddler's death a secret, but he knew there was no hope of doing that for very long, not without waiting until the middle of the night and then sneaking the body into the undertaking part of Tom Nunnley's business, behind the hardware store.

Even then, any secrecy would only be temporary. Word of what had happened was bound to get out, and once one or two people knew the truth, it would spread like wildfire through Big Rock.

Monte sighed and stepped down off the porch. "Do I want to ask what happened to him?"

"I reckon you can probably guess. Cal and I were out . . . hunting . . . when we came across his wagon. He wasn't with it, but we found him in a thicket not too far off."

"And there was evidence of . . . ?"

"There was," Smoke said.

The curious townspeople had backed off a bit when the wagon stopped in front of the sheriff's office, but one man was close enough to hear what Smoke and Monte were saying and understand the implications. He turned his head toward the crowd and shouted, "It was the bear! That rogue grizzly got old Doc Endicott!"

Instantly, an uproar filled the street. The commotion drew even more people from the nearby buildings. One of Monte's deputies hurried up to see what was going on.

"Go inside and get a shotgun," Monte told the man. "You won't need it, but just the sight of it will make folks stay back more. Then climb on that wagon next to Cal and ride with him down to Tom Nunnley's place. Cal, take it on around back so Tom can get to work."

Cal nodded.

"Smoke, stay here with me, if you wouldn't mind," Monte went on.

"Sure," Smoke said. He swung down from the saddle and looped the horse's reins around the hitch rail, then he and the sheriff stepped back onto the porch.

Some of the crowd started to follow the wagon as Cal turned it toward the undertaker's, but Monte shouted, "Everybody get back here! There's no reason for you to go along and get in the way. I want all of you to hear me out!"

"There's no time to listen to any speechifyin'!" one man objected. "I'm goin' home to get my rifle, and then I'm gonna find that damn bear and kill it!"

Whoops of agreement went up from at least a dozen men. Another said, "If everybody in the valley goes out, we can't help but find that blasted bear!"

Monte raised his arms. "Settle down, settle down!" he ordered. "Forming an armed mob to go rampaging through the valley is the *last* thing you need to do!"

"Well, then, what do you think we ought to do, Sheriff?"

"Sit around waitin' until the bear gets us, too?"

"I got kids, and I'm gonna protect 'em, by grab!"

Monte let the angry shouts go on for a minute or so. There was nothing else he could do. He looked over at Smoke, who just shook his head. He didn't have any helpful suggestions, either.

Finally, Monte yelled for quiet again. When the crowd gradually fell silent, he said, "Smoke has been trying to track down that bear, and he'll keep on—"

Phil Clinton had made his way to the front of the crowd. The newspaperman interrupted Monte by saying, "Smoke, you know nobody around here respects you more than I do, but you've been hunting that bear for weeks now and haven't found anything except more victims!"

"That's true enough," Smoke allowed. "I won't deny it, but you know me, Phil. Once I set out to do something, I stick with it until I get it done. I'm stubborn that way."

"Maybe so," yelled another member of the crowd, "but how many folks will have to die between now and then?"

Smoke's jaw tightened. He didn't like what was happening. He was as frustrated as he had been in a long time, and that feeling ate at him.

"All I can say is I haven't given up on trying to find that bear and deal with it, once and for all."

"Unless somebody beats you to it!" More eager whoops filled the air. "Come on, boys, let's go over to the Brown Dirt Cowboy and make some plans. This is gonna be the biggest hunt this valley has ever seen!"

Most of the men stomped off toward the saloon, yelling excitedly. Monte sighed and said, "More like the biggest disaster this valley has ever seen."

"More than likely," Smoke agreed.

"You think I ought to threaten to arrest all of them if they set foot outside of town with a rifle?"

"Is your jail big enough to hold most of the men in Big Rock?"

Monte shook his head and said, "You know it's not."

"Then it seems like all you can do is hope that nobody gets killed when the shooting starts."

"Because when you get that many liquored-up idiots out there looking to kill something . . . it's only a matter of time until it turns into a slaughter."

That wasn't quite the way things played out over the next week, but not for lack of effort from the incensed citizens of the valley.

Every man in the area who had some time on his hands and friends to egg him on became a bear hunter. Groups of heavily armed men rode out of Big Rock and scoured the valley from one end to the other. More than once, they

spotted something suspicious, got excited, and began
blazing away at it, only to discover that they were shooting
at another group of hunters.

"A few fellas have been winged," Monte said when he
told Smoke about it, "but nobody's been killed yet. That's
pure luck, though, and I don't know how long it can hold
up. Are you and Pearlie and Cal still looking for that bear?"

Smoke nodded. "We've ridden out every day, although
Pearlie says we're fools to risk our necks that way. He's
convinced somebody's going to mistake us for the bear and
throw lead at us."

"I wouldn't be a bit surprised."

They were on the porch and loading dock in front of
Goldstein's Mercantile, Big Rock's biggest and best
general store. Sally needed to pick up some supplies and
was inside the store at the moment. Smoke had ridden into
town with her that day instead of searching for the killer
grizzly again. He had told Pearlie and Cal to take a break
from the unsatisfying quest, as well.

Maybe one of the other hunting parties would have more
luck than Smoke and his friends had had.

The drumming of rapid hoofbeats made both men look
around. A small figure on horseback was moving along the
street. The urgency of the horse's gait reminded Smoke of
the day Roy Ford's family had brought his body into town.

"Who's that?" Monte asked as he frowned toward the
approaching rider.

"The Jackson boy's the only one I can think of who's
that much of a carrottop," Smoke said.

The youngster on the fast-moving horse appeared to be
about twelve years old. His hair was a bright orange/red,
exactly like a carrot, as Smoke had commented, and very
visible because he wore no hat.

He was clad in overalls and a homespun shirt, suitable

garb for farming, which was what he and his family did on a small homestead about five miles southeast of Big Rock.

Monte stepped to the edge of the porch and lifted a hand to flag down the hurrying boy, but the lad was already veering his mount in that direction anyway, having spotted the lawman.

"Sheriff!" he cried. "Sheriff Carson!"

"Slow down, son," Monte said as the boy pulled his lathered mount to a stop. "Why are you in such an all-fired big hurry? What's wrong?"

"It's that bear, Sheriff! The bear that everybody keeps talkin' about!"

Smoke's spirits sank at the thought that they were about to hear another grim tale of violent death, but he wasn't the sort to give in to emotions like that. He stepped forward, too, next to Monte, and said, "Tell us what happened, Emery." He had remembered the boy's first name after a moment's thought.

Emery Jackson's chest rose and fell rapidly as he leaned on the saddle horn and tried to catch his breath after the hard ride. He said, "We were out in the patch where we grow corn . . . my pa and my little brother and me . . . when all of a sudden he was just there, like he came out of nowhere!"

"A bear?" Monte said.

"Not just a bear, Sheriff. *The* bear! The biggest critter I ever laid eyes on!"

"Did it attack you?" Smoke said. "Did it hurt your pa or your brother?"

He had noticed already that there were no bloodstains on Emery's clothing and he appeared to be unharmed, just shaken.

"No, he . . . he didn't charge us or anything like that, thank goodness. He just stood up on his hind legs and roared real loud. Loud enough to make my ears hurt. And he waved those big paws around. I swear, they were like tree trunks with claws on 'em, Mr. Jensen."

"What did you do?" Monte asked.

"Pa told me and my brother to run back to our cabin and make sure our ma and our little sister were inside and the door was barred. He said he'd keep the bear from hurtin' us."

"Did he have a gun?" Smoke asked.

"His rifle was leanin' against a tree at the edge of the field, but it ain't big enough to be good for shootin' much of anything except squirrels and possums and raccoons and suchlike. But he was sidlin' over to get it anyway when that bear went to flailin' around and knockin' down cornstalks. We all ran then, even my pa."

"Did the bear come after you?"

Emery had caught his breath and calmed down a little. He frowned and said, "No, sir, he never did. He just acted like . . . well, like he was tryin' to scare us by showin' off how big and fierce he was. And then when we yelled and run off, he got back down on all fours and lumbered away through the cornfield. We watched him go."

"What happened then?" Monte wanted to know.

"My pa told me to throw my saddle on my pony, since it's the fastest horse we got, and rattle my hocks into town so I could tell you about the bear, Sheriff. He said you might want to bring a posse out there and try to follow its trail. He forted up in the house with my ma and my little brother and sister."

Smoke said, "Your pa hasn't been out hunting that bear?"

Emery shook his head. "No, sir, we heard about it, of course, but he said he's a farmer, not a hunter, and anyway, like I said, his rifle ain't near big enough to bring down a bear, and it's the only gun he's got. So he said somebody else'd have to find that dang bear and kill it. Only he didn't say dang bear, he said something a lot worse, and my ma shushed him."

Monte nodded and said, "You did a good job of riding in to let us know what happened, son. Why don't you tie up your pony and let it rest a spell before you start home? While you're waiting, you can go on in the store and tell Mr. Goldstein I said for him to give you a couple of pieces of candy. I'll stand good for it."

Emery scrambled down from the saddle and said, "Gee, thanks, Sheriff!"

Once the boy had gone inside, Monte looked at Smoke and said, "That whole family is lucky the bear didn't wipe them out."

"Maybe," Smoke allowed, nodding slowly.

"There's something funny about it, though," Monte said. "The Jackson farm is southeast of town, and so far all the bear sightings have been west or northwest of Big Rock."

"Not that funny," Smoke said. "Bears can range for quite a distance. Maybe he's bored and looking for new territory."

Monte grunted. "New victims, you mean."

"From the sound of young Emery's story, the bear didn't make any effort to hurt them. Now *that's* a little odd."

"Come to think of it," Monte mused, "the first ones who spotted him were Nelse Andersen and Dean McKinley, and he didn't attack them, either. He chased McKinley, but a lot of animals will chase something that runs from them. It's just instinct."

Smoke agreed with that but said, "There's no doubt, though, that it killed Chuck Haskell, Roy Ford, and old Doc Endicott. Once a predator goes rogue and gets a taste for human flesh, it hardly ever goes back to its old ways."

"Well, I may not understand it," Monte said, "but I'm just glad Tom Nunnley doesn't have any new bodies to get ready for burying." A little shudder ran through the lawman. "I hate to think about what that beast might've done to those children."

Smoke didn't want to think about that, either, so he was glad when Sally came out of the mercantile just then with a couple of Goldstein's clerks following her, carrying the crates of supplies she had bought. They loaded the goods in the back of the wagon, Smoke helped Sally to the seat, where she took up the reins, then he swung up into the saddle of the horse he had ridden into town. They said their goodbyes to Monte and headed back to the Sugarloaf.

Sally commented to Smoke later that he was quieter than usual during the drive.

He just nodded, not explaining that he had some unexpected thoughts stirring around in his mind. He'd been trying to make sense of them.

He didn't mention that he hadn't had much luck with that effort, either.

CHAPTER 9

Graham Blake was tying his horse to the hitch rail in front of the Brown Dirt Cowboy Saloon when the red-headed kid went galloping past him like savage Indians were after him.

Blake watched with interest as the youngster reined in and talked to two men standing on the front porch of a mercantile. Sunlight glinted from the badge pinned to the vest that one of the men wore.

That would be the local law, Blake thought. A middle-aged, weathered man who still gave off an air of competence and vitality. A man to watch out for, Blake decided. He wouldn't forget when it came time for him and his men to carry out their business in Big Rock.

There was nothing special about the man standing with the lawdog, other than the fact that his shoulders were broader than most men's. He wasn't wearing a badge, so he wasn't a deputy. Blake dismissed the man from his mind.

He went into the Brown Dirt Cowboy and headed for the bar, seemingly intent on nothing more than getting a drink.

Blake took a half-dollar from his pocket and tapped the bar with it, not loudly or peremptorily, but the gesture was enough to catch the attention of the heavyset, balding, middle-aged bartender anyway. He ambled up on the other side of the hardwood, smiled, and asked in a deep, gravelly voice, "What can I do for you, mister?"

"I'll have a beer," Blake said.

"New in Big Rock, ain't you?" the bartender asked as he filled a mug from the tap on a keg. "I don't recall seein' you before."

"I just rode in," Blake admitted.

Foam spilled over the top of the mug as the man set it on the hardwood. "I got a good memory for faces, if I do say so myself. Name's Pudge. Well, that's not really my name, but that's what everybody calls me. You can see why."

He patted the rounded belly under the apron he wore and grinned.

"My ma named me Horace, but to tell you the truth, mister, nobody's called me that for years and that's just fine with me. Never cared for it, no, sir. Pudge suits me just fine. For a while when I was in the army, some of my friends tried to call me Slim, since it's just the opposite. You know, like how sometimes a really tall fella will be called Shorty. But it never seemed to stick, so they decided on Pudge and that worked just fine. What do they call you?"

Clearly, this bartender was in love with the sound of his own voice. That might get annoying in a hurry if somebody had to listen to him all the time, but for now, Blake was glad the man was so garrulous. That might be a stroke of luck.

"My name is Blake."

"First or last?" Without giving Blake a chance to answer, Pudge went on, "Never mind, it don't really matter, does it? If you're like me, you'll answer to just about anything anybody calls you, as long as it ain't late for dinner!"

Blake smiled and drank some of the beer while Pudge haw-hawed at his own joke. He was wondering about the best way of steering the conversation in the direction he wanted it to go when the bartender took care of that problem for him.

"What brings you to Big Rock, Mr. Blake? I'll bet you heard about that bear and came to hunt it, didn't you?"

"Bear?" Blake repeated, as if he had no idea what Pudge was talking about.

"Yeah, that killer grizzly. There's been stories about it in the newspapers all over the state, from what I've heard. Mr. Phil Clinton, he's our newspaper editor here, he wrote a story about it, and then the papers in Denver printed it, too, and then the whole thing just spread out all over. It's big news."

Blake took another drink and said, "You know, it seems like I have heard something about that."

"I don't see how you could've missed it. It's big news all over. This giant bear has been roamin' around the valley killin' folks. Killed a bunch so far. Well, three dead men, so maybe not a bunch, but still, that's pretty bad."

"Sounds like it," Blake agreed mildly.

"It's just a matter of time until somebody finds the blamed bruin and kills it, though. There are huntin' parties all over the valley lookin' for it. I'd say half the men in town are off on a bear hunt. Maybe more."

Blake nodded and said, "I thought the town looked a little empty when I rode in. Is there a bounty posted on this bear?"

"No, not that I know of, but say, that's a dandy idea! Some of the men who own businesses here in town, like my boss, Mr. Emmett Brown, ought to get together and put up a bounty. I might just say somethin' to Mr. Brown about it. I'd be happy to give you credit for the idea, though, Mr. Blake."

"No, no, don't worry about that," Blake said as he shook his head. "Don't even mention me. Tell him you came up with it on your own, Pudge."

"Really? Well, that's mighty nice o' you, sir, mighty nice! Although, when you stop and think about it, even if there ain't no actual bounty on that bear, the fella who finally tracks it down and kills it will do all right for hisself, let me tell you. Why, his money won't be any good anywhere in town for a while, folks'll be so grateful to him. Yes, sir. But a ree-ward would make it even better, wouldn't it? You sure you don't want any credit for the idea?"

"No," Blake said, smiling faintly. "I think I've already gotten what I came to Big Rock for."

"Oh? What's that?"

Blake lifted the mug. "A good cold beer and a pleasant conversation."

And confirmation of the idea that had been in his head ever since he'd looked at that blood-spattered newspaper he'd taken from the dead bank president in Gridley, Wyoming.

The next day, Smoke and Pearlie rode to Big Rock, on through town, and then out the trail to the Jackson farm. This was the area where the valley gradually opened back out and the mountains and foothills fell behind to the west. While the area was still well suited for ranching, the less rugged terrain made it more amenable for farming, as well, and a number of homesteaders had moved in during recent years.

That day, just in the five miles between Big Rock and the Jackson place, Smoke and Pearlie saw several large groups of mounted men riding back and forth, clearly looking for something.

Smoke had no doubts about the object of their search: those riders were on a bear hunt, just like he and Pearlie were.

"I don't like the looks of this, Smoke," Pearlie said when they were about halfway to their destination. "I know how mobs like that work. Those fellas are actually scared, but they don't want their friends to know that. So they get some courage out of a bottle and pound themselves on the back and do a lot of loud talkin' about how they're gonna go out and bag themselves a killer grizzly."

Smoke nodded. "They're all keyed up and ready for trouble, and when they see something moving on the other side of some trees or hear something moving in the brush, they haul out their guns and start shooting without taking the time to see what they're blazing away at."

"Yep. I'm surprised we haven't heard any guns goin' off—"

As if it had been waiting for that cue, a volley of shots suddenly rattled to their left. Smoke and Pearlie both tensed in their saddles as they reined in. Smoke didn't hear any bullets whining in their direction, but those shots had been aimed at something.

"We'd better go see if anybody got hurt," Smoke said as he turned his horse in the direction of the shooting, which had died away by now.

"If they did, it was likely their own blasted fault for bein' out here," Pearlie grumbled as he rode alongside Smoke.

"We're out here," Smoke reminded him, "and there are innocent folks who live around here, too."

They hadn't gone very far when more gunfire thundered ahead of them. Smoke could tell that rifles, handguns, and possibly shotguns were going off.

"That sounds like a dang war just broke out!" Pearlie exclaimed.

"Come on!" Smoke called as he urged more speed out of his mount.

The two men rode hard around a knoll and came in sight

of a line of trees. Smoke knew a creek meandered through that growth, with aspen and cottonwoods growing thickly on both banks.

Half a dozen men lay on that side of the creek, stretched out on their bellies as they fired toward the trees. Their horses were milling around skittishly farther back, except for one animal that lay on its side, unmoving.

Smoke had a pretty good idea what had happened. Those men had been riding along the creek when someone opened fire on them from the other side of the trees. One of the horses had been hit and evidently killed. The men had gone to ground and returned the fire, and now the two sides were continuing that fierce exchange of bullets.

Smoke and Pearlie reined in before they came too close. "The loco fools!" Pearlie yelled. "The other bunch must've thought they were shootin' at the bear, but they have to know by now they were wrong. Bears don't shoot back!"

"They're probably half drunk and don't really know anything except that they're being shot at," Smoke said. "And both sides will keep shooting until somebody gets killed. We need to put a stop to this."

"How are we gonna do that without gettin' in the middle of all that flyin' lead?"

Smoke looked around and then said, "Come on."

He put his horse up the slope to the top of the knoll that overlooked the tree-lined creek. It was brushy and had several outcroppings of rock. Smoke dismounted and started gathering dry, broken branches. He piled them on top of a fairly level slab of rock that jutted out from the ground to form a blunt promontory.

Pearlie said, "You're gonna build a bonfire, ain't you?"

"We've got to get their attention somehow."

Pearlie joined in gathering firewood. When they had a good-sized stack of it on the rock, Smoke took out his knife and shaved enough curling slivers off one branch to serve as kindling. He fished out a lucifer and used it to get a small fire going at the base of the pile. The flames licked upward and soon caught some of the larger branches on fire.

"We'll need to keep a close eye on the blaze and make sure it doesn't start to spread," he warned. "We don't want to start a wildfire."

"It'd serve those crazy varmints right if they got caught in such a thing," Pearlie said. "But you're right, we don't want to burn up half the country."

The blaze continued to grow. Soon, a thick column of gray smoke rose into the air. The wind carried the smoke toward the creek and the two groups of men shooting at each other. Even with all the powder smoke in the air, Smoke expected that they would smell the burning wood and start looking around for its source. Frontiersmen were always alert to the danger of an uncontrolled fire.

Sure enough, Smoke saw one of the men push himself up a little higher on his elbows and twist his head around to peer over his shoulder toward the knoll. Even at this distance, Smoke's keen eyes saw him jerk a little in surprise at the sight of the fire on the rocky point.

The man yelled at his companions and waved an arm. More of them looked around.

"I see some fellas over yonder in the trees on the other side of the creek," Pearlie said. "They're comin' closer and lookin' to see what's on fire, too."

"And the shooting has stopped," Smoke said.

A few echoes from the gun-thunder could still be heard as they rolled away across the landscape, but other than that, silence had fallen over the former battleground. The crackling from the burning branches seemed loud in that hush.

While Pearlie waved his hat over his head to make sure

the men below were paying attention, Smoke cupped his hands around his mouth and shouted, "Hold your fire! No more shooting! You men on the other side of the creek, come out into the open! Hold your fire!"

"You reckon they're gonna listen to you?" Pearlie asked.

"I don't know. But you keep an eye on the fire while I go down there and talk to them. If I wave my hat, you can go ahead and put the fire out."

Pearlie nodded toward the creek and said, "Looks like the other bunch is startin' to come on out like you told 'em to. But I'll bet their trigger fingers are still pretty itchy, so be careful when you ride down there."

"I intend to," Smoke assured his old friend.

He mounted and rode down the slope, watching as the men on the other side of the creek began to emerge from the trees. But they were holding rifles and had an air of tension about them, as if they were ready to duck back behind cover and start shooting again at a second's notice.

The men on this side of the stream got to their feet but looked just as wary, Smoke noted. They divided their attention between him as he approached and the men they'd been swapping lead with a few minutes earlier.

"Ward Stephens, is that you?" Smoke called as he drew nearer and recognized one of the men.

The man he'd addressed looked a little embarrassed that Smoke had called out his name. He said, "Howdy, Smoke. Had any luck findin' that bear?"

Smoke reined in and gave the men a stern look. "No, but at least I'm not shooting at my friends." He gestured toward the men on the other side of the creek. "I think I see Bennie Gardner over there. Don't the two of you go fishing together all the time?"

Stephens, who worked at the wagon yard in town, and Gardner, who was a carpenter, were indeed friends, Smoke knew. Gardner stepped forward more and called, "Dang it, I didn't know Ward was over there. We thought it was crazy men shooting at us and figured we'd better defend ourselves!"

One of the men with Stephens said, "They started it! They killed my horse! Shot it right out from under me! We had every right to throw lead back at 'em!"

Smoke said, "You're all out here looking for that grizzly bear, aren't you?"

Stephens directed a surly frown at Smoke and said, "Somebody's got to find it and kill it, before it wipes out half the folks in the valley!"

"No offense, Smoke," another man said, "but you ain't had the least bit of luck doin' that yet."

Smoke nodded. "That's true, and I'm sorry I haven't been able to track down that beast, but I haven't given up. I won't give up as long as it's threatening the safety of the people in this valley. I can understand why you fellas feel exactly the same way. But when you get so many large groups of armed men prowling around, looking to shoot something, there's bound to be trouble, even though you all want the same thing."

"Damn right we do," another man said. "We want that thousand dollar bounty!"

Smoke frowned. "What are you talking about?"

"I don't reckon you've been in town today, Smoke, or you would have heard about it," Stephens said.

"Pearlie and I rode through Big Rock but didn't stop."

"Well, there's a thousand dollar reward now for whoever kills that bear," Stephens explained. "Emmett Brown came up with the idea, or one of his bartenders did, anyway, and he put up some of the money. A bunch of the other business owners in town chipped in, too, and got the total up to a thousand dollars. That's a lot of money for doing something that needs to be done anyway."

"And it's going to bring out even more men who want to find that bear," Smoke said grimly.

Stephens shrugged. "Most of the able-bodied fellas in Big Rock will be out looking before the day's over, I reckon."

Smoke took his hat off, turned in the saddle, and waved the hat over his head in the signal for Pearlie to extinguish the fire up on the knoll.

As he put the hat back on, he said, "You boys aren't going to start shooting at each other again, are you?"

Stephens shrugged and said, "Talk to Bennie and those other hombres across the creek. They're the ones who started this fandango."

"My horse is still dead," complained the man whose mount had been shot. "Somebody's got to pay for that!"

"You can work that out without trying to fill each other full of lead," Smoke snapped. "And if you've got any sense, you'll all go home before somebody else starts shooting at you."

"I'm not passin' up a chance for that reward!" yelled one of the men across the creek. Several others in both groups echoed that sentiment, loudly and enthusiastically.

Smoke shook his head and didn't try to conceal the irritation and frustration he felt. He pulled his horse around and rode back toward the knoll. The fire was out now, although a little smoke still curled into the air from the embers. Pearlie had slapped out the flames with a rolled-up blanket.

"I could tell you were tryin' to talk some sense into their heads," Pearlie greeted Smoke. "But it didn't work, did it? Everybody's too eager to be the fella who finds that dang bear."

"It's even worse than that," Smoke told him. "Emmett Brown and some of the other business owners in town got together and put up a thousand dollar reward for the man who kills it."

Pearlie let out a low, surprised whistle. "That much dinero will bring everybody who wasn't already huntin' the varmint right outta the woodwork. And wild, senseless gunplay just like what we just put a stop to here will be goin' on all over the valley."

"I'm afraid you're right," Smoke said, "but short of the governor declaring martial law and sending in the army, I don't know how we're going to keep it from happening. For now, let's head on out to the Jackson farm and see if we can pick up the trail there."

CHAPTER 10

Smoke was well-known in the area. Fred Jackson and his wife, Thelma, were pleased to have him visiting their farm, even under these less-than-ideal circumstances. Carrot-topped Emery and his little brother and sister looked up to Smoke, and Pearlie, too, as if they were heroic characters from a storybook.

The two visitors accepted the cups of coffee Thelma offered them. Fred explained what had happened the day before, essentially the same story his son Emery had told Smoke and Monte Carson.

"I wish I could be more help, Mr. Jensen," Fred concluded, "but I didn't see where that blasted bear went. I don't mind telling you, right then I was just trying to put some distance between it and me and my boys."

"I don't blame you a bit for that," Smoke assured him. "I'd be trying to protect these fine youngsters, too." He took a sip of the coffee as he and Pearlie sat at the table with the farmer. "We'll go out and have a look around here in a bit, if that's all right with you."

"Sure. I'm honored to have you on our place."

"We'll try not to mess up your cornfield," Smoke said with a smile.

Fred shook his head. "Shoot, that bear's already trampled through there. He knocked down a goodly portion of the stalks."

"I'm curious about a few things," Smoke went on. "How far away was the bear when you first saw him?"

Fred frowned in thought and then said, "Maybe fifty yards. That sound about right to you, Emery?"

"Yes, sir, Pa," the boy replied. "Fifty yards is just about right."

"And it didn't charge you?"

"Nope. Just reared up out of the corn and roared at us and waved its front legs around. Never came any closer, even when it started slashing at the corn with those big ol' paws."

"Does that strike you as a mite odd?" Smoke asked.

"Well . . . it didn't at the time. I was just thinking about getting me and my boys out of there. Fact of the matter is, I was prayin' mighty hard that it *wouldn't* charge us."

Pearlie said, "I reckon I'd have been doin' the same thing, Fred."

"But the bear charged those fellas it killed, didn't it?" Fred went on. "Or do you reckon it jumped 'em from behind?"

"There's no way of knowing that," Smoke admitted. "The sign didn't prove anything one way or the other. It seems to me that if the creature was looking to kill more humans, though, that was a mighty good chance for it."

"I'll say," Fred agreed fervently. "A man can't outrun a bear. That's why I was going to stay and fight it, to give Emery and Mickey a better chance to get away. I just wanted to slow it down long enough for them to make it back here to the cabin."

"But Pa," Emery objected, "it would'a killed you!"

Smoke said, "That's the kind of thing brave men do for

their children, Emery, and I can tell that your pa is a mighty brave man."

"It's an honor to have you to say something like that about me, Mr. Jensen," the lanky farmer said. "I wasn't really thinking much at the time, though. It was all just instinct."

"That's the biggest part of being a hero, most of the time. Good instincts," Smoke said and then moved the conversation back to the bear and its actions. "So after roaring all loud and scary-like and waving its paws around, the bear just left?"

"Yes, sir, that's what he did. When I looked back, he was down on all fours again and disappearing into the taller corn. I couldn't see where he went. You can track him, though. He's bound to have left quite a path through those plants."

"You ain't been back out there?" Pearlie asked.

"No, I haven't. I'd like to see how much damage was done, but I figured the sheriff or somebody would be coming from town and I'd go take a look with them."

Smoke drank the last of his coffee and set the empty cup on the table. "Come along with us, then. That's what we're here for."

Fred led the way to the cornfield, which was several hundred yards from the cabin. Smoke and Pearlie led their horses. When they reached the field, it was easy to see the swath of destruction the bear had left behind. Numerous cornstalks were bent over and broken. Some had been uprooted.

The soft dirt of the field yielded the best paw prints so far. Smoke knelt beside the tracks and studied them until he had committed everything about them to memory. He felt confident that if he saw these particular prints again, he would recognize them.

"That's a mighty big bear," Pearlie said. "You can tell that by lookin' at these prints. You're wonderin' how come it didn't go after Fred and his youngsters, aren't you, Smoke? I got to admit, I'm a mite curious about the same thing."

"Usually once an animal starts attacking people, it doesn't stop. Any time I run across something unusual, it makes me stop and think."

"You got any answers?"

Smoke shook his head and smiled ruefully. "No. And unfortunately, when we do find the bear, we can't ask it. So we may never know." He came to his feet. "And until we find it, those questions don't matter. The important thing is putting a stop to the madness that's going on around here before a lot of people get hurt. The quickest way to do that is to find the bear."

Smoke and Pearlie shook hands with Fred Jackson, thanked him for his help, then mounted up to follow the bear's trail. The paw prints led north once they left the cornfield.

This trail was the easiest to follow that Smoke had found so far. In addition to the prints, the bear had left other sign, including claw marks on trees and other places where it had rubbed against the rough bark, scratching an itch and leaving behind quite a few tufts of hair.

Eventually, the bear's course curved back to the northwest, toward the mountains. Smoke and Pearlie were able to follow it into the rugged terrain for another hour before they lost the trail.

"Dadgum it!" Pearlie said. "I thought for sure that this time we were gonna find the blasted thing."

"So did I," Smoke said as he leaned forward in his saddle to ease weary muscles. His eyes ached a little, too, from straining to pick out the increasingly fainter and fainter tracks. His voice revealed the frustration he felt as he went on to say, "But somehow he's given us the slip again."

"What now?"

"You head back to the ranch. I'm going to Big Rock and talk to Monte. There's got to be some way we can talk sense into all those gents who are roaming around eager to shoot something."

"You might start by tryin' to get those fellas to take back that reward," Pearlie suggested. "As long as that bear's got a bounty on his head, even more folks are gonna be huntin' him."

"You're right about that. I can't very well tell Emmett Brown and the others what they can or can't do with their own money, but maybe I can reason with them."

"What do I do if I run into that critter on the way back to the Sugarloaf?"

"Use your best judgment," Smoke said. "If you take a shot, aim for the eyes. Putting a bullet in its brain will be the quickest way to stop it."

"That'd be some fancy shootin'," Pearlie said. "More like the sort of thing you could do, but I'll sure give it a try if I get the chance."

The two men said their farewells and split up.

Graham Blake had been in Big Rock early that morning, eating breakfast in the City Pig Restaurant and listening to the excited chatter of the diners around him. They were all buzzing about the big news that had been announced the previous evening.

A group of local businessmen had gotten together and donated money for a reward to be paid to whoever ended the threat posed by the rogue grizzly. A thousand dollars was a huge amount of money for most folks. Blake overheard several men making eager plans to go hunting for the beast together. They agreed they would split the reward money, no matter which of them actually fired the fatal shot.

That would probably lead to arguments and perhaps even fights. Blake didn't care about any of that. He was just glad the seed he had planted with Pudge the bartender had grown as he hoped. He had his sights set on something much larger.

The bank might have as much as ten thousand dollars in its vault. Several of the stores appeared to be quite lucrative, too, and might have considerable amounts of cash on hand.

With nearly all of the able-bodied men out vying for that reward, the settlement would be wide open for him and his men, Blake thought with satisfaction. They would empty the bank vault and loot as many of the stores as they could.

This promised to be the biggest job they had ever pulled. The payoff might add up to enough to get them the rest of the way to Mexico without even having to stop and carry out more robberies along the way.

Blake lingered in the café over a second cup of coffee, then hung around town for another hour, watching as man after man rode out, some alone but many together, all of them heavily armed.

"Armed for bear," Blake murmured to himself, smiling as the exodus from Big Rock continued.

A short time later, his men began drifting into the settlement one by one, according to the plan Blake had outlined that morning in their camp west of town. If he had decided to call off the raid for any reason, he would have returned to camp before now to let them know.

When he didn't show up, the others knew that the job was on and they should start heading for Big Rock.

This was a bigger town than most of the ones where the

gang had struck, and while that promised more loot, it also entailed greater risks. Blake was sorry that Harry Dunning had gotten himself killed up there on the Wyoming/Colorado border. Dunning would have been one more gun on this job.

He would make do with what he had, Blake told himself. Frank Holt and Lester Stoughton would accompany him into the bank. Paul Deere, Ken Bennett, and Bob Kramer would remain outside as lookouts, in case any trouble developed on the street.

The bank was their main target, so they would strike there first. Blake's plan called for him and his men to tie and gag everybody in there so they couldn't raise the alarm.

Then the three of them would rejoin the men outside, and they would all move on to Goldstein's Mercantile. Blake figured the take there would be good, too.

Once again, they would tie and gag everybody in the store and move on to the next business on the list. It wasn't a physical list—Blake hadn't written the names down—but the order was etched in his brain.

Naturally, it was too much to hope that they would be able to empty the whole town of loot. Something would go wrong somewhere. It always did, because human nature could be predicted only to a certain extent.

Then the shooting would start, and Blake and his men would be forced to flee, fighting their way out of town if they had to. But with luck, they would clear a considerable payoff before that happened.

Those thoughts raced through Blake's mind as he stood on the boardwalk in front of Earl's Barber Shop, his shoulder propped against the thick, red-and-white-striped pole that traditionally advertised a haircutting establishment. His freshly shaved cheeks stung pleasantly from the bay rum Earl had splashed on them a few minutes earlier.

Getting his beard stubble scraped off *before* a job was breaking with tradition. A part of Blake's mind was uneasy about that, but he put the worry aside as being silly superstition. He'd had an impulse and had given in to it, and now he was glad he had.

The talkative barber had confirmed everything Blake had supposed about the town. Nearly all the men had abandoned their homes and jobs to hunt the bear.

"I'd be out there myself if I didn't have a bad ticker," Earl had said. "Can't stand much excitement. And I tell you, this old heart would be beating a mile a minute if I ever found myself lookin' at a giant, killer grizzly bear!"

Blake was glad most of the men in Big Rock didn't feel that way.

So far Deere, Kramer, and Holt had ridden into town, tied their horses near—but not in front of—the bank, and wandered into various businesses to kill time. Stoughton and Bennett showed up while Blake was loitering in front of the barber shop. They rode in from opposite ends of town and dismounted, but hesitated before looping their horses' reins around hitch rails.

Instead, they looked at Blake.

The other three men emerged from the buildings where they had been waiting. They had all been keeping track of the time. They turned their gazes to Blake, as well.

Slowly, Blake reached into his pocket and pulled out a turnip watch attached to a chain. He lifted it and thumbed the catch that opened it. What the hour was didn't really matter. Blake looked at the watch for a couple of seconds, then snapped it closed and replaced it in his pocket.

That was the signal.

Blake started walking toward the bank. From the corner of his eye, he saw Frank Holt start in the same direction.

By turning his head slightly, he saw Lester Stoughton advancing from the other way. Both men frowned, probably noticing that Blake had been shaved.

The two of them slowed down slightly so that Blake reached the double doors leading into the bank first. He opened the one on the right side and was about to step through it when the left-hand door swung open, too, and a man stepped out, almost bumping shoulders with Blake.

Blake stopped short but recovered from his surprise almost instantly. He moved aside a little, smiled, and said, "Pardon me, Sheriff."

The man coming out of the bank was the badge-toter Blake had noticed the day before. He stopped for a moment, too, returned Blake's smile, and said, "Sorry, mister. Should've been watching where I was going."

"Not at all. Just bad timing we almost bumped into each other, but no harm done, eh?"

"Not at all." The lawman nodded. "You have a good day."

"Same to you, Sheriff," Blake said.

He saw that Holt and Stoughton had stopped their approach to the bank and turned aside rather abruptly when the sheriff emerged. Now they were standing nearby, apparently idly, but their casual stances didn't look entirely convincing to Blake. He hoped the sheriff hadn't noticed the same thing.

The lawman didn't show any signs of being suspicious. He started across the street without looking back. Blake hesitated for only a heartbeat before he went on into the bank.

The lobby was cool and dim compared with outside. Blake's keen-eyed gaze flicked around the room. There were four teller's cages, three of them occupied. Each of those three tellers was helping a customer, but no one was waiting in line.

An elderly couple stood at the counter where the various forms were. The man was writing on one of the forms laboriously while his wife stood at his elbow saying something in a whiny voice and poking a clawlike finger at the paper, clearly telling her husband how he was filling it out all wrong.

A beefy, well-fed hombre in a frock coat sat at a desk in the back. He scowled as he studied some documents spread out in front of him. Probably figuring out how many loan requests he could turn down and how many properties he could foreclose on, Blake thought.

As far as he could see, no guard was on duty in the bank. That was a little unusual in a town this size. Maybe the man who normally held that post had abandoned it to go after that killer grizzly. Whatever the reason, Blake would gladly accept that stroke of luck.

Footsteps behind him told him that Holt and Stoughton had entered the bank, too. As one of the men at the tellers' cages finished his transaction and turned to leave, Blake drew his gun and said in a calm, clear voice without shouting, "Everyone stand still. Just do as you're told, and nobody will get hurt."

The man who'd been about to leave stopped short. He looked like a storekeeper of some sort, tall and skinny with a pair of rimless spectacles perched on his nose. He didn't look like he'd give the least bit of trouble. In fact, he raised both hands to elbow level without being told to.

The well-fed gent at the desk got to his feet and blustered, "What's the meaning of this?"

Stoughton stepped forward, thrust a gun at him, and said,

"You ought to be smart enough to figure that out, fat boy. This is a holdup."

The old woman poked her husband in the side and demanded, "Do something, Hiram!"

Her husband, who was tall and mostly bald, with a turkey neck and prominent Adam's apple, said, "What do you want me to do? They've got guns!"

"That's right, old-timer, we do," Blake said. He motioned with the revolver he held. "All of you come over here. Stand there by the desk. You tellers, you do the same. Come on."

An idea had occurred to him. He could force the townspeople to tie one another up, until only one of them was left free. That man would then be easy to handle.

"This isn't the first time somebody's tried to rob this bank," the beefy gent said. "You'll be sorry."

"I don't think so," Blake replied. He gestured with the gun again, sharper this time. "Come on. Don't make me lose my patience."

The bank employees and customers shuffled together into a fairly compact group. Blake and Holt were able to cover them all without any trouble, leaving Stoughton to clean out the cash drawers in the cages. He stuffed paper money and gold and silver coins into a large canvas bag that had been folded up and concealed under his coat for that purpose.

While Stoughton was doing that, Blake told the banker, "We're going to need to get into that vault."

The man shook his head. "It's locked, and I'm the only one who knows the combination."

"Don't make me shoot you," Blake threatened.

"I just told you, I'm the only one who knows the combination. Kill me and you'll never get in there without blowing the door off, and I don't think you'll have time for that."

"I didn't say I'd kill you. I said I'd shoot you." Blake struggled to keep a tight rein on his temper. "After I put a bullet through your knee, I'm betting you'll do anything I tell you to."

The banker paled a little at that, but he shook his head stubbornly.

"I won't do it," he said. "I won't cooperate with you."

"Well, then . . ." Blake swung his gun a little to one side and aimed at the old woman's head, instead. "Maybe I'll just blow this old bat's brains out. I'm betting there's no vault combination or anything else worthwhile in her head. Hell, I'd probably be doing her husband a favor by shutting her up. Isn't that right, you old pelican?"

"Hiram . . ." the old woman said in a high, quavery voice as she stared in horror down the barrel of Blake's gun.

The old man swallowed hard, causing his Adam's apple to bob up and down grotesquely.

"Mister," he said in a reedy but resolute voice, "you harm one hair on my wife's head, I'll hunt you down and kill you if it takes the rest of my life."

Blake laughed. "Looks to me like that won't be all that long. Now, what do you say, banker man? You going to do as you're told?"

One of the tellers said, "Don't do it, Mr. Montgomery. I just saw Mr. Jensen ride by outside."

Behind one of the tellers' windows, Lester Stoughton suddenly stiffened and jerked his head up in surprise.

"Jensen!" he repeated. "*Smoke* Jensen?"

A cold ball of apprehension suddenly formed in Blake's belly. The name was familiar, although he didn't recognize it immediately. Stoughton obviously did, though.

Stoughton rushed out from behind the cages, carrying the now heavily stuffed canvas bag.

"Forget the vault," he said. "We need to get out of here right now."

"Damn it, I'm in charge here," Blake began, worried that things were falling apart already but also angry that Stoughton would presume to start giving orders. He eared back the Colt's hammer. "Open the vault or I'll kill her!"

Before the banker could respond, the scrawny old man let out a surprisingly deep bellow of rage and charged Blake, who pulled the trigger.

CHAPTER 11

Smoke hadn't seen any more signs of the bear on his journey into Big Rock to pay a visit to Monte Carson, but he had noticed a number of men on horseback riding here and there, sometimes alone but usually in groups.

He wondered if Pearlie had run into any trouble on his way back to the Sugarloaf. It seemed unlikely . . . but everything seemed unlikely these days.

It was almost as if that bear had brought an atmosphere of unreality with it when it had drifted into this part of the country and that eerie sensation had settled over the whole valley.

Nothing was what it seemed, Smoke mused.

The fact that Big Rock's main street was practically empty didn't help the feeling of uneasiness that had Smoke in its grip.

On a normal day, a dozen wagons and buckboards would be parked in front of the various businesses. Men on horseback would be coming and going, and pedestrians would be headed up and down the boardwalks.

Smoke didn't see any wagons. A few horses with empty saddles were scattered here and there, tied at hitch rails. Women in dresses and bonnets chatted with one another and moved along the boardwalks, but no men.

A laughing kid ran across the street in front of Smoke with a small brown dog chasing him and barking happily. That common sight made the rest of the scene seem even odder by comparison. Smoke veered his horse toward Monte's office and hoped he would find his old friend there.

Monte came out of the office before Smoke got there. He had a shotgun tucked under his arm. The weapon made Smoke quirk an eyebrow quizzically. He didn't figure Monte would leave his office carrying a Greener unless he expected trouble.

Smoke reined in at the hitch rail as Monte paused on the boardwalk in front of the office.

"Smoke," he said, "I'm mighty glad to see you."

"Something wrong, Monte?"

"Maybe, maybe not. But when I came out of the bank a few minutes ago, I nearly bumped into a stranger who was going inside."

Smoke shrugged. "Strangers ride into Big Rock, and sometimes they need to visit the bank."

"Yeah, but there were two more strangers hanging around right outside, and they seemed a little startled when they saw me. They turned away so they didn't have to look me in the face."

"That does sound a mite odd," Smoke admitted.

"Then they both went in the bank behind the other fella. I didn't make a big production of it, but I was watching to see what they did. None of them have come back out. I gave it a few minutes, just in case nothing out of the ordinary was going on, but it's been long enough now that I want to take a look for myself."

"Probably a good idea." Smoke swung down from the saddle and tied his horse's reins to the hitch rail. "I'll come with you."

"I sure won't say no to that offer."

The two men walked toward the bank. They didn't get in any hurry, so there was nothing about their actions to draw attention. They had a clear view of the establishment's front doors and would know right away if anyone came out.

"Town's mighty quiet today," Smoke observed. "Most of the men seem to be gone."

"Yeah, and that's just the sort of thing that might make Big Rock a tempting target for any hombres who are up to no good."

"Like those fellas who went in the bank."

"I've got a bad feeling about them," Monte said.

Smoke trusted his old friend's instincts. Monte might not have set out to be a lawman, but he had packed a star for a long time now and done an excellent job of keeping the peace in Big Rock.

That peace was shattered suddenly as a gunshot blasted inside the bank.

The next instant, Smoke heard another shot to his left and from the corner of his eye saw a garish jet of muzzle flame.

Graham Blake was so surprised to have the old-timer lunge at him that his hand jerked just slightly as he pulled the trigger.

That threw his aim off enough that the bullet whipped past the old man's ear. It flew on to the back of the room, where it clanged off the vault door and ricocheted somewhere with a high-pitched whine.

Hiram plowed into Blake. His left hand wrapped around the gun's cylinder while the right closed on Blake's wrist and shoved his arm up so the Colt pointed at the ceiling.

That left Blake's left hand free. He balled it into a fist

and hammered a blow to the side of Hiram's head. The old man groaned, and his grip slipped off Blake's gun arm as his knees buckled.

But the skinny bank customer who'd looked so harmless a moment earlier had taken advantage of the chance to rush Blake, as well. Screaming like a crazed ape, his features distorted so that he *looked* like an ape, too, he flailed away with both fists and managed to land a solid punch on Blake's jaw that rocked the outlaw backward.

Blake shoved the Colt's barrel into the man's midsection and pulled the trigger again. The bullet ripped through his belly, smashed his spine, and exploded out his back. The dying man fell backward to land in a bloody sprawl.

That .45 slug traveled a few more feet and struck one of the tellers in the arm, knocking the man halfway around. He cried out in pain as he clutched the wounded arm.

All the other prisoners dived to the floor as Holt and Stoughton opened fire, as well. The bank president grabbed the old woman on his way down and dragged her out of the path of the bullets.

The panicky, deafening fusillade lasted only a few seconds. As the room still rang with echoes from the gun-thunder, Stoughton yelled, "We gotta get out of here!"

Blake knew Stoughton was right. He wanted to kill that crazy old man for ruining everything, but it was more important to get away.

They wouldn't be leaving empty-handed. From the looks of the bag Stoughton had filled from the tellers' drawers, it contained a tidy amount.

Only a patch on what he'd hoped to gain from this job, though, Blake thought bitterly as he wheeled around and started toward the doors.

* * *

Smoke's instincts and reflexes took over as he realized someone on the street was shooting at him. He whirled toward the muzzle flash he had seen. His gun came out of leather too fast for the eye to follow. It roared and spat flame, seeming quicker than was possible according to the laws of nature.

However, the man who had fired the shot at Smoke had started moving as soon as he pulled the trigger, so the bullet from Smoke's gun narrowly missed and chewed splinters from the wall of the building behind him.

Smoke fired again as the man threw himself headlong behind a water trough. His hat flew off. Smoke didn't know if that was from the dive or if he had shot the hat off.

Either way, the hat's owner was still alive and in the fight. He slammed three shots past the end of the trough and forced Smoke to hunt some cover of his own.

Unfortunately, he and Monte had been in the middle of the street when the ball opened. There wasn't any cover close by, and they were caught in a crossfire, to boot. A man on the other side of the street opened up with a Winchester. Smoke hit the ground and rolled as bullets kicked up dust around him.

A part of Smoke's brain was still cool and collected. It wasn't hard to figure out what was going on. The three strangers who had aroused Monte's suspicions were robbing the bank, and they had at least two confederates out in the street guarding their backs.

Monte had dropped to one knee. He brought the shotgun to his shoulder and fired at the man with the rifle, the Greener going off with a loud boom.

At the same time, the Winchester cracked sharply again. Monte dropped the shotgun and went over backward. Smoke knew the sheriff was hit but didn't have time to check and see how bad the injury was.

Stretched out on his belly, Smoke triggered a round at the rifleman. The man jerked to the side, either hit or spooked by how close the bullet went past him. He didn't fall, though. He stayed on his feet and ran toward a horse tied at a nearby hitch rail. He fired several more times as he ran, blasting with the Winchester as fast as he could work the rifle's lever.

The man on the other side of the street was still a threat, too. As Smoke rolled over and snapped a shot toward the water trough, he caught a glimpse of a third man running along the boardwalk toward him and Monte. That man had a gun in his hand, but it was possible he was coming to help Smoke and the lawman.

No, that was too much to hope for, Smoke realized a second later as the newcomer opened fire on them.

Closer at hand, three men burst out of the bank and headed for horses. They were brandishing guns, too, and as they caught sight of Smoke and Monte out in the open, they started shooting, as well. Bullets whistled toward the two men in the street from all directions.

Luck might have run out for both of them if a couple of new players hadn't taken hands in the game. Louis Longmont, who had been drawn out of his restaurant by the commotion, stood on the boardwalk, drew a bead with the gun in his hand, and coolly drilled the bank robber carrying a canvas sack that was probably full of money.

At the same time, Tom Nunnley stepped out of his hardware store holding a shotgun. The third man who had joined the attack on Smoke and Monte was about thirty feet away on the same side of the street with his back to Nunnley, who could have cut him down from behind.

Instead, Nunnley's basic decency prompted him to yell, "Drop your gun!"

The outlaw whirled around rather than follow the order.

Flame lanced from his gun muzzle. Nunnley fired both barrels of the Greener.

The man jerked backward as buckshot tore through his left leg. He dropped his gun but managed to stay on his feet as he hobbled frantically toward the closest horse. He jerked the reins loose from the hitch rail and hauled himself into the saddle as the skittish horse took off.

The wounded outlaw hung on for dear life. Nunnley thumbed fresh shells into the shotgun's chambers, but by the time he snapped the weapon closed, the man he'd shot was more than a block away.

Farther along the street, the bank robber who'd been carrying the loot when Louis shot him had fallen to his knees. He still clutched the canvas bag in one hand as he pressed the other to his side.

Two of his companions each grabbed an arm and pulled him upright, then half-carried, half-dragged him toward the horses while still firing at Smoke and Monte, who kept their heads down and returned the fire as best they could.

Louis squeezed off two more rounds, but the range was long and the bullets missed. The other outlaws made it into their saddles, even the man Louis had wounded, and all five of them galloped out of Big Rock, following the one who had already fled. They threw a few wild shots behind them to discourage pursuit.

Smoke was already thinking about going after them, but first he had to find out how badly Monte was hurt. He pushed himself to his feet, ran over, and dropped to a knee beside his friend.

Monte had rolled over onto his back and was lying there with lines of pain etched into his rugged face. Smoke saw blood on the right leg of the sheriff's trousers.

Smoke pouched his iron and pulled his knife from the

sheath at his waist. "Are you hit anywhere else?" he asked as he started cutting away the bloody fabric from the wound.

"I don't think so," Monte replied through clenched teeth. "And that's nothing but a blasted scratch. My leg just wouldn't work anymore."

"I'm not surprised, because it's more than a scratch," Smoke told him. "Looks like the bullet went clean through. I can't tell if it broke the bone or not."

Running footsteps made him glance up. Tom Nunnley hurried toward them, holding the shotgun ready in case the bank robbers doubled back.

That seemed pretty unlikely, though. With at least two of them wounded, they were probably trying to put as much distance between themselves and Big Rock as they could.

"Are you all right, Smoke?" Nunnley asked.

"Yeah. They weren't very good shots."

"Good enough, I'd say," Monte put in. "I'm glad they weren't any better!"

Despite the seriousness of the situation, Smoke had to chuckle at that. "I reckon it does all depend on your perspective," he said.

Nunnley said, "How bad is the sheriff hurt?"

"I'll live," Monte answered for himself.

Louis Longmont had trotted up on the other side in time to hear that. He said, "It appears you may be laid up for a while, though, Monte."

"Not hardly! I've got to get a posse together and go after those blasted—"

"We'll let Dr. Spaulding decide about that," Louis interrupted. "I've already sent for him."

The medico arrived on the scene just a few moments later, hatless and carrying his black bag. By that time, Smoke had laid bare the entrance and exit wounds after rolling Monte onto his left side to keep the bullet holes out of the dirt.

"How many times have you been wounded in the line of duty, Sheriff?" Spaulding asked as he hunkered next to Monte. "It seems like I've patched you up at least a dozen times."

"It's not that many," Monte replied curtly. "Being a lawman's a dangerous business."

"I'd say so, but I'd also say that you should survive this injury, assuming that you don't get blood poisoning. And I think I'm a good enough doctor to prevent that from happening." Spaulding looked at the bystanders. "Smoke, Tom, can you carry him to my surgery?"

Several men had come out of the bank and from other businesses to gather in the street, but the crowd was a lot smaller than it would have been if so many hadn't been out searching for the rogue grizzly.

Smoke and Nunnley were the most capable of carrying Monte, though, so Smoke took his shoulders and Nunnley got him by the feet.

"Careful," Spaulding warned. "We don't want to make those wounds bleed any more than they already are."

It didn't take long to get Monte onto the operating table in the doctor's surgery. Spaulding and his nurse set to work cleaning the wounds in preparation for closing them with stitches.

"Thank you, gentlemen," he said without looking up at Smoke and Nunnley. "We can handle this from here. I suggest you go see if anyone else in town was wounded in that exchange. It sounded almost like a war."

"It was pretty hot and heavy there for a minute or two," Smoke agreed. "Thanks, Doctor. We'll go check on the townspeople."

Louis was in the forefront of the group of people waiting

outside the doctor's office. Smoke asked him, "Is anyone else hurt? Dr. Spaulding wants to know."

Louis shook his head. "I've asked around, and as far as I've been able to determine, there was one other serious injury, a gunshot wound to one of the bank tellers. Some of his friends have gone to get him and help him to the doctor's office."

The gambler's expression was grim as he went on. "I'm afraid there was one more casualty, but Dr. Spaulding can't do anything for him. Edmond Norris was killed in the bank. One of the robbers shot him."

Smoke's jaw tightened. Norris hadn't lived in Big Rock for long, only a few months. He'd worked as a law clerk for Judge Proctor, the local justice of the peace.

"Hiram Krepps was assaulted, struck in the head by the same robber who killed Norris," Louis went on, "but he insists he's all right. He's more worried about his wife. Mrs. Krepps has a severe case of the vapors." Louis allowed himself a faint smile, then grew more serious as he went on, "How's Monte?"

"The doctor says he'll live, more than likely."

"Yes, it'll take more than getting drilled through the leg to send Monte Carson across the divide," Louis agreed.

Smoke spotted Joel Montgomery, the banker, in the crowd and asked, "How much did they get away with, Joel?"

"I honestly don't know yet," Montgomery replied. "I'll have our tellers start making a count. I wanted to see how Sheriff Carson was doing first. I can tell you this much: the thieves got only what was in the cash drawers in the cages. It might add up to a few thousand dollars, but the rest of the funds are still secure in the vault."

"Well, that's good news, anyway."

Louis asked, "Are you going after them?"

Smoke nodded. "I don't care if they stole less than they might have. They killed a man, viciously attacked an old-timer, wounded our sheriff and another man, and did their best to kill both him and me. It's the next thing to a miracle that we both survived, and we've got you, Louis, and you, Tom, to thank for that. If you hadn't pitched in when you did, we never would have made it out of that street alive."

Smoke drew in a breath and looked around at the crowd, then went on, "So yes, since our sheriff is laid up with that bullet wound and won't be doing any riding for a while, I'm going after those outlaws and bringing them to justice, and any man with a horse and a gun is welcome to join me."

Chapter 12

The horses were lathered with sweat and their sides were heaving when Graham Blake called a halt a couple of miles outside of Big Rock.

Blake didn't want to stop. He would have preferred to keep riding, but killing the horses wouldn't help them. In the long run, it would just put nooses around their necks. They all knew that.

Without dismounting, Blake looked over at Stoughton and asked, "How bad are you hit, Lester?"

"Bad enough," Stoughton replied through clenched teeth. "It hurts like blazes!" He lifted his bloody hand from where he'd been holding it tightly to his side. "But I think it's just a deep crease. I don't reckon I'm killed."

"Good," Blake said. He meant it even though he would have abandoned Stoughton in a second without any qualms if the man had been hurt badly enough to slow them down.

"I'm hurt, too, damn it," Paul Deere complained. His right leg hung all but useless. Several pieces of buckshot had struck it, and his trousers were dark with blood.

"You're lucky that townie was a mighty poor shot," Bob Kramer told him. "At that range, with a scattergun, he should have blown you to doll rags."

"Maybe so," Deere said as he glared at Kramer, "but that don't make my leg hurt any less!"

Soft-spoken Ken Bennett, who barely said anything under normal circumstances, pointed out, "We can't stay here, Graham. There's liable to be a posse after us any time now."

"It won't be much of a posse," Blake replied with a shake of his head. "I'm not sure the sheriff could round up a dozen able-bodied men in that town right now, even if he wasn't wounded. And he looked like he was hit pretty hard. Who's even going to lead a posse?"

Stoughton said, "Smoke Jensen will, that's who."

"Jensen again! You seemed to recognize the name back there, Lester."

"You don't?"

"The name's vaguely familiar," Blake admitted, "but I don't know who he is."

"Probably the deadliest gunfighter who ever strapped on a Colt," Stoughton said. "Some years ago, he waltzed into a town up in Idaho where nineteen gun-wolves were waiting just to kill him. When he rode out, all nineteen of them were dead, and that was just the start. He's cleaned out other towns where the odds were sky-high against him."

"Legends like that are almost always exaggerated," Blake scoffed.

"Not in Jensen's case. If anything, the stories folks tell don't do him justice. Now that I think about it, I saw him over in Kansas a few years ago. He tackled a gang of rustlers in the streets of Abilene and wiped them out. Once I heard his name, I recognized him. He was the fella in the street with the sheriff."

"He's still just one man," Blake insisted.

"One man or not, and no matter how big the posse is, we need to put some more distance between us and this place,"

Frank Holt said. "The horses have had a chance to blow for a few minutes. We ought to get moving."

Once again, Blake experienced the irritation he felt when one of the gang started trying to give orders. That was what Holt's suggestion sounded like to him, but he also couldn't argue with the logic of what Holt said.

"Yeah, let's move out," he said. "Hold the horses down a little. We can't afford to wear them out before we find a place we can swap them for fresh mounts."

There were a number of ranches in this valley. They just needed to find one isolated enough with some decent horse-flesh on hand. Then they could switch out, at gunpoint if necessary.

"Which way are we going?" Kramer asked. "I know the plan was for us to head south . . ."

"The terrain's more rugged to the north," Blake said. "It means doubling back, but I think we'll stand a better chance of giving a posse the slip if we go that way. Once we're sure they're not on our trail anymore, we can circle around and start south again."

"As long as we can stop somewhere long enough to patch up these holes in my leg," Deere said.

"And the one in my side," Stoughton added.

"We'll have to start thinking about another job, too," Holt said, "since we didn't get near as much in this one as we figured we would."

Blake glanced at the canvas bag full of money, which was tied to Stoughton's saddle horn.

"We don't know how much the take was," he snapped. "You boys are making this sound like a total disaster."

"What would you call it?" Holt asked.

Frank was getting too damned big for his britches, Blake thought. If this kept up, he might have to take him down a notch.

And if Holt didn't like being reminded of his place in the gang . . . Well, Blake could deal with that, too.

For now, he led the way as they heeled their horses into motion again and rode north toward the mountains.

Half an hour after the shooting stopped in Big Rock, the posse was ready to ride. Smoke looked the men over as they stood in front of the sheriff's office, holding their horses.

There were ten of them. Half of them were older, business owners who had things to take care of and couldn't go chasing off after a bear and a reward, no matter how much of a frenzy the valley was in, and half were younger, clerks and keepers of smaller shops who weren't exactly seasoned fighters and frontiersmen.

It was a pretty unimpressive bunch. Smoke had to admit that.

At the same time, they were all brave enough to step up and volunteer to go after the bank robbers. Courage wasn't everything, of course. A brave man could still die because he wasn't fast enough, smart enough, strong enough.

Having sand counted for a lot where Smoke was concerned. He gave the men a firm nod as they looked at him.

"I appreciate all of you being willing to come along after those robbers," he told them. "You know that tracking them down and dealing with them will be a dangerous job."

"We know, Smoke, but those varmints killed a man, shot up our town, and stole our money. We're not going to stand by and let them get away with that."

The rest of the men nodded and muttered agreement with the speaker.

"We may be out on the trail for several days," Smoke warned them. "We have a couple of pack horses loaded with supplies donated by Goldstein's Mercantile and Foster and Matthews Grocery Store. We're taking along plenty of extra ammunition, too, thanks to the mercantile. So we're well equipped for a long chase if it's necessary. Now, I need to go check with Sheriff Carson one last time, then we'll ride out."

The posse members looked nervous but ready to pick up the trail of the bank robbers.

Smoke hoped all of them would return safely to Big Rock. He knew there was a significant chance that wouldn't happen . . .

Spaulding stood in the front room of his practice, wiping his hands on a blood-stained cloth, when Smoke came in.

"How's the other man doing?" Smoke asked. "The bank teller who was shot in the arm."

"He'll live," the doctor replied, "but the bullet shattered a bone, so he'll probably never have the full use of that arm again. Taking that into consideration, he should still make a reasonably good recovery."

"I'm glad to hear it. How about Monte?"

"The entrance and exit wounds have been thoroughly cleaned and disinfected, and I stitched them up so they'll heal. The bullet *may* have nicked the bone. I'm not sure, but the leg isn't broken and should heal just fine. Sheriff Carson lost quite a bit of blood and is weak from that. I've given him a sedative to help him rest."

"He's not knocked out, is he?" Smoke asked with a frown.

"Well, he may not have dozed off yet. Did you need to speak with him?"

"Yeah, just for a minute."

Spaulding nodded. "You'd best do it quickly, then, if he's not already asleep."

"Come with me, Doctor, if you don't mind," Smoke said.

"Of course. He's in this room here at the end of the hall."

Monte had been moved into a small, plainly furnished

room that the doctor used for patients who were recuperating. He lay in bed, propped up slightly on pillows, with his heavily bandaged leg stuck out straight in front of him.

For a moment, Smoke thought Monte was out already from the sedative Spaulding had given him, but at the sound of footsteps, the lawman opened his eyes. He had a little trouble focusing for a second. Then he said, "Smoke . . . Thought you'd already be after those owlhoots by now."

"We're just about to ride out, Monte," Smoke told him. "Before we go, you need to deputize me, so it'll be legal for me to lead that posse."

"No need to . . . worry about that. You know you've always got . . . my authority to act on behalf of the law . . . Consider yourself . . . sworn in."

"Good enough for me. Thanks, Monte." Smoke looked at Spaulding. "Doctor?"

"I assume you want me to act as witness. Certainly, Smoke. If it ever becomes necessary, I can swear that you're acting in a legal and duly appointed manner."

"We'd better ride, then. We have some bank robbers to catch."

When he got back to the sheriff's office a couple of minutes later, Smoke saw that another volunteer had arrived, bringing the posse's membership to an even dozen counting himself.

"I'm glad to see you," he told Louis Longmont. "I can't think of anybody else I'd rather have riding along with us."

"I always intended to come along," the dapper former gambler said. "I just had some business to wrap up first, before I leave Poke in charge. But I'm ready to ride."

"So are we, Smoke," another man said. "Let's get after those outlaws."

"Sounds good to me," Smoke said with a nod. "Mount up, men. Let's ride!"

CHAPTER 13

Desperation was growing inside Graham Blake, and he didn't like the feeling.

His two wounded men needed medical attention. Lester Stoughton and Paul Deere both swayed more than usual in their saddles, clearly weakened by loss of blood.

They didn't complain—much—but if they didn't get a chance to rest soon and have their wounds tended to, they might pass out and fall off their horses.

The horses weren't in good shape, either. Blake had tried not to push them too hard, but with the threat of a posse led by Smoke Jensen looming behind them, they couldn't afford to waste any time.

Normally, with the sheriff shot down and probably wounded seriously, Blake wouldn't have worried too much about pursuit. But according to what Stoughton said about him, this Jensen was a ring-tailed roarer and might be able to handle them all by himself, without a posse's help.

Blake still believed Jensen's reputation was probably inflated beyond the reality of his abilities, but it didn't pay to take unnecessary chances.

With all that weighing on Blake's mood, it didn't help matters when Ken Bennett suddenly asked, "What about that bear?"

"What bear?" Blake said without thinking.

"The one that caused all those fellas to rush out of town looking for him. The one you told us about that killed folks."

"What about him?" Blake asked impatiently.

"Well, if we see him, what do we do? You said there's a thousand dollars bounty on his head."

Maybe the reason Bennett didn't talk much was because he was stupid as a rock, Blake thought.

"We can't ride back into Big Rock and claim any reward," he said, keeping his voice level so as not to reveal the annoyance and frustration he felt. "If we do happen to see the beast, we'll stay away from it. Let somebody else worry about the damned thing."

"I'm surprised we haven't run into any of the men hunting for it," Frank Holt said.

"The last time it showed up was southeast of town," Blake explained, growing more exasperated that they were even talking about this. "I suppose a lot of the hunters went that direction today."

Bob Kramer spoke up, pointing and saying, "Look there. Is that smoke from a chimney?"

Blake was grateful for the distraction, as well as hoping that Kramer was right. Chimney smoke meant a cabin or ranch house. Maybe they would be able to get some fresh horses there.

He studied the gray tendril curling into the sky and decided it did come from a chimney.

"Let's take a look," he said.

"I hope whoever it is has some fresh horses," Holt said.

Kramer said, "I hope there's a good-looking woman or two around the place."

Blake resisted the temptation to take off his hat, ride alongside Kramer, and start swatting at him with it. He said, "I hope there's a woman there, too, because they're usually better at patching up injuries, but we don't have time for anything else. Do all of you understand me about that?"

"Maybe we could take the gals with us," Kramer suggested with a hopeful leer.

"We don't even know if there are any women where that smoke's coming from, and if there are, we're not taking them with us. Prisoners would just slow us down, and we can't afford that."

"Hell, Graham—"

"Blake's right about that," Holt interrupted. "There'll be time to worry about women when we're well away from the posse that's bound to be looking for us by now."

Blake appreciated the support from Holt but still didn't care for the man's tone. He pushed that out of his mind for the moment and concentrated on where they were going.

They lost sight of the smoke when they entered a wooded area, but Blake knew which direction they needed to go and didn't require the smoke to steer by.

Sure enough, when they broke out of the trees, they found themselves looking down at a bend in a creek. The bend enclosed an area a couple of hundred yards wide that ended in a shallow bluff dropping off to the water.

A log cabin sat within that bend. The smoke the outlaws had spotted rose from the stone chimney at one end of the structure, which was built Texas-style, with a roofed but otherwise open dogtrot in the middle between the two rooms.

The smoke confirmed that somebody was there. More importantly, a large pole corral stood beyond the cabin, with eight or ten horses milling around inside it. They were aware of strange horses approaching, and that had them worked up a little.

"That looks like just what we need," Holt said as they drew closer to the place.

"Let me do the talking," Blake said. "We don't want any more trouble than is necessary."

"Oh, it's gonna be necessary. These folks won't just let us swap horses without trying to stop us."

"They may not like it, but I'm betting when they see that they're outnumbered, they won't try anything."

Blake hoped he was right about that.

A couple of big brown dogs were lying in the open area between the cabins. There was a good reason it was called a dogtrot, Blake thought. The curs stood up and started barking as the riders came toward them.

A man stepped out of the cabin to the right and said to the dogs, "What are you loco varmints carryin' on about n—"

He stopped short as he saw the men on the tired horses.

"We've got company, Bella," he said, glancing over his shoulder.

The rancher wasn't carrying a rifle or wearing a gun belt, Blake noted. But as he and his men drew rein and stopped in front of the dogtrot, a woman stepped out of the cabin with a Winchester in her hands. The man partially shielded her from Blake's view, but he could see the rifle, all right.

The woman had blond hair pinned up on her head with several strands that had worked their way loose to dangle around her face. She was reasonably young and good-looking.

A hardness around her mouth and eyes told Blake that she might have been a soiled dove at one time. There was nothing unusual in that. A lot of doves got out of the business by marrying one of their customers.

A certain number of men were always going to fall in love with a whore.

This fellow was tall, broad shouldered, and dark haired.

He nodded and said, "Howdy, boys. Need to water your horses in the creek? You're welcome to do that."

Blake gave him a friendly smile and patted his mount's neck.

"I reckon they're pretty thirsty, all right," he said.

"Had a hard ride?"

"You could say that."

The rancher's eyes narrowed as he studied the strangers.

"Yeah, you look like you've been in a hurry," he said. "In fact, those horses look plumb worn out, but they appear to be decent mounts, if they were to be rested good and proper." He waved a hand lazily toward the corral. "Got some good animals in there, if you'd care to swap."

The suggestion took Blake completely by surprise. He had figured they would have to take the fresh horses at gunpoint and probably even kill the folks who lived there.

He tried not to look as thunderstruck as he felt as he said, "You want to swap horses with us?"

"Well . . . maybe not an even swap. You could throw in, say, fifty dollars."

Holt growled in his throat and leaned forward slightly in the saddle.

"Why, you—"

Blake lifted a hand to forestall whatever obscene insult Holt was about to spew. He didn't know anything about this couple, but an uneasy feeling stirred inside him, telling him it might be better to play along with them.

He didn't like the look in that woman's eyes as she stared past her husband's shoulder straight at him. The two of them couldn't hope to survive a shootout, but it was as if she were telling him, *Go ahead . . . but you'll die first.*

"That offer sounds fair to me, friend," Blake said, "but we need a little something extra, too. As you can see, two of my friends have been hurt. Is there any chance your beautiful wife there could tend to their injuries?"

The woman answered the question, saying, "I've patched up a few men in my time. They can come inside, and I'll do what I can for them."

"Be better if the rest of you stayed out here," the man added.

Blake hesitated, but only for a moment, as Deere said, "This leg of mine is hurting like a son of a gun."

"What you said is fine, mister," Blake told the rancher. "Your wife can see to my men, and you and the rest of us will figure out that horse trade."

"All right." The man turned slightly toward his wife, revealing that he had a pistol stuck in the waistband of his trousers at the small of his back. So he hadn't been unarmed, after all, Blake thought. The rancher said, "Take them in one at a time, Bella."

"Yeah, that was my thought, too," she said. She looked at the riders. "Which of you men is hurt the worst? You're each just about as bloody as the other one."

"Paul, you go first," Stoughton said to Deere. "I'm just creased. You had several pieces of buckshot go clean through your leg."

"I'm obliged to you," Deere said. His face had gotten rather pale and drawn during the ride. The shock of the wounds and the blood he had lost were starting to take a toll on him.

The blonde called Bella moved out from behind her husband and kept the Winchester leveled as she said, "He'll need help getting inside. A couple of you men give him a hand, then come back out here."

Blake nodded to Kramer and Bennett. "You boys handle that."

They dismounted, lifted Deere down from his saddle,

and wrapped an arm each around him. Deere walked a little, but mostly they carried him inside the cabin.

"Put him on the table," Bella told them. "Take that linen tablecloth off of there first, though!"

When Kramer and Bennett came out of the cabin a few moments later, Blake said to Bennett, "You stay here in case somebody needs a hand. The rest of us will go see about those horses."

Blake and Holt dismounted, joining Kramer on the ground. The young rancher moved closer to study the horses they'd been riding.

"These are decent saddle mounts. They've been ridden hard. You came from the direction of Big Rock."

"Where we came from is our business," Blake said.

The man nodded. "Truer words were never spoken, as the old saying goes. Walk over to the corral with me, and you can pick out which animals you'd like to swap for."

"We can take any of them in the corral?" Holt asked.

"That's right. I started this ranch to raise horses, and they don't do me any good unless I make a profit on them."

"You ain't all that particular who you trade with," Kramer said.

The rancher laughed. "I can't very well cast the first stone, like they talk about in the Good Book."

"Ridden some dark trails, have you?" Blake asked.

"I've heard a few owls calling in my time, let's put it that way." They had reached the corral. The man put a hand on the top rail and went on, "But sometimes a fella gets tired of living that way and decides he'll try to stay on the right side of the law for a change. That doesn't keep me from having some sympathy for men I might've shared a campfire with, back in other times and places."

"We never met," Blake said.

"No, but that doesn't keep us from recognizing each other."

"Well, we're obliged to you for helping us out."

"No, I'm obliged to you. You could have come in shooting." The man shrugged. "Bella and I would have put up a fight, of course, but I reckon the odds would've been against us." He chuckled. "We'd have whittled them down considerable before going under, though."

Blake didn't doubt that for a second. Now that he had gotten a better look at this man and talked to him some, he was glad he'd decided to be cautious. If they'd bulled in and tried to take what they wanted, they might have lost two or three men.

And Blake might have been one of them. He was glad things hadn't worked out that way.

He leaned on the corral fence, too, and said, "Let's take a look at these horses."

By the time they walked back to the cabin, having settled on which horses they were going to swap for, leaving the worn-out ones in the corral and leading the freshly saddled mounts, Deere was sitting on a backless bench in the dogtrot with his back propped against the cabin wall. Bandages were wrapped tightly and tied around his leg.

He bounced a tiny lead ball in the palm of his hand as he said, "No wonder it hurt so bad. Most of the buckshot went on through, but this piece was still in there. The lady dug it out and patched up all the holes."

Stoughton emerged from the cabin's open door, leaning on the blonde as he came out. Blake could tell from the stiff way he moved that he was heavily bandaged, too.

"Well?" Blake asked. "Are my friends going to live?"

"For now," Bella replied. "I wouldn't venture a guess as to how long, if you're on the run from the law." She glanced at her husband. "We know how dangerous that can be, don't we, Danny?"

He smiled. "We don't need to talk about that." With a nod to Blake, he went on, "I'm just glad we were able to do a little business without having any trouble."

"Trouble's something we don't need," Blake said. He drew some gold coins from his pocket and passed them over to the rancher. He hadn't had to dig into the loot from the bank in order to pay the premium on the horse trade, but what he'd just handed over represented most of the funds he had left without doing that.

"Obliged to you," the man said as he pocketed the coins. "And good luck."

Blake nodded to him and gestured for the other men to mount up. They swung into their saddles and rode away.

Once they were out of earshot of the cabin, Kramer said, "That sure was a mighty sweet-looking woman, Graham. I still think we should've brought her with us. We could've knocked her man on the head when he wasn't lookin'."

Bennett surprised them all by laughing.

"You damn fool," he said to Kramer. "That was Dan St. Cloud. You wouldn't have taken him by surprise. If you'd tried it, he would have killed you. And if you *had* managed to grab the girl, she'd have cut your guts out the first chance she got. She went into the roughest whorehouse in Texas and came out running the place."

"Well, look at you talking up a storm," Blake said. "If you knew those folks, you should have spoken up."

Bennett shook his head. "I don't know them. St. Cloud was pointed out to me on the street one day in a settlement down there, and I heard talk about Bella but never laid eyes on her until today. St. Cloud robbed banks and held up trains and stagecoaches all over Texas, New Mexico Territory, and Arizona. Hard to believe he's gone straight.

I suppose maybe some fellas just aren't cut out to be owlhoots, even though they're good at it."

Holt said, "You make it sound like we're lucky those two didn't kill us all and take that loot for themselves."

Bennett just looked at him and didn't say anything.

"We've got good, strong horses under us again, Lester and Paul are patched up, and it didn't take long," Blake said. "I'm going to consider all that good luck and not complain about it. Come on, I want to be deeper in the mountains by nightfall so we can find a good place to hole up."

CHAPTER 14

The bank robbers had been in too much of a hurry as they were leaving Big Rock to worry about trying to cover their tracks. They had just stampeded out of town as fast as possible.

Because of that, the trail they had left was easy to follow at first. Smoke had no trouble tracking the six horses. The outlaws had ridden out of town and then fled north, taking out across country without following any road or trail.

Smoke and Louis Longmont rode side by side, a little ahead of the others. Quietly, so the words wouldn't be heard over the hoofbeats of the posse's mounts, Louis said, "We may have that bunch outnumbered two to one, but if it comes down to a gunfight, these men won't match up very well with them."

"I know that," Smoke said. "A man has to work with the tools he has, though."

"If we swung by the Sugarloaf and picked up Pearlie and Cal and a few of your other hands, it would go a long way toward making the odds truly even."

"It would," Smoke agreed, "but it would also take too long. Those bank robbers already have a lead on us. If we give them an even bigger one, they'll get up into the mountains where it'll be harder to root them out."

"I see your point," the gambler and former gunman said. "You and I should be able to take care of most of the gunplay."

"That's what I'm counting on." Smoke glanced over his shoulder at the men following them. "Besides, you never know how well a man will do under fire until the time comes. Those fellas might surprise you."

"I hope you're right," Louis said, but he didn't sound as if he were actually convinced.

A short time later, Smoke found a place where the gang had stopped for a few minutes to rest their horses. He could tell that by the amount of droppings on the ground.

When the outlaws had resumed their flight, they were no longer moving in a headlong rush. Whoever was leading them seemed to be making more of an effort to travel over rocky stretches of ground that didn't take prints, as well.

Because of that, Smoke, Louis, and the others had to slow down, too, and be more careful not to miss the tracks.

The more deliberate pace gnawed at Smoke's nerves, but there was nothing he could do about it. If they lost the trail, their quarry would stand an even better chance of getting away from them.

"Well, there's one good thing you can say about this, I suppose," Louis mused as they rode.

"What's that?"

"Everybody's forgotten about that bear."

Smoke let out a grim laugh. "Not everybody," he said. "I've been keeping an eye open for bear sign."

"What will you do if we find it? Go after the bear or stay on the trail of those outlaws?"

"That's a good question. The bear never robbed a bank."

"Give him time," Louis said. "From what I've heard

about the way he acts, he's more intelligent than most bears. Who knows what he's capable of?"

"A bank-robbing bear," Smoke said, nodding. "Now that would be something."

A short time later, the trail led them to a small ranch. Alerted by the hoofbeats, two big brown dogs loped out to greet them, barking loudly.

Smoke had already spotted a tall, dark-haired man standing beside a corral. The man picked up a Winchester that was leaning against the pole fence and walked toward them. He didn't hurry, but his movements had a brisk efficiency about them.

Smoke motioned for the posse to stop, then rode forward slowly with Louis at his side. He glanced toward the cabin. In the afternoon sunlight, the dogtrot was in shadow, but Smoke could tell the door on one side was open.

He was pretty sure he caught a glimpse of another rifle barrel sticking a few inches out of that door.

Smoke wore a smile on his face as he reined in and nodded to the man who now stood in front of him and Louis.

"Howdy," Smoke said.

"Afternoon," the man said back, his face carefully expressionless.

Smoke rested easy in the saddle and thumbed his hat back. He was trying to show this man that they meant no harm, but he didn't know if the effort would do any good.

Something about the man told Smoke that he seldom, if ever, let down his guard.

"My name is Smoke Jensen," Smoke said, plainspoken as always. "I own a ranch called the Sugarloaf."

The man nodded and said, "I've heard of you and your ranch, Mr. Jensen." The Western code of conduct impelled him to introduce himself. "My name is Dan . . . Miller."

He hesitated just slightly before saying the last name, barely noticeable but enough to tell Smoke it probably wasn't his real name.

That was all right. Out on the frontier, a man had the right to call himself whatever he wanted. For a good long while, when he'd been wanted on those phony legal charges, Smoke had called himself Buck West. His brother Luke had gone by the name Luke Smith for several years, too, before reclaiming the Jensen name.

So if this fella wanted to call himself Miller, that was fine.

"It's been a while since I've been in this part of the valley," Smoke went on. "The last time I was, this spread belonged to an old-timer named Henry Browne."

Miller nodded. "I bought the spread from Mr. Browne about six months ago. My wife and I are raising horses."

Louis said, "I remember Browne saying something about wanting to sell out, the last time I talked to him. I'm Louis Longmont, by the way."

"Heard of you, too," Miller said. "What brings you fellas out this way?"

"We're on the trail of some outlaws who robbed the bank in Big Rock earlier today." Smoke didn't see any reason to be deceptive about it. "They killed a man and wounded two others, including our sheriff."

"And that's why you and Mr. Longmont are leading a posse after them?"

"That's right." Smoke watched Miller closely as he asked, "Have you seen them?"

For a moment, Miller didn't answer. Smoke could tell he was thinking things over, deciding what to say.

Even so, Smoke was a little surprised when the man said, "They were here," then inclined his head toward the corral.

"The horses they rode in on are over there with some of mine."

"You swapped with them?" Louis exclaimed.

"There were six of them," Miller said curtly. "My wife and I are here alone. They didn't look to cause trouble. They just wanted fresh horses. What the hell was I supposed to do, shoot it out with them?"

"They'd have killed you and taken the horses anyway," Smoke said.

"That's what I thought. We would have gotten two or three of them, mind you . . . but we'd still be dead."

Smoke nodded toward the cabin and said, "Is that your wife over there, poking a rifle out the door?"

"That's right." Without taking his eyes off Smoke and Louis, Miller called, "Bella, step on out."

An attractive blond woman moved out into the dogtrot. From the way she handled the rifle, Smoke could tell it wasn't the first time she'd had her hands on a Winchester.

"We're not looking to make trouble for you," Smoke said. "What you did was reasonable, I reckon. I appreciate you telling us the truth."

Miller's shoulders rose and fell a little. "You'd have looked at those horses in the corral and figured it out anyway. You can tell that they've been ridden pretty hard recently. It'll take a while for them to recover from being run like that."

Smoke smiled faintly. "Yeah, that's probably the way it would have played out."

"We could tell they were on the dodge, but we didn't know about the bank robbery, and we sure didn't know they'd killed anybody."

"It should have been a reasonable assumption," Louis said. "Especially since at least two of them were wounded."

Miller nodded and said, "It was just those two. The others weren't hurt."

"I suppose they asked for medical assistance, and you gave them that, too," Smoke said.

"Bella tended to their wounds. We just wanted them to ride on and leave us alive, Mr. Jensen."

Louis said bluntly, "You're lucky they didn't take your wife with them."

"Well, now, if they had tried that . . . there would have been shots exchanged. Neither of us would have allowed that to happen."

Smoke thought for a moment, then said, "I don't mean to be insulting, Miller, but I suppose you can prove you bought this spread from Henry Browne?"

"The bill of sale's inside the cabin. I can get it and show it to you, if you insist."

"No, that's all right," Smoke said, figuring that Miller wouldn't have made that offer if he couldn't follow through on it. Unless he was bluffing.

But Smoke's instincts told him this man wasn't the bluffing sort. He said what he meant and meant what he said. Smoke recognized that quality in other men because he possessed it himself.

"I'll take your word for it," Smoke went on. "Just one more question. Do you want to come with us?"

"After that gang?" Miller shook his head. "No, thanks. It's not my fight."

Louis said, "You don't have any money in the bank in Big Rock?"

"As a matter of fact, I don't, and I didn't know the fella who was killed. I'm sorry for his death, but he was no friend or relative of mine."

"Fair enough," Smoke said. "Are you willing to point out which direction they headed when they left?"

For the first time, a shadow of a smile touched Dan Miller's lips.

"You said one more question. That's the third one since you said that. But you'll follow their tracks anyway, and I don't owe *them* anything, either." Miller nodded toward the mountains. "They rode north. I reckon they're going to try to get up in the high country and give you the slip there."

"That may be their intention, Mr. Miller, but they're not going to get away," Smoke said. He pulled his hat brim back down and pinched it as he nodded to the blond woman in the dogtrot. "Good afternoon to you, Mrs. Miller."

She just gave him a cool, level stare in return.

Smoke turned his horse and rode past the corral toward the creek. Louis was beside him, and the other members of the posse trailed closely behind. Their horses splashed through the stream. As the men rode toward a line of trees in the distance, Louis said quietly, "That fellow may claim to be peaceable, but he still has plenty of bark on him."

"I've got a feeling the lady does, too."

"You think he used to be an outlaw and gave it up to start a horse ranch?"

"Seems likely," Smoke said, "but whether it's true or not, it's none of our business."

"He gave that gang a better chance to get away by swapping horses with them."

"Like he said, what else was he supposed to do? We'll still catch up to them, sooner or later."

They rode a little farther before Louis mused, "I think Mr. and Mrs. Miller would be bad folks to have for enemies."

"More than likely," Smoke agreed, "but under the right circumstances, they might make good friends, too."

* * *

Once they had fresh horses under them, Blake and the other outlaws were able to move faster again. Blake didn't know the mountains in these parts, but he figured he would recognize a good spot to hole up when he saw it.

"You really think we can give that posse the slip?" Holt asked as they began to climb into the foothills.

"I'll be honest with you, Frank. I don't know. Most of them are townies. They probably don't have the sand for a long chase. It just depends on how hard Jensen is able to push them and for how long."

"Men like that are scared rabbits," Holt said dismissively. "If they had any guts and ambition, they would have been out looking for that bear so they could collect the reward and be heroes. Having most of that sort gone from Big Rock was what we were counting on, wasn't it?"

"Yeah, it was," Blake agreed, wondering what Holt was driving at.

"Then it stands to reason that if a few of them were to be killed, the rest of the bunch would turn tail and run. Especially if this Jensen fella is one of those who die."

"You think we should fort up somewhere and ambush them," Blake said as understanding dawned on him. It wasn't a bad idea, but he was annoyed with himself that Holt had come up with it instead of him.

"If we can find a good place for it. I've been keeping an eye out."

"So have I," Blake lied. "The same thing occurred to me a while back. I didn't want to say anything until we found somewhere it might work."

He didn't know if Holt believed him or not, but he didn't particularly care, either. Nobody could read his mind and prove anything either way.

He definitely kept his eyes open for a suitable spot, though, as they climbed higher.

The posse had to slow down and let the horses rest. While they were at the Miller ranch, Smoke had considered swapping some of their horses, too, but Miller didn't have enough mounts on hand for the entire group. Swapping out a few of the animals really wouldn't have accomplished anything.

Louis knew that, too, but it bothered him that the outlaws were increasing their lead. He said as much to Smoke during one stop to let the horses blow, then he sighed.

"I know it can't be helped. I just don't want them to get away, that's all."

"None of us do," Smoke said. "We'll run them to ground sooner or later."

Louis glanced at the men who had dismounted and were standing around, holding their horses' reins, getting drinks of water from their canteens, and talking among themselves. Some wore suits and vests, and they all had on shoes. Not a pair of riding boots among them.

"You think these men can stand up to a lengthy pursuit?"

"Their hearts are in the right places, I'm sure of that. I warned them before we left town that we might be out on the trail for several days."

"But can they hold up to the strain?"

"I reckon we'll find out," Smoke said. "We'll push on in a few more minutes."

Louis looked at the sky. "It'll be dark in two more hours."

"I know." Smoke was worried about that, but there was nothing he could do to stop the world from turning.

One thing they had on their side, Smoke thought as they rode on a short time later, was that he knew the high country they were headed for. He figured there was a good chance he was more familiar with it than the outlaws they were pursuing.

There were some blind canyons up there, he recalled. If the bank robbers happened to find themselves in one of those, they would be trapped.

That would be a stroke of luck, but if the posse could get close enough to their quarry to harass the outlaws with some rifle fire, they might be able to push the fugitives right into one of those dead ends.

That was the plan vaguely forming in the back of Smoke's mind, anyway. A lot of things would have to break the right way for it to work.

A big, rocky shoulder bordered by steep-sided bluffs jutted out from the base of one of the peaks up ahead. The sky still had enough daylight in it for Smoke to make out the tracks they were following. The trail led toward that shoulder.

He knew that to the right of the big bluffs, a ledge curled around and led to the top. It was a natural path, and if the outlaws had found it, they would more than likely follow it. That was the easiest way into the lower reaches of the mountains.

But that way held dangers for the posse. As few as two well-armed men could put up quite a fight and hold the trail against a larger force.

As soon as that thought went through Smoke's mind, he slowed his horse and signaled for Louis and the other men to do likewise.

"What is it, Smoke?" Louis asked.

"I want you boys to wait here while I do a little scouting."

"I think I should come with you."

"No, you stay here," Smoke said in a flat voice that brooked no argument. His tone eased a little as he added,

"If anything happens to me, you'll have to take over, Louis. You're the only one who can, and you know it."

Louis frowned, but he nodded in acceptance of Smoke's decision. He knew his old friend was right.

"I'll be back," Smoke said confidently. While the others sat there with worried expressions on their faces, he rode toward the spot where the trail leading up and around the promontory began.

CHAPTER 15

Graham Blake looked back down the sloping trail. He could see about fifty yards of the broad ledge before it curved and went out of sight.

To Blake's left was an almost sheer cliff that dropped seventy or eighty feet to the ground below. To his right was a cleft in the rock maybe ten feet wide and twenty feet deep. That opening was big enough for two men and horses to hide inside it. Some brush growing across the gap and just outside it made concealment even easier.

Behind Blake, the ledge continued, rising and curving until it reached the top of the rocky shoulder that thrust out from the mountain. Frank Holt had scouted up there already and reported that the trail opened onto a broad, fairly level bench that they could cross easily before reaching the next slope leading higher into the mountains.

Satisfied that they wouldn't find a better spot for an ambush, Blake nodded to Bob Kramer and Ken Bennett and said, "All right, boys, you'll stay here and deal with that posse when it comes around the bend."

"Just the two of us?" Kramer said. He sounded like he didn't care for that idea.

Blake waved a hand at the trail. "Look at it! It's like a shooting gallery, boys. You can't miss. Just hide in that brush, and when the whole bunch comes in sight, you open up on them with your Winchesters. Hell, you can probably kill every one of those possemen before they even figure out what's going on."

"But Smoke Jensen—" Bennett began.

"You know what he looks like," Blake interrupted. "Besides, he'll probably be right in front, leading the way. Just shoot him first! Once he's dead, the others won't put up much of a fight."

Kramer rubbed his jaw, made a face, and said, "That's a heap of killin', Graham. More than we've killed in all our jobs put together, I reckon."

"They made the choice to come after us," Blake said in a flat, hard voice. "Whatever happens to them, they've got it coming."

Bennett asked, "Why'd you pick the two of us for this ambush?"

"Lester and Paul are wounded."

"You and Frank aren't," Kramer said.

"Everybody does his part," Blake said, feeling frustrated again. "We all shot those folks up in Wyoming, remember, and I gunned that fool who jumped me in Big Rock."

"Why are you boys worried about how many you kill?" Holt rasped at Kramer and Bennett. "They can only hang you once, can't they?"

None of them could argue with that.

"How far behind us do you reckon they are?" Kramer asked.

Earlier, while checking their back trail with a spyglass he took from his saddlebags, Blake had spotted the posse, barely visible in the distance behind them.

In answer to Kramer's question, he said, "At least an hour. More likely two. So you'll have plenty of time to get settled in while you're waiting."

"Plenty of time to worry, you mean," Bennett said. He held up a hand to forestall any recriminations. "But that's all right, Graham. We'll take care of it, won't we, Bob?"

"Sure," Kramer agreed, then narrowed his eyes. "You'll wait for us up there on that bench, won't you? You're not getting any ideas about runnin' off with the loot and leaving us here, are you?"

"We wouldn't do that," Blake assured him.

Kramer and Bennett nodded but didn't look completely convinced by his denial.

Lester Stoughton and Paul Deere had remained in their saddles while the others were discussing the ambush. Bandaged up as they were, climbing off and on a horse was just too much trouble and too uncomfortable unless it was absolutely necessary.

With the details settled, Blake and Holt swung up into their saddles again while Kramer and Bennett led their mounts into the cleft in the rock. A few clumps of hardy grass grew in there, so the horses had something to graze on while their masters waited for the posse to show up.

The others rode on, leaving the two men there.

They rolled quirlies and smoked, talking quietly now and then. After a while, Kramer got a flask from his saddlebags, and he and Bennett passed it back and forth, taking swigs of the whiskey it contained.

"I reckon if Graham was here, he'd complain about us drinkin'," Kramer said as he handed over the flask.

Bennett tipped it to his lips for a moment. When he lowered it, he said, "As long as we get that posse off our trail, I don't think he'll have a right to say much."

"That never stopped him before!"

Both men shared a laugh at that.

When they stopped laughing, they heard the faint sound of hoofbeats drifting up from somewhere below.

Both men stiffened for a moment, then Bennett shoved the flask back into Kramer's hand.

"They're coming," he said. "We'd better get ready."

Kramer screwed the cap back on the flask and put it away. He pulled his Winchester from its saddle scabbard. Bennett did likewise. Earlier, they had both worked the levers on their rifles, so they knew each weapon had a bullet in the chamber, ready to fire.

They had tied their horses to the brush, too, just inside the opening. Despite what Bennett had just said, there really wasn't much to do to get ready for the ambush. They crouched in the thick growth just outside the spot where the cleft opened onto the ledge.

After they had both listened intently for a moment, Bennett grated a curse and said, "That's not a whole posse headed this way!"

"No, it sounds more like one horse," Kramer agreed.

"Jensen must have sent a man ahead to scout the trail. What do we do now?"

Kramer chewed his lip in thought, then said, "If we shoot him, it'll warn the others and they won't come up the trail. They'll find some other way around and still be after us."

"Maybe we should wait until he rides past and then jump him," Bennett suggested. "Then we can kill him without making much racket."

Kramer considered for a second and nodded.

"That seems like our best bet," he said. "I'm bigger'n you, so whoever it is, I'll grab him and pull him off his horse, then you move in, quick-like, and get him with your knife."

"All right."

"Just don't stab me by mistake!"

"I don't know, you're a pretty big target," Bennett said, grinning to show that he was just joking.

The two outlaws drew back into the opening and leaned their rifles against the rock wall. Bennett got a sheathed Bowie knife from his saddlebags.

Crouching even lower, they moved out where they could part the brush carefully and peer down the trail again. The sounds of the approaching horse had grown steadily louder. As they watched, the lone rider came around the bend and started up the ledge toward them.

Bennett slid the blade free. The late afternoon sun winked off the metal for a second as he breathed another curse and whispered, "That's him! That's Smoke Jensen!"

"You mean he came ahead to scout himself, instead of sending one of the others?"

"I tell you, it's him!" Bennett insisted in a hissing under-tone. "Now what do we do?"

"We can still jump him, just like we planned," Kramer said. "He's just one man."

"If even half the things I've heard about Smoke Jensen are true, I don't know if the two of us can handle him, Bob. I think we should go ahead and shoot him, like we planned to start with."

Kramer shook his head. "That'll warn the others."

"It doesn't matter," Bennett insisted. "Like Graham said, if Jensen is dead, the rest of the bunch will give up. They're just a bunch of storekeepers and clerks, maybe a lawyer or somebody like that. When they hear the shots and Jensen doesn't come back, they'll know he's dead. And they'll know the same thing is waiting for them if they keep coming after us."

Kramer rubbed his heavy jaw and frowned in thought. He looked like the process was painful.

Finally, he said, "You might be right. Anyway, even if they don't turn back, Jensen's the most dangerous one of the bunch, ain't he?"

"Smoke Jensen's always going to be the most dangerous one in any bunch he's part of."

Kramer nodded. "Then I reckon you're right. Let's go ahead and kill him while we've got the chance."

Bennett sheathed the knife and shoved it into the waistband of his trousers. Both men grabbed the rifles they had leaned against the wall just inside the opening and catfooted out far enough to kneel and peek through the brush again.

The horse's hoofbeats were louder now. It wasn't far off.

As Bennett leaned forward and ever so cautiously parted the branches so he could peer through the narrow gap, what he saw made his heart suddenly slug harder in his chest.

The horse was there, all right, still walking slowly up the trail toward the ambush site.

But the saddle on its back was empty, and the reins were looped around the horn.

Where in blazes was Smoke Jensen?

It was just the faintest, most fleeting flicker of light that warned Smoke as it darted across the ledge in front of him, a good distance up the trail near some brush. Most men never would have seen it.

As it was, Smoke's keen vision barely registered the sight.

That was enough. The sun had just reflected off something up ahead. It might not be anything threatening, might be something natural and not man-made . . .

But if it wasn't, then why had the tiny reflection moved?

Although that clump of brush didn't look big enough for any bushwhackers to hide behind, Smoke honed in on it as the most likely source of a potential threat. The growth was thick enough he couldn't see through it, but somebody could be watching him through tiny gaps between branches.

Following his instincts, he quickly looped the reins around the saddle horn, kicked his feet free of the stirrups, and slid to the left, off the horse.

As his feet hit the trail, he grabbed his hat off his head and lightly swatted the horse's rump. The animal kept moving.

Smoke put his hat on, pressed his back against the rock wall, and drew his Colt. He held it alongside his right ear, pointed the barrel at the sky, and waited.

Flattened against the bluff as he was, the slight curve in the trail meant he couldn't see all of the brush, only the very edge of the clump. But it moved suddenly, and he heard boot leather scrape on the ground.

Just as he had thought it might, the sight of the empty saddle had drawn the ambushers out. He stepped forward, turned, and leveled the revolver.

Forty feet away, two of the outlaws stood with rifles in their hands, their legs and the lower halves of their torsos hidden by the brush. They stared down the trail in utter confusion.

That confusion vanished as soon as they saw Smoke and realized the trick he had played on them.

"Drop the rifles and get your hands up!" he called to them.

Instead, the men flung the Winchesters to their shoulders and opened fire.

Smoke crouched slightly and squeezed the Colt's trigger. His horse was between him and the outlaws, which made shooting tricky. The big bay was a dependable mount, and he didn't want to lose it.

The two bushwhackers weren't worried about that. They sprayed lead along the trail, perfectly willing to kill the horse if it meant getting Smoke, too.

Smoke's first bullet whistled past the bay's shoulder.

One of the outlaws' slugs burned along the horse's right hip and made it scream in pain, then rear up and paw at the air with its hooves.

Smoke took advantage of that, crouching and moving to his left so he had a clearer shot past the rearing horse at one of his targets. He fired again, and this time the .45 caliber round punched into the upper left chest of the bank robber closest to the edge of the trail.

The impact knocked the man halfway around and caused him to drop his rifle. He pressed both hands to his chest. Blood welled between his splayed fingers. Hard hit, probably dying, he reeled forward . . .

Then shrieked as the ledge disappeared under his feet and he pitched forward into empty space. That scream ended abruptly a moment later.

Smoke's horse, momentarily maddened by the pain of the bullet burn, charged into a gallop as soon as its front hooves hit the ground again. It ran up the wide ledge toward the top, past the brush where the ambushers had been hidden.

The second bushwhacker stopped his wild shooting. As Smoke fired again, the outlaw ducked back and disappeared into what had to be an opening in the rock wall that Smoke couldn't see from where he was.

Smoke ran up the trail toward the spot where the bushwhacker had vanished, watching intently for any sign of movement. He was ready to fire in a split second if he needed to.

Then a riderless horse burst into the open. It was being crowded to the right, down the ledge toward Smoke, by another mount that charged into the open a split second later. The riderless horse, spooked by all the gun-thunder and out of control, barreled directly at Smoke. He had to hold his fire and leap toward the rock wall to get out of the way.

By the time the runaway horse had passed Smoke, the escaping outlaw was well up the trail, riding for the top as hard as he could. He bent far forward over his mount's neck so he didn't present much of a target.

Smoke tried a final shot anyway, but the curve of the trail carried the bushwhacker out of sight and the bullet didn't hit anything except empty air.

Smoke couldn't see his horse anymore, either. It might have been most of the way to the top by then.

He punched the expended cartridges out of the Colt's cylinder and replaced them with fresh rounds. That was always the first thing he did after a dustup like this one, as soon as he got the chance.

Then, holding the revolver at his side just in case the surviving outlaw doubled back to make another try for him, which seemed highly unlikely, he moved to the edge of the trail and looked down.

The man he had shot was sprawled at the base of the slope, lying face down in a dark pool of blood. If Smoke's bullet hadn't killed him, the fall would have. Either way, Smoke was confident the hombre would never move again.

He could still hear the stampeded horse heading toward the bottom of the ledge. Those hoofbeats stopped, but then started up again a moment later, accompanied by the sounds of many more horses. Smoke wasn't surprised when Louis Longmont and the rest of the posse came into view after a few minutes.

Louis was in front, leading what Smoke assumed was the dead outlaw's horse, since the one who'd gotten away had taken the other mount. Louis rode up, reined in, and asked, "Are you all right, Smoke?"

"Yeah, they threw a whole heap of lead my way, but they managed to miss with all of it except for one round that creased my horse."

Louis looked around. "Where is your horse?"

"Took off for the top of the trail at a dead run. So did one of the varmints we're after, when he saw that their ambush wasn't going to work."

"How many were there?"

"Just a couple."

Louis lifted an inquisitive eyebrow.

Smoke nodded toward the edge of the trail and said, "The other one went off there, with some of my lead in him."

"Well, that's one we don't have to worry about, anyway," Louis murmured.

"Yeah, we'll whittle 'em down one at a time if we have to," Smoke said.

He glanced at the sky. No sunlight reached the ledge anymore. Shadows had crept over it as the fiery orb dropped behind the peaks to the west.

"But we won't do it today," he went on. "As soon as we find out what's at the top of this trail, we'd better hunt for a good place to make camp."

CHAPTER 16

During the late afternoon and early evening, more than a hundred men who had spent the day fruitlessly combing the valley for the rogue grizzly drifted back into town.

They were shocked to hear about the bank robbery in which one man had been killed and two more wounded, including Sheriff Monte Carson. The only good news was that the outlaws hadn't gotten away with all the money in the bank.

The heavyset bartender called Pudge was in his element, standing behind the hardwood and telling everybody who came into the Brown Dirt Cowboy Saloon in colorful detail about the holdup and the resulting shootout in which the sheriff and Smoke Jensen had been trapped in a crossfire in the middle of the street.

"I wouldn't have bet money that either of them fellas would come outta that fracas with a whole skin, not even Smoke," Pudge declared in his deep, gravelly voice as he wiped the bar with a rag and looked around at the eagerly listening customers. "The air was so thick with lead I don't reckon a fly could'a buzzed through there without gettin' ventilated." He frowned and paused in his circular wiping. "Although, come to think of it, I don't rightly reckon you could ventilate anything that small. If a bullet was to hit a fly, it'd just plumb smoosh the little critter to nothin'.'"

"If anybody could shoot the wings off a fly, it'd be Smoke Jensen," one of the men said.

"Nobody's talkin' about shootin' the wings off a fly," another complained. "Pudge was tellin' us about the bank robbery."

"How many robbers were there?" a third man asked.

Pudge shook his head and replied, "I couldn't say for sure. I don't know if anybody ever got a good count, the way so many wild shots were buzzin' around and everything was all confused. Most folks ducked for cover right at the start of the ruckus and kept their heads down until it was all over."

"You've got to have some idea."

"Half a dozen would be my guess," Pudge said with a solemn nod. "At least that many."

"And Smoke's gone after 'em, you say?"

"Him and Louis Longmont," Pudge confirmed. "And some other fellas who weren't out huntin' that bear."

One of the men groaned. "Don't mention that blasted bear. All day in the saddle and not a sign of the damn thing. And today's not the first day a lot of us have gone out lookin' and come up empty."

Pudge said, "I heard a few fellas who were in here earlier talkin' about how some of the bunches wound up shootin' at each other. Nobody was killed, but I reckon that was pure luck."

"I would have bet almost anything that Smoke would've tracked and killed that varmint by now."

Emmett Brown walked up in time to hear that comment from one of the saloon's patrons. Brown hooked his thumbs in his vest pockets, scowled, and said, "Smoke Jensen's not superhuman. He's a man like any other man. Sometimes he fails."

The saloonkeeper got along well enough with Smoke, but Smoke was good friends with Louis Longmont and Longmont's was the Brown Dirt Cowboy's fiercest competition in Big Rock, so it was natural that Brown might resent hearing his customers singing Smoke's praises.

"Maybe so, but I still reckon Smoke's got the best chance of doin' it," the customer insisted.

"He'll have to get back from leading that posse after those bank robbers first," Brown said. "In the meantime, with Sheriff Carson laid up, the town's pretty much defenseless."

"The sheriff's got a couple of deputies keepin' an eye on things. He told them to stay here instead of goin' with the posse just so the town wouldn't be defenseless," one of the customers contradicted.

Pudge could tell that his boss had his dander up. Brown was liable to keep arguing with the customers until he lost his temper. That wouldn't be good for business, so Pudge decided it might be wise to change the subject.

"Speakin' of shootin' the wings off of flies," he began, "back durin' the war we had a fella in our outfit who could do that, I'll bet. I never saw such a good long-range shot, not even Smoke Jensen. I swear, this fella could hit a man-sized target at a mile, the way that buffalo hunter Billy Dixon is supposed to have done down yonder in Texas durin' that big fight with the Comanches. I've seen him do it."

"I don't believe that story about Dixon," one man scoffed. "That's just a windy that somebody spun."

"Lots of men claim to have been there and seen it."

"Any time somethin' happens, a whole heap more men claim to have been there than possibly could've been. I've even heard there are some gents who claim to have been at the Little Big Horn with Custer and survived."

Several men nodded sagely and muttered agreement.

"Well, we know that's not true," Brown said. "Might as well claim you were at the Alamo with Davy Crockett and Jim Bowie!"

"Jamie MacCallister was," another man pointed out. "Colonel Travis sent him out to deliver dispatches before the final attack. That's a plumb fact."

"Well, it's not the same thing at all," Brown said. "MacCallister wasn't there for the final fight."

"Reckon it would've made any difference if he had been?"

"One more man against six thousand Mexicans? I don't see how it could have!"

The conversation about famous frontier battles continued. Pudge was pleased that he had maneuvered the discussion away from Smoke Jensen and Brown had calmed down.

Eventually, the men who had spent the day unsuccessfully bear hunting began to drift out, tired and ready to go home. Some of them would go back out again the next day, more than likely, but a dispirited air hung over the Brown Dirt Cowboy Saloon and Big Rock in general. Between that killer bear and the bloody bank robbery, Big Rock just seemed to be flat out of luck.

Pudge mused on that as he closed down the saloon at midnight. The soiled doves had retreated to their rooms upstairs, alone now since their customers were gone for the night. Brown was holed up in his office, going over the books or whatever it was he did in there.

Pudge cleaned up the bar and wiped out glasses while the swamper, Jimmy Malone, put the chairs up on the tables and swept. When Jimmy was finished, Pudge told him, "Go on home, Jimmy, and watch out for that bear along the way."

"Why, ye don't think th' creature would come right into town, do ye, Pudge?" the elderly Irishman asked.

"No, bears don't like towns. More than likely he'll steer clear of Big Rock, I reckon."

"Maybe before I go, a wee dram o' whiskey, perhaps, to settle my nerves?" Jimmy suggested. "So I can be more watchful, ye know."

Pudge chuckled as he reached for a bottle and glass.

"Just a small one," he told Jimmy.

He poured the drink for the swamper, then one for himself and tossed it back. The whiskey was pretty raw, since Brown didn't see any need to spend extra money on the good stuff. Most of the patrons of the Brown Dirt Cowboy never knew the difference.

The whiskey landed in Pudge's belly with a burst of welcome warmth. He wasn't a big drinker, which was an advantage in his profession. He was able to keep a clear head while he was working, but now and then he enjoyed a wee dram, as Jimmy put it.

The swamper expelled a satisfied sigh and set the empty glass on the bar.

"'Tis thankin' ye I am, Pudge," Jimmy said, then he went out through the batwings. Pudge closed the actual doors behind him and locked them.

He went behind the bar, took off his apron, and hung it on a nail. His coat was folded neatly and placed on a shelf underneath the bar. He took it out, put it on, and went through a door into the storage room. He let himself out through another door that opened into the alley behind the saloon and locked it behind him with a key Brown had given him.

It was dark back here, mighty dark, and as Pudge walked along, he thought that maybe he should have brought a lantern from the saloon to light his way to the rooming house where he lived.

Most nights that idea never even crossed his mind, because he knew the route so well that he had no trouble finding his way. The only real danger was that sometimes a drunk might wander into the alley and pass out. Pudge had stumbled over such human obstacles now and then.

That night, though, it might have been nice to be able to see. He believed what he had told Jimmy: it was unlikely that bear would venture anywhere close to town. Wild animals didn't like civilization. It had been a long time since a bear or a mountain lion had been spotted in the vicinity of Big Rock.

The bear plaguing the area now was different, though. It seemed to do things that bears normally wouldn't. That meant it was unpredictable. Maybe he should have warned old Jimmy to be careful after all, Pudge told himself.

That was when he smelled something wild and rank and heard a rapid scuffling noise behind him. He started to turn, but as he came around, something struck him across the face with terrific force, rending flesh and gouging deep and exploding agony through Pudge's brain. The force of the blow drove him to his knees and then he was bowled over onto his back . . . not an easy thing to do to a man of Pudge's size.

Screams filled the deep shadows and shredded the peaceful night.

Dr. Spaulding had stepped out onto his front porch a few minutes earlier to enjoy a few breaths of crisp night air. Even though he kept his house well ventilated because he knew fresh air was good for his patients, it was inevitable that medicinal odors lingered in there, along with other, more unpleasant smells at times.

He had checked on Monte a few minutes earlier and found the lawman sleeping soundly. He wouldn't have expected anything less because he had given Monte a draught to help him slumber. The rest would do him good.

The sheriff was the only patient Spaulding had recuperating at his house at the moment. He had made the rounds of the others in town currently under his care and found them all to be doing well.

Then he had returned to his house, updated his notes on the cases, and spent some time reading articles in the latest medical journals that had arrived in the mail bag on the train.

It had been a good, productive evening, and now he was ready to relax a bit before turning in.

His collar was loose and his sleeves were rolled up. He brought out his pipe and a pouch of tobacco and soon had the old briar going. Fragrant clouds of smoke wreathed his head.

That smoke did nothing to muffle the screams that suddenly came to Spaulding's ears. It was late enough at night that Big Rock was dark and quiet . . . except for the shrieks of a man in terrible pain.

Spaulding stiffened in alarm. His teeth clamped down harder on the pipestem. He jerked it out of his mouth as the screams died away into a softer, gurgling sound that faded completely after a tense moment.

Spaulding jerked the pipe out of his mouth and whirled around to plunge back into the house. For a second he considered trying to wake Monte and seek the sheriff's advice, but he knew that wasn't going to work. Sedated as he was, Monte couldn't be roused into any kind of coherent state.

The doctor's medical bag was sitting on a table just

inside the doorway, ready for the next time it was needed. That time was now, Spaulding decided. He grabbed the bag's handle.

He didn't know what had happened, but somebody was hurt. Those screams had left no doubt of that. It was his duty to find out what had happened and render whatever aid he could.

He went quickly down the porch steps and trotted through the night in the direction the agonized cries had come from. They had sounded as if they originated several blocks away.

Also disturbed by the sounds, a few dogs had started barking. That was all Spaulding heard. He wasn't sure if he'd be able to find the source of the screams.

A big figure loomed out of the shadows ahead of him. Spaulding stopped short as fear surged through him. He liked to think he was as courageous as most men. He had faced danger with his eyes wide open on several occasions in the past.

But now he thought about the bear that had the whole valley in a state of panic, and even though it seemed very unlikely that the beast would have ventured into Big Rock, for a moment Spaulding was paralyzed by the possibility that he was about to be attacked by a lumbering behemoth with razor-sharp teeth and claws.

Instead, a familiar voice called worriedly, "Who's there?"

"Tom!" Spaulding exclaimed. "Is that you?"

Tom Nunnley moved closer. Now, in the faint light from the stars, Spaulding saw that the local undertaker carried something in each hand. Nunnley had a lantern in his left hand and a shotgun in his right.

"Doc? Doc Spaulding?"

"Yes, it is. Do you know what's going on, Tom?"

"All I know is that I was working late and heard somebody

doing some awful caterwauling. It sounded like they might be hurt pretty bad, so I figured I ought to see if I could find them."

"I thought the same thing," Spaulding said. "From the sound of it, my services may be required." He sighed. "But I fear it may be more likely your talents will be called into play."

"Building a coffin, you mean." Nunnley's voice was grim in the darkness. "I hope not, but let's go find out."

"Why haven't you lit that lantern?"

"Well, I grabbed it when I rushed out of my place, but I was in such a hurry I didn't realize until too late that I don't have any matches on me."

Nunnley sounded a little embarrassed to make that admission.

"I can take care of that," Spaulding said. "I have a tin of matches in my pocket."

He set down his medical bag for a moment, took out the tin, and struck a lucifer on its roughened side. Nunnley leaned his shotgun against the wall of a nearby building and opened the lantern so Spaulding could light it.

Even though the shadows were still thick around them, the small circle of light made the doctor feel a little better. He said, "Let me take the lantern, Tom. That way you'll have both hands free to use that shotgun if you need to."

"If we run into that blasted bear," Nunnley said.

"Do you think that's what we're dealing with?"

"I don't know. Whoever screamed sure sounded like something bad was tearing into him."

The two men set off again. Windows glowed with yellow light here and there. Spaulding knew he and Nunnley weren't the only ones who had heard the cries.

They seemed to be the only ones who were investigating them, however. After everything that had happened,

Spaulding couldn't blame the citizens for being hesitant to come out of their homes.

"How's the sheriff doing?" Nunnley asked quietly.

"Sleeping. I gave him something to make sure of that."

"That's good, I reckon. Otherwise, he'd be out here with us, bad leg and all."

"He's better off where he is," Spaulding agreed. "He needs the rest."

"Yeah. I'd feel a mite better about things if we had him siding us, though."

Spaulding would have, too, although he didn't see any point in admitting that.

After a minute or so, Nunnley said, "Could you tell where the screams were coming from?"

"Not exactly, but I feel like it was somewhere around here." The two men were in front of the Brown Dirt Cowboy Saloon, which was dark and closed for the night. Spaulding lifted the lantern higher, so its light spread out a little more, and said, "I don't see anything in the street."

Nunnley swallowed hard. Spaulding didn't see it, but he heard it.

"Maybe in the alley back there?"

Nunnley's tone of voice made it clear that he didn't care much for the idea of exploring the dark alley behind the row of businesses.

"Perhaps," Spaulding said. "We should probably take a look."

Nunnley lifted the shotgun and cocked both hammers.

"Stay to the side and a little bit back of me, Doc," he said. "If I have to cut loose with this Greener, you don't want to be in the line of fire."

"No, I certainly don't," Spaulding muttered as the two men started along the narrow passage beside the saloon.

When they reached the alley, Nunnley said, "Which way?"

"Right, I think," Spaulding answered. That was mostly just a hunch on his part.

They spread out a little more, and Spaulding made sure to stay a step behind the burly undertaker. Nunnley stalked forward, crouching slightly as he thrust the shotgun's twin barrels ahead of him.

They hadn't gone very far when Nunnley stopped short and let out a startled exclamation.

"Doc! Do you see it? Up ahead there?"

Spaulding had spotted the huddled shape on the ground at the same time Nunnley did. Immediately, he didn't like the looks of it. He had seen too many bodies in the past. He recognized the shape of death.

At least the man on the ground appeared to be alone. Spaulding didn't see anything else moving around. He had stopped when Nunnley did, but now he said, "We'll have to get closer."

"Yeah, I guess so. Keep back, just in case . . . but keep that light shining in front of us."

The two men advanced slowly. The man-shaped thing on the ground resolved itself into the body of a man, definitely, as they came closer.

"I know who that is," Nunnley said abruptly. "That's Pudge, one of Emmett Brown's bartenders."

"I think you're right." Spaulding wasn't a regular customer at the Brown Dirt Cowboy, but he had been in there often enough to recognize the heavyset bartender.

"His clothes are torn to pieces and there's blood all over them," Nunnley said in a voice tinged with horror.

"And a pool of blood around him," Spaulding said as the lantern light touched the dark, reddish-black circle surrounding the body. "Stop, Tom. We'd better stay back."

"But he might need help!"

Spaulding shook his head. "I'm afraid Pudge is beyond

help. No human being can lose that much blood and still be alive. There may be tracks around the body, though, and we don't want to disturb them."

"Tracks . . . ?"

Spaulding moved to the side, circling to keep his distance from the corpse while shining the light on Pudge's face.

Nunnley saw it, too, and began cursing under his breath, although something about the hushed words almost made them sound more like a prayer than an oath.

"It tore him up," Nunnley said. "That damn bear. It ripped him to pieces." A hollow tone came into his voice as he went on, "It was right here in Big Rock. It's coming for us, Doc, and nothing's going to stop it!"

CHAPTER 17

Although Graham Blake had promised Kramer and Bennett that the rest of the gang wouldn't go off and leave them behind, the thought *had* crossed his mind. They had the loot from the bank robbery, after all—what there was of it—and it would be easy enough to slip away from the two bushwhackers instead of waiting for them.

Blake wasn't the only one who had considered it. As they rode across the pine-dotted bench toward the mountains, Frank Holt brought his horse alongside Blake's and asked quietly, "Are we really going to hang around until those two catch up?"

"We said we would . . ."

Blake put a little hesitation in his voice to show that he might be willing to be talked out of it.

"You know there's a chance they won't even survive that ambush," Holt went on.

Blake shrugged. "As long as they slow Jensen down long enough for us to get away, that's the main thing I'm worried about."

"If we keep going higher, we can hole up somewhere they'll never find us."

Blake glanced at the sky and said, "The problem with that is we don't have a lot of light left. Night might catch us still on the trail, and we don't know what it's like up there. We might ride into a ravine and not ever see it. I think we're going to have to find a decent place and make camp whether we want to or not."

"Yeah, I suppose that's the smart thing to do," Holt said, with obvious reluctance. Blake knew he was thinking that a four-way split was better than divvying up the loot six ways. Nobody could argue with that.

Blake didn't want to double-cross Kramer and Bennett, though. It was hard to betray somebody who had ridden with you through danger and hard times . . . although thinking about it never hurt anything.

The sun was touching the peaks to the west and throwing a magnificent golden arch upward into the sky when the four outlaws reached the far side of the bench. A thickly wooded, fairly steep slope led upward. As the riders stopped, Blake's eyes searched for a good trail, but in the fading light, he couldn't see any.

"I think we're going to have to stop here and wait until morning to push on," he said.

Holt looked like he wanted to argue. "You think Jensen and that posse will stop—" he began.

At that moment, gunfire sounded in the distance. All four men looked around.

"That'll be Bob and Ken cuttin' down on that posse," Stoughton said.

"I hope they kill every last one of those damn townies," Deere said. "Especially the one who put that buckshot in my leg!"

"We don't know that he came along with the posse," Blake pointed out. He was listening to the sounds and had heard both the sharp cracks of rifle fire and the heavier booms of a revolver.

The flurry of shots ended quickly, though, which caused Blake and Holt to exchange a worried glance.

"That didn't sound like enough shooting to wipe out that posse," Holt said.

After a moment, a pistol blasted again, and then silence fell as the echoes rolled away. Evidently, the fight was over and Holt was right.

The ambush hadn't ended the way Blake had hoped it would.

"Now what do we do?" Stoughton asked.

"Hold on," Blake said. "We'll wait a few minutes and see what happens."

They didn't have to wait very long before they heard a horse galloping toward them across the bench. The swift rataplan of hoofbeats drew steadily closer.

"That's just one man," Holt said. "Damn it, can't anything turn out right anymore?"

The angry glare he cast toward Blake made it plain that he blamed their leader for everything that had gone wrong that day. Anger welled up inside Blake, but he fought down the urge to pull his Colt and blow a hole through Holt.

Before this was over, they would likely need every gun they had, Blake told himself. But that wouldn't always be the case . . .

The rider galloping toward them came in sight. After a moment, Blake recognized Ken Bennett. He couldn't make out many details at this distance, but he knew the rider wasn't big enough to be Bob Kramer.

"What do you think happened?" Deere asked.

"I'll tell you what happened," Lester Stoughton said. "I heard two rifles and one pistol. I think Smoke Jensen killed Bob, and Ken took off for the tall and uncut before Jensen could kill him, too!"

That sounded like a reasonable explanation to Blake, but

he said, "Two men should have been able to hold that trail against an army."

"Smoke Jensen's an army all by his lonesome," Stoughton said.

Bennett arrived a moment later and slowed his horse's thundering hoofbeats to a stop. He was breathing hard, just like his mount. He leaned forward and rested his hands on the saddle horn as he dragged in air.

"What the hell happened?" Blake snapped.

"Bob's dead," Bennett said. The news came as no surprise to any of the outlaws. "Jensen killed him. He came up that trail by himself and left the rest of the posse down below."

"So the odds were two to one, and you not only failed to kill him, you lost a man."

"Don't blame me! We did our best." Bennett frowned. "How'd you know we didn't kill Jensen?"

Holt let out a disgusted snort. "If he was dead, you wouldn't have come riding this way like all the bats of hell were right behind you."

Bennett shrugged in acceptance of that statement.

"Did you even wing him?" Blake asked.

"I, uh, don't think so." Bennett hurried on, "I never saw anybody who could shoot like that, Graham. He plugged Bob without even seeming to aim. And he came close enough to me that I don't reckon I'll ever forget how those bullets sounded."

"Yeah, but he missed or you wouldn't be here," Holt said.

"I got lucky. That's it, pure and simple."

"I'd say Jensen is the one who's lucky," Blake responded, "but he won't be next time." He paused. "Did you even see the posse?"

"No, just Jensen."

"Then for all we know, the posse's already turned back."

"Well . . . maybe. I can't really say, one way or the other."

Holt said, "That seems like a lot to hope for, Graham."

"It never hurts to hope. Where's Bob's horse?"

Bennett shook his head. "I stampeded him down the trail at Jensen. That was the only thing that gave me a chance to get away. Jensen was dismounted, and his horse bolted up the trail ahead of me. I didn't see it when I came out on the bench, though. If I had, I would've grabbed it."

Blake wasn't sure about that. Bennett had been in such a hurry it was unlikely he would have slowed down long enough to catch Jensen's horse.

But it didn't matter. Their mounts were still reasonably fresh after swapping earlier in the day, and the horses would get to rest again tonight.

"We need to get out of the open," Blake said. "Come on, we'll ride up into the trees a ways and find a place to make camp. It'll have to be a cold camp, though. We won't want to risk a fire that would give away our position."

None of the others grumbled about that, which surprised Blake a little. But at this point, the way things had been going, a little discomfort was probably just what they expected.

"Are we going to push on through the night after them?" Louis Longmont asked as the posse stopped at the top of the trail to rest the horses, which give Smoke and Louis time to discuss their next move.

Smoke considered the question for a moment and then shook his head.

"This bench is a couple of miles wide," he said, "and flat enough that they'd see us coming. We know they like ambushes. They could hole up in good cover in that timber on the far slope and have half a dozen rifles waiting for us."

"Five," Louis corrected with a grim chuckle. "You did for one of them, remember?"

"That's true."

"If they keep going, they'll have an even larger lead on us in the morning. That means it'll take even longer to catch them."

"The chances of them doing that are pretty small," Smoke said. "That high country is plenty rugged, and it's hard, dangerous traveling in the dark. They might be desperate enough to try that, but I think it's more likely they'll hole up for the night. That's what I'm counting on, anyway."

"What do you mean by that?"

Smoke smiled. "We'll make camp here, and when it's good and dark, I'll go have a look and see what I can find out."

"Taking a page from Preacher's book, eh?"

Louis had met Smoke's mentor, Preacher, on a number of occasions and knew what Smoke was talking about. When the old mountain man had been a lot younger, at the height of the fur trapping era in the Rocky Mountains, Preacher had been mortal enemies with the Blackfoot tribe. Many times, he had slipped into a Blackfoot camp in the middle of the night, cut the throats of half a dozen warriors, and then slipped back out without rousing any of the others from their sleep.

It had been morning before the survivors found the bodies of the slain warriors and realized that the man known as Ghost Killer had paid them a visit in the night . . . and it was only sheer luck that they were still alive while others had died.

"I don't plan to cut anybody's throat while he's sleeping," Smoke said. "For one thing, I'm not sure I could ever match the level of stealth Preacher was capable of back then, but I can find out where they are and make sure of their numbers."

"I'd offer to go with you," Louis said, "but I think you understand that sneaking around through the woods isn't my strong suit."

"And what I said before still holds true. If anything happens to me, it'll be up to you to take over."

Louis shook his head. "No gang of two-bit bank robbers is going to be any match for you, Smoke."

"I appreciate that vote of confidence, but you never know what's going to happen."

A short time later, the posse moved on. Smoke kept his eyes open for a good campsite. At that elevation, once the sun had set, night descended quickly.

They found a spot where some rocks formed a rough circle. Smoke told the men they would spend the night there. Some of them got busy unsaddling and tending to the horses, while a couple of others began gathering firewood.

"It's all right to have a fire, isn't it, Smoke?" one of them asked.

Smoke nodded. "Yeah, it's not like we're trying to fool those hombres we're after. They know we're back here. I caught a glint of light a time or two during the afternoon that was probably the sun reflecting off a pair of field glasses. There's a good chance they've been watching us."

Building a fire served another purpose that he didn't elaborate on. When the outlaws saw the pinpoint of orange light flickering in the distance, they would know that the posse wasn't closing on them.

That might make them overconfident and less alert, which is just what he wanted if he was going to be sneaking up on their camp later that night.

Although the odds of the outlaws doubling back to attack the posse were small, Smoke posted guards and worked out a schedule where all the men would take turns. With that done, after they had supper from the supplies they had brought with them, he stretched out on a blanket, used his saddle for a pillow, and got a couple of hours of sleep, dozing off almost immediately, as most frontiersmen were capable of. Out there, a man learned to sleep when and how he could.

Smoke didn't need anyone to rouse him from that slumber, either. He woke when he wanted to, instantly fully alert, as if he had an alarm clock in his head. That was another talent men who had ridden the dark trail cultivated.

Louis was awake, too, even though it wasn't his guard shift yet.

"Are you going after them on foot?" he asked Smoke.

"That's the safest way. Sound carries a long distance at night, especially in this thin air. No matter how quiet I tried to be, they'd be liable to hear me coming on horseback."

"Assuming they're alert."

"If you'd robbed a bank, killed a man, and shot a sheriff earlier today, and you knew there was a posse after you, wouldn't you be alert?"

Louis laughed softly. "Indeed I would." He grew more serious as he went on to say, "Be careful, Smoke."

"That's what Sally always says to me."

"And I'm sure you'll pay just as much attention to my warning as you do to your wife's," Louis said dryly.

Smoke left the camp, moving within a few yards of one of the posse members standing guard. The hombre never knew he was there.

The moon hadn't risen yet. Smoke had made sure to put his plan into motion before that happened. The stars gave him plenty of light to see by as he moved across the bench toward the wooded slopes on the far side.

He had taken off his boots, tied them together, and looped the rawhide thong around his neck. Those high-heeled boots were made for riding, not walking.

He had also pulled on an extra pair of socks to protect his feet, which were pretty tough-soled to begin with. His gait was a long-legged, easy stride that covered the ground efficiently.

He slowed when he neared the slopes. They stretched to the right and left for miles, and he had no way of knowing which way the outlaws had gone.

It was entirely possible, maybe even likely, that he wouldn't be able to find them. He'd been watching for a campfire but hadn't spotted one. He supposed that they'd had sense enough to make a cold camp.

When he reached the trees, he stopped and stood stock-still for several long minutes with every sense he possessed functioning at its top level. He didn't expect to see anything, so he concentrated mostly on listening and smelling.

A smile touched Smoke's lips when the faintest whiff of tobacco smoke drifted to his nostrils.

The outlaws had been smart enough not to build a camp-fire to announce their presence, but it hadn't occurred to them that the smell of a quirley could travel a considerable distance, too. Smoke turned so that the night breeze was in his face and started in that direction.

As it turned out, his instincts had guided him well while he crossed the bench by dead reckoning. He had reached the far slope less than half a mile east of the outlaws' current position.

That assumed the smoke he smelled came from them, of course. It was always possible somebody else was out and about up there that night.

But not likely, he told himself. Not likely at all. That wasn't good grazing country. None of the spreads in the valley ran their cattle up there or had line shacks in that area. No heavily traveled trails cut through there, and certainly there weren't any roads.

No, the only people likely to be up there that night were bank robbers on the dodge and the posse that was pursuing them.

Now that he was close to his destination, Smoke paused and drew his boots on. He entered the trees, little more than a shadow drifting through shadows, and catfooted his way forward. He tested every step before letting his weight down to make sure he wasn't about to step on a branch that might crack with a sound that would seem almost as loud as a gunshot.

He couldn't smell the tobacco smoke anymore. Whoever had been nursing that quirley had pinched out the butt.

That didn't matter. The damage had already been done.

Smoke heard men's voices talking quietly in front of him.

CHAPTER 18

Attempting to dull the pain of their wounds, Lester Stoughton and Paul Deere had guzzled down enough whiskey that they passed out.

So the treatment had worked, if you wanted to look at it that way, Graham Blake thought as he sat with his back propped rather uncomfortably against a tree trunk.

Frank Holt was only a few feet away, leaning against another tree. Ken Bennett, who'd kept to himself since returning from the failed ambush that had gotten Bob Kramer killed, sat on the other side of the little clearing, not far from the horses.

Holt had just pinched out the cigarette he'd rolled earlier. He snapped the little remnant away into the darkness and said, "Maybe after the horses have rested a little longer, we ought to move out on foot and lead them. We could go slow enough we wouldn't risk falling into a ravine or running into any other trouble. Hell, every foot we put between ourselves and the posse is that much longer it'll take them to catch up to us."

"That's true," Blake agreed, "but Lester and Paul have drunk themselves into a stupor, and besides, if we start wandering around in the dark, we run the risk of going in circles. Even worse, we might get turned around and blunder right into that damn posse from Big Rock."

"So, what do you think we should do, just sit here and wait for Smoke Jensen and the others to catch us?" Holt's tone held a bitter edge. "That'd be the simplest thing, I reckon."

"Nobody said we ought to do that, Frank," Blake snapped. "And to tell you the truth, I don't much cotton to the way you've been talking to me lately. Especially today."

"You mean since that robbery got ruined and all we got for our time and trouble was a few dollars?"

"We haven't counted the loot yet, and you know that. There ought to be enough to keep us going for a while."

"But not enough to get us all the way to Mexico! That was what you talked about, Graham, how we'd grab ourselves a big enough payoff to get us to the border—"

Bennett surprised them by saying, "Will both of you just shut up? I swear, you bicker like an old married couple!"

Blake drew in a sharp breath and said, "What the hell? You can't talk to me like that."

"Yeah," Holt said, "if you'd shot a little straighter, Jensen would be dead now and Bob would still be alive. If anybody's to blame for what's gone wrong, it's you."

Bennett had been hugging his knees to him, but now he stood up quickly and cursed.

"It's not my fault, damn you!" he yelled in a rage. "Get on your feet, Frank. Get on your feet and go for your gun!"

Holt started to surge upward, but Blake shot out a hand and pulled Holt back down.

"Stop it, you two! Ken, you back off. Frank, settle down. You want to make it easier on that posse by us killing ourselves off? Because that's what's going to happen if we keep on blaming each other!"

"I did the best I could, I tell you," Bennett insisted. "If

we'd all stayed down there on that trail and bushwhacked Jensen, we would've gotten him. I'm sure of it."

"There wasn't room to hide all the horses, or us, either," Blake pointed out. "What we did made sense."

Bennett snorted. "You'd say so, since it was you calling the shots."

For a second, Blake was almost angry enough to tell Holt to go ahead and shoot the blasted loudmouth.

Then he remembered everything he'd said earlier about needing every gun they had if things came to a showdown. That was still true, since it was a distinct possibility.

"We all need to stop this squabbling," Blake said. He kept his voice calm and level. "Fighting among ourselves won't change anything."

"You're right," Holt said, then he surprised Blake by adding, "Sorry I put a burr under your saddle, Ken. I wasn't there, so I don't reckon I've got any right to talk."

"Well . . . fine," Bennett said without much grace. As if trying to save face, he went on, "If I ever get another crack at Smoke Jensen, I won't miss again. I can promise you that."

"If everything I've heard about Jensen is true, you'll get that crack at him," Blake said. "Because he sure doesn't sound like the sort of man to give up once he's started after something!"

In the brush a few yards away, a wry smile curved Smoke's lips. He didn't care whether he got compliments from an outlaw, but he liked to think that what this one had just said was true. When he went after a goal, he was determined to stick with it until he achieved that goal.

Sally would call that tendency mule-headed stubbornness, more than likely.

Either way, Smoke wouldn't be turning back until these owlhoots had been brought to justice and he'd recovered the stolen bank money.

Two of them were sound asleep. He heard the different snores coming from them. There were three others, he decided, because he'd heard that many voices. It was too dark in the shadows underneath the trees to be sure about the number, even with Smoke's keen vision, but he was confident about that estimation.

If he'd been able to see, he might have gone ahead and tried to take them.

As it was, he waited and listened to what they had to say as the air of tension and impending violence gradually eased.

"What do you think we ought to do next?" the man called Frank asked. Smoke had pinned down three names from the conversation: Frank, Graham, and Ken. Graham seemed to be the leader.

He was the one who answered. "That posse will expect us to keep going north. We might be able to give them the slip if we cut east tomorrow."

"I thought the plan called for us to circle west."

"It did, starting out," Graham admitted, "but now that I've gotten a better look at the mountains in that direction, I believe that would be a mistake. The country's just too rugged that way. We can make better time by going east until we're out of the mountains and then make a run south."

"Toward Mexico," Frank said.

"Yeah. Toward Mexico." Graham chuckled. "We'll still get there. I give you my word on that, boys. We'll throw that posse off the trail, then the next time we stop to pull a job, everything will go perfectly and we'll grab enough loot to get us the rest of the way to the border."

A moment of silence followed that confident declaration.

Then Frank said, "I think you're whistling in the dark a little, Graham. But you've been right more often than you've been wrong since we started riding together, so I reckon we ought to give you the benefit of the doubt."

"Well, thank you most to death," Graham replied with a sarcastic note in his voice.

"No, I mean it. We'll go along with whatever you say . . . for now. Right, Ken?"

"Yeah, I reckon," the one called Ken answered sullenly.

That feeling of tension was back in the air, but it didn't last long before Frank said, "I'm gonna get some sleep."

"Go ahead," Graham told him. "You try to sleep, too, Ken. I'll stand guard."

"You'll be able to stay awake?"

"I said I would, didn't I?"

That snappish exchange was the last conversation for a while. When Smoke heard more deep, regular breathing, he figured the other two outlaws had gone to sleep, leaving Graham the only one who was awake.

Smoke considered trying to grab him and take him prisoner, but he knew he couldn't do that without making enough racket to wake the others. Then it would be five against one.

Although he had faced odds worse than that many times and emerged victorious, it didn't seem like a worthwhile risk under these circumstances, when he already knew what the gang planned to do.

Besides, he was acting as Monte Carson's deputy, sort of, which meant he had a duty to capture those outlaws, if possible, and take them back to Big Rock to face being tried for bank robbery and murder.

They would still wind up dead, swinging from a hangman's noose, but nobody would ever be able to say that sending them to their rightful rewards in hell hadn't been done all legal and proper.

With that thought in mind, Smoke eased back, away from the darkened campsite, and once he was clear, he headed across the bench to rejoin Louis Longmont and the rest of the posse.

He was eager to share with Louis the plan that had begun to form in his mind . . .

The next morning, before the sun was up, the men from Big Rock broke camp following a hearty breakfast cooked over a large fire.

Smoke wanted to make sure the bank robbers knew where the pursuit was.

Once the fire was out and the eastern sky had begun to turn gray, instead of starting across the bench the way their quarry had gone, the posse withdrew quietly down the trail, back to the flats below.

Smoke's horse, which had stampeded up the trail to the bench the day before and then disappeared, had wandered into the posse's camp during the night, drawn by the scent of the other horses, no doubt.

Smoke was mounted on the bay again as he led the way back down the ledge. Since the trail was wide enough for two men on horseback, Louis Longmont rode beside him.

"If anyone other than you had come up with the idea, Smoke, I'm not sure the men would have gone along with it," Louis commented. "It's a gamble, abandoning the trail of those outlaws and trying to outguess them."

"There's some risk involved, all right." Smoke chuckled, "but you've spent most of your life running risks and figuring the odds."

"Oh, I didn't say *I* would have objected. Your plan

makes perfect sense to me. I was talking about the other fellows, who are a bit more . . . straightforward, shall we say . . . in their thinking."

Smoke's plan called for the posse to pull back down to the valley and head east, sticking close to the foothills so they wouldn't be as likely to be spotted from the slopes high above where the outlaws would be traveling.

This was where Smoke's familiarity with the region was to the posse's advantage. If the gang headed east, as he had overheard them planning the night before, only a few trails existed that they could follow. All of them eventually descended to the plains east of the Front Range.

Smoke figured he and his companions could get there ahead of the bank robbers. He recalled hearing about the Civil War general who had said the battle usually went to those who "got there fustest with the mostest."

That was what he planned to do that day.

To accomplish that, they would have to ride hard and push their horses. That was where the gamble came in: if their quarry got past them, they wouldn't be able to give chase because their mounts would be played out.

Smoke knew the most likely route the outlaws could follow. He headed toward where he thought the posse would intercept the fugitives.

The sun rose and splashed light over the foothills where the riders maintained a steady, ground-eating pace. Smoke called a halt only when he thought it was absolutely necessary for the horses to rest for a few minutes.

He was less worried about the men, although this long chase had most of them looking gaunt and hollow-eyed and sweated, too. Even though it had been less than twenty-four hours since they'd left their homes in Big Rock and they'd had a few hours of sleep during that time, this was still more hard riding than they were used to. They wouldn't hold up to a long chase, and Smoke knew it.

It wasn't their fault. It was just the way things were.

So the gamble he was taking now was actually their best chance of bringing the bank robbers to justice, he told himself. If it didn't work . . .

Well, he would just have to send the posse home and run the outlaws to ground by himself. Yeah, mule-headed. Sally was right about that.

By early afternoon, the stops had become more frequent. Even so, the horses were starting to flag. They wouldn't be able to keep up more than a walk for much longer.

But they wouldn't have to, because clearly visible up ahead, the hills ended and the ground dropped to long, level plains that seemed to stretch endlessly eastward.

Those plains did end, Smoke knew, because he'd been to the other side numerous times. He'd traveled all the way to the home of Sally's parents in New England and seen the great cities of the eastern United States. He liked it a lot better out in the West, but he was glad he'd had the opportunity to visit those other places.

He slowed the bay, pointed, and said to Louis, "See that long bluff running north and south?"

"Of course."

"There's an opening in it. Looks like a big door."

Louis nodded. "I've heard of it. The Devil's Gateway, isn't that what people call it?"

Smoke grinned and said, "They used to, when the Indians hid in there and waited for the wagon trains to come along so they could jump them, but those days have been over for quite a while."

"Yes, five or six years, at least," Louis said dryly.

"The point is, that's where the trail I think those bank

robbers are following comes out. I figure we'll be waiting for them when they show up."

Several of the other men were close enough to overhear what Smoke and Louis said. One of them asked, "What if they don't come this way, Smoke?"

"We'll have to try something else, I suppose," Smoke answered, sounding confident and nonchalant. He wasn't quite that casual inside, but he really did feel like he had guessed right on what the outlaws were going to do.

"I don't mean to doubt you, Smoke," the posseman said. "We're all ready to follow you to hell and back. Isn't that right, boys?"

Words of agreement came from the other men.

"I appreciate that," Smoke said. "We ought to know in the next hour or so if it's going to work out."

The posse's course curved to the northeast. From this distance, a man could get a good view of the mountains and really grasp their vast, epic sweep. Smoke could only imagine what it must have been like for those first settlers to lay eyes on those magnificent peaks. And before them the mountain men such as Preacher, who had dubbed them the Shining Mountains and referred to their era as shining times.

So it must have been, Smoke thought.

He and his father hadn't headed west until later, not long after the Civil War, by which time the settlers had come and established towns and had brought with them both civilization and progress . . . and rot and decay.

Smoke pushed those thoughts out of his head. Lawlessness was a fact in the West now and had to be dealt with. That was what he and his companions had set out to do.

By late afternoon, they faced the Devil's Gateway. The bluff in which that gap opened was about five hundred yards from the small, dry wash where the posse had concealed their horses.

The men waited in the wash, too, except for Smoke and Louis, who knelt at the edge and watched the opening in the bluff, alert for any signs of movement. Time stretched by, drawing Smoke's nerves taut along with it.

The men and the horses welcomed the chance to rest after covering so much ground. Smoke knew that was a good thing, but every minute that passed increased the odds that he had guessed wrong and the outlaws were long gone.

As if sensing his old friend's tension, Louis said, "We would have made much better time than they did. They didn't know where they were going. So I'm not surprised that they're not here yet."

"Neither am I," Smoke admitted. "But a thing doesn't always sit well in a man's guts, even when it makes sense."

"That's true. Well, I suppose we can give them the rest of the afternoon—"

"No," Smoke broke in.

"No? We can't?"

Smoke was smiling as he said, "We won't have to. Here they come now."

CHAPTER 19

Smoke's hawklike vision had spotted the riders emerging from the Devil's Gateway first, but when Louis peered in that direction, he said, "Ah, yes. I see them, too. Five men, I make it?"

"That's right, five men, and two of them are wounded."

"Well, then, we have them outnumbered by quite a bit. If they have any sense at all, they'll surrender once they see how badly the odds are stacked against them."

"Maybe," Smoke said, "but they're bound to know that they'd be going back to a rope, so they're liable to decide it's better to fight." He looked over at the gambler. "You and I will handle most of that."

"I understand. You're liable to get an argument from the men, though. They came to do their duty as they see it."

"It could well be that they'll have to, but I'm hoping it won't come to that." Smoke glanced toward the oncoming riders again, then said, "Keep an eye on them. Let me know if they change the way they're going."

"Of course."

Smoke slid back down into the wash, where the members of the posse were waiting with their horses. They had been talking quietly among themselves. Some had wanted to fill pipes or roll quirleys, but Smoke had forbidden that, not wanting the outlaws warned by the smell of tobacco as he had been, the night before.

"Men, gather around and listen up," Smoke told them. His voice wasn't loud, but it was clear and powerful and each man heard him plainly. "Those bank robbers are headed this way. Louis and I are going to meet them out there in the open and give them a chance to surrender."

"Ah, hell, Smoke, they're not gonna do that," one of the men said.

"More than likely they won't," Smoke agreed, "but we're a legal, duly sworn posse, and we have to give them that chance." He shrugged. "But if they start the ball . . ."

"You'll call the tune," another man said.

Smoke didn't respond to that. Instead, he went on, "What I want you men to do is line up here along the edge of the wash. Stay low, and have your guns ready. If there's shooting and Louis and I go down, you open fire, but don't take a hand unless Louis and I are out of the game."

He looked around at the men and settled on the one he thought was the steadiest, Ben Gardner, who worked in the freight office at the railroad depot.

"Ben, you keep a close eye on Louis and me. You give the order to fire if we're out of the fight. The rest of you, listen for Ben's order."

Men nodded understanding and muttered agreement. They began lining up at the edge of the wash, standing on the gently sloping bank and thrusting their rifle and shotgun barrels over the rim.

Smoke rejoined Louis, who still knelt low enough that the prairie grass mostly obscured him. The grass waved back and forth a little in a gentle, late afternoon breeze.

"How close do we let them get?" Louis asked quietly.

"A little closer," Smoke replied. "We want the other

fellas to have a good chance of hitting them, if it comes down to that."

"As long as our own men don't shoot us in the back," Louis said with a wry smile.

"I warned them about that," Smoke replied with a chuckle of his own.

Neither man felt as casual as they acted, but they had gone through enough of these tense moments in their lives, waiting for violence to erupt, that they knew how to keep the mood light and not allow tension to stretch their nerves too tight.

A nervous man often wound up dead.

Graham Blake was starting to feel pretty good about their chances. They had moved at a brisk pace all day. The terrain through which they had traveled was rugged, but not rough enough to slow them down too much.

Now they were out of the mountains and foothills, moving onto the plains. Before too much longer, it would be time to start looking for a suitable place to make camp. Blake knew there were some old buffalo wallows out there, and he thought that one of them might provide a good spot.

"Where do you think Jensen and the rest of that posse are, right about now?" Frank Holt asked.

Blake laughed. "I'd say there's a mighty good chance they're wandering around in the high country, ten or fifteen miles behind us, and wondering where the hell we went to."

"I hope you're right," Lester Stoughton rasped.

Blake looked over at him and frowned. "Lester, you're not looking so good."

"I'm not feeling so good, either," Stoughton said. "I think that crease in my side is starting to fester. I know that pretty little blonde cleaned it yesterday before she bandaged it up, but sometimes that doesn't always take. A wound can still go bad on you."

It appeared that might well be the case. Stoughton's face was gray and drawn, without much color except for two round, bright-red spots on his beard-stubbled cheeks.

He was feverish, Blake realized. Blood poisoning from the bullet wound was the most likely explanation.

"There's bound to be a town somewhere up ahead," Blake said. "We'll find a sawbones and get you some medical attention, Lester."

"I hope so, because I'm not sure how much farther I can ride."

Blake looked at Paul Deere. "How are you doing, Paul? You're wounded, too."

"You reckon you're tellin' me anything I don't already know?" Deere said. He spat off the side of his horse. "I'm all right, I think. In better shape than Lester, anyway. I wouldn't mind having an actual doc take a look at this leg of mine, though, just to make sure it's not showing any signs of going bad. And it could sure use some rest, too, after bouncing in this saddle all day."

"Soon," Blake promised. "Just as soon as we can."

"Let's ride ahead a ways and take a look around," Holt suggested.

Blake had a hunch that Holt wanted to say something out of earshot of the others. He looked over his shoulder at Bennett, who was bringing up the rear, and told him, "Keep an eye on our back-trail, Ken."

"I have been," Bennett said, still sounding a mite peevish. He hadn't completely gotten over the argument from the night before.

Blake and Holt nudged their horses ahead of the others, until they were far enough away that they could talk quietly without being overheard.

"I know what you're going to say, Frank," Blake said. "You think we ought to leave Lester behind since he's getting sick."

"Stoughton and Deere both," Holt replied. "They're slowing us down, Graham. You know that as well as I do." Holt snorted. "Hell, I don't care whether Bennett comes along, either, if he's gonna keep acting like a sulled-up old possum. However much money is in that bag, it'll divvy up a lot nicer two ways than it will five."

"Or even three or four, eh?"

An ugly grin creased Holt's face. "You said it, pard, not me."

Blake turned the idea over in his head. He remembered the old saying about there being no honor among thieves. He'd always believed that to be untrue. A certain loyalty existed among the outlaw fraternity. It had to, otherwise life as an owlhoot would be pure anarchy and it would be impossible for anyone to ever work together.

But a man had to be practical, too. Numbers didn't lie when it came to dividing the loot, and Holt was right about the wounded men slowing them down.

"How about this?" he said, keeping his voice pitched low. "We find a settlement, or even just some ranch, and leave Lester and Paul there. That bag's still tied to Lester's saddle. We can get it while they're being patched up. If we try to just take it from him, he'll know what's going on and put up a fight."

"As sick as he is, you really think he could stop us from doing whatever we want to?"

"Probably not," Blake allowed, "but even so, any time lead starts getting thrown around, you never know what's going to happen."

"I suppose. If we take their horses, too, they can't follow us."

"That's right."

"What about Bennett?" Holt's voice was sharp with dislike as he asked the question.

"We can make out like he's coming with us, just so he won't cause any trouble. Then, when we're well away from wherever we leave the other two . . . you can solve that problem however you want to, Frank."

Holt grunted. "I reckon I know the best way." His fingers rasped over his stubbly chin. "I don't much cotton to the idea of leaving those two alive behind us."

"Lester and Paul, you mean?"

"Yeah. Seems like we'd be making two enemies we don't have to. Stoughton'll probably get sick and die from that wound, but Deere might not. Then we'd be looking over our shoulder for him the rest of our lives."

"Well, you've got a point there," Blake admitted. "I hate to think about taking the double cross all the way, but . . ."

"It's the safest thing to do. Makes the most sense."

Blake half-turned in his saddle and looked back at the three men behind them.

"Yeah, you're right—" he began.

Then Holt interrupted him by ripping out a curse and clawing at the holstered gun on his hip.

Smoke had frowned as the two outlaws rode out ahead of the other three and began what appeared to be an earnest conversation. With the gang separated like that, it would be more difficult to deal with them if any shooting broke out.

Now that he had gotten a better look at the men, Smoke was under no illusions that they would surrender. They weren't the type, and he knew it.

He and Louis crouched even lower now. They had taken their hats off so that the outlaws wouldn't spot them as easily. They listened to the horses' hoofbeats coming closer and closer until Smoke finally glanced over at Louis and nodded.

As one, they straightened to their feet, their guns already in their hands.

"Elevate!" Smoke shouted. "In the name of the law!"

The man on the right ignored the command. He was already pulling his gun. Louis fired as the outlaw's weapon came level.

The bullet punched into the man's chest. He got a shot off as his finger jerked the trigger involuntarily, but the slug plowed into the ground well in front of Smoke and Louis.

The fight could have ended there, if the bank robbers had been willing, but the other man who had been out in front drew his gun, too, with a smooth, fast movement.

But the draw wouldn't have been anywhere near fast enough to beat Smoke, even if Smoke's gun wasn't already clasped in his hand. Smoke triggered the Colt. It boomed and bucked against his palm.

The outlaw rocked back in the saddle as the bullet drove into him. His horse, spooked by the shooting, wheeled around in a circle. The rider swayed back and forth wildly but managed to stay mounted. He swung his gun toward Smoke again.

Smoke fired a second time. This round struck the outlaw just above his left eye, bored on through his head, and exploded out the back of his skull in a grisly pink shower of blood, brain, and bone.

He dropped his gun and toppled off the horse in a loose sprawl. His right foot hung in the stirrup, though, so when the horse took off, the corpse bounced along beside its flashing rear hooves for several yards before coming loose.

The next two men had been riding side by side about twenty yards behind the pair in front. They reined in and looked for a second as if they were going to yank their horses around and try to flee.

But they must have decided at the same instant not to do that, because they yelled curses, clawed guns from their holsters, and opened fire as they charged together at Smoke and Louis.

They couldn't have seen the men in the wash yet, didn't know the actual odds they were facing. Maybe they figured they had the advantage, two against two, since they were mounted and Smoke and Louis were on foot.

Powder smoke and flame jetted from their gun muzzles as they thundered toward their two adversaries.

Smoke and Louis remained cool-nerved, despite the bullets that whipped around them, narrowly missing. They fired calmly and steadily. They were close enough that Smoke saw dust puff from the front of one man's shirt as the lead pounded into him.

Both men fell, riddled by the deadly accurate fire of the two gun-wizards. Their panic-stricken mounts galloped on, forcing Smoke and Louis to move hurriedly aside to keep from getting trampled.

The horses didn't stop until they spotted the wash ahead of them, where the members of the posse were now scrambling into the open despite the orders Smoke had given them.

With four of the five outlaws down and pretty clearly dead, they must have thought the fight was over.

But there was a fifth man still on his horse, hanging back from the others, and he threw a rifle to his shoulder and opened fire, spraying bullets along the wash as fast as he could work the repeater's lever and pull the trigger.

One man cried out in pain and fell backward into the

wash. The others let out alarmed yells and dived to the ground.

The surviving outlaw, who was out of effective handgun range, whirled his horse and lit a shuck.

Smoke pouched his empty iron, turned toward the posse, and called, "Ben! Winchester!"

The freight man rose up on his knees and tossed his rifle toward Smoke, who caught it deftly. In a continuation of the same smooth movement, Smoke whirled around, socketed the rifle's butt against his shoulder, and laid his cheek against the smooth wood of the weapon's stock. He drew a bead on the escaping outlaw.

Smoke didn't hesitate. The bank robbers were all equally guilty in his eyes. He squeezed the trigger.

The Winchester cracked and kicked. Smoke lowered the barrel and saw the distant rider keep going for a second, then the man jerked, flung his arms out to the side, and fell forward over his horse's neck. He slid off, hit the ground, and bounced in the loose-limbed way that signified death.

"And that will conclude matters," Louis said as the echoes of the gunfire rebounded faintly from the bluff to the west.

"You and I will make sure of that," Smoke said. He added over his shoulder, "Ben, see to that man who was hit."

"I will, Smoke. He's not dead. I don't think he's hurt too bad."

Smoke hoped that was the case. He had brought these men out there and considered them his responsibility, whether they followed his orders to the letter or not.

As soon as he and Louis had thumbed fresh rounds into their guns, they strode forward and checked on the fallen outlaws. Their Colts were ready if they needed to fire again.

That turned out not to be necessary. The four outlaws

closest to the wash were all dead. They wouldn't rob any more banks or gun down any more innocent men.

Smoke got his horse, swung up onto the bay, and rode out to see about the man he'd downed with the long shot from the Winchester.

That owlhoot was dead, too. The rifle bullet had struck him squarely between the shoulder blades and drilled on through to exit from his chest.

Smoke caught the man's horse, which had come to a stop and started grazing about fifty yards away.

By the time he rode back, leading the riderless mount, Louis had untied a canvas sack from the saddle of one of the gang's other horses.

"Here's the loot from the bank, Smoke," he announced as he displayed the bag. Louis pointed at the second pair of men he and Smoke had killed. "Those two are the ones who were wounded back in town. You can see the bandages the Miller woman put on them."

Smoke nodded and said, "Nobody's going to hold that against Mrs. Miller. She and her husband didn't have any choice but to cooperate with those killers."

He spoke loudly enough that everybody in the posse could hear him. He wanted them to carry that message home with them, so that Dan and Bella Miller wouldn't have any problems over what had happened.

The man who'd been wounded by outlaw lead had a clean hole drilled through his upper left arm. It appeared that the bone wasn't broken. Dr. Colton Spaulding would give the wound some proper medical attention once they got back to Big Rock.

For now, the bullet holes had been cleaned with whiskey and bound up to stop the bleeding. The fellow would wish he had listened to Smoke, but in the long run, he would recover.

"Are we going to leave those miscreants where they fell or take their bodies back to Big Rock?" Louis asked.

Smoke considered the question. Plenty of times, he had left the evil men he'd been forced to kill right where they lay. As he'd heard Preacher say, the wolves and buzzards had to eat, too.

But this time, they were close enough to town that they would be back the next day, and the outlaws could be laid to rest in paupers' graves in the local cemetery.

Monte Carson might have wanted posters on them in his office, too, and names could be put to faces. In the long run, it didn't matter, but of such traditions, civilization was made.

"Load them up on their horses," Smoke ordered. "Might be some bounties posted on them, and if there are, you fellas can share them."

"Well, that wouldn't be right," Gardner objected. "You and Louis did all the work."

"You men rode out here and risked your lives when you didn't have to. One of you was hurt. That deserves some sort of reward."

"But the two of you—" Gardner began.

"Don't worry about that," Louis told him, with a smile. "For fellows like Smoke and me, it's all in a day's work."

CHAPTER 20

The possemen, along with five horses carrying grim, blanket-wrapped burdens, reached Big Rock in the early afternoon of the next day.

Their entry created quite a stir, of course. People came out of the buildings onto the boardwalk to watch the weary, beard-stubbled riders pass.

"You and some of the men take those corpses around back of Tom Nunnley's store," Smoke told Ben Gardner. "Tell him to get them ready for burial but not to plant them yet. Not until I've had a chance to check the wanted posters in the sheriff's office. I'll take care of that as soon as I look in on Monte and find out how he's doing."

"I understand, Smoke," Gardner replied.

"I'm headed for my place," Louis told Smoke, but before he did so, he glanced around and said, "Does it seem like there are more people in town than there were when we rode out a couple of days ago?"

Smoke frowned slightly as he looked up and down the boardwalks.

"Yeah, I think you're right," he said. "I don't see a bunch of strangers, though. Looks more like some of the men who went out looking for that bear have given up the hunt and are sticking closer to home."

"Do you think that's because they found the thing and killed it?"

"I don't know, but when I talk to Monte, I'm sure I'll find out."

As Smoke rode past the bank on his way to Dr. Spaulding's house, Joel Montgomery came out onto the boardwalk and raised a hand.

"Smoke, it's good to see you," he said. "Was anyone who went with you hurt?"

Smoke liked the fact that the banker inquired about the health of the posse members before asking if they had recovered the money. He said, "One man got winged, that's all. He should be all right."

The wounded man was passing by on his way to the doctor's house, flanked by two of his friends to make sure he got there. Smoke nodded to them as they rode by.

Then he untied the canvas bag from his saddle horn and tossed it to Montgomery.

"What they took is all there," he said, "and we won't have to bother putting those varmints on trial."

Montgomery nodded. "Yes, I saw the little procession headed for the undertaking parlor. Thank you, Smoke."

"Seems like things have changed a mite here in town since we left," Smoke observed.

"You're on your way to see Monte?"

"That's right. That's where I'm headed next."

"Then he can tell you all about it." The banker shook his head. "But it's not good, I'll say that much."

Slightly annoyed that Montgomery hadn't just explained what was going on, Smoke heeled the bay into motion again and rode on toward his destination.

He found Monte sitting up in bed in the room he occupied at Dr. Spaulding's house. The lawman had an anxious look on his rugged face.

"I was hoping you'd stop by here to see me before you headed out to the Sugarloaf, Smoke," he said once the two men had exchanged greetings. "I overheard some of the talk from the fellas who just brought in that wounded man for the doc to take a look at. You got those bank robbers, didn't you?"

"We did," Smoke said. "They're over at Tom Nunnley's."

Monte grunted. "Best place in the world for them. You didn't lose any of the posse?"

"Just had the one man wounded, that's all. We were lucky. Those outlaws tried to ambush us at one point, but it didn't work out for them, and then we finally caught up to them just the other side of the Devil's Gateway."

Monte nodded and said, "Good work. Of course, I'm not surprised by that."

Smoke couldn't curb his impatience any longer. He said, "What happened here while we were gone, Monte? Joel Montgomery told me it wasn't good, but he didn't give me any details. Did that bear get somebody else?"

"You know that fella called Pudge who tended bar at the Brown Dirt Cowboy?"

"Sure." Smoke's eyes narrowed. "*Tended* bar, you said?"

"Yeah. Night before last, that bear killed him. His funeral was yesterday."

Smoke's jaw tightened in anger. He hadn't known the garrulous bartender very well, but Pudge was a likable gent and Smoke was sorry to hear he was dead.

But Smoke was puzzled, too, so he said, "I wouldn't have thought Pudge was the sort of hombre to go out hunting a killer grizzly."

"He wasn't." Monte sighed. "The bear got him right here in town, when Pudge was on his way home after the saloon closed."

Smoke wasn't one to show much of a reaction to unexpected news, but he felt like he'd just been punched in the belly. He said slowly, "The bear came into Big Rock?"

"That's right. Pudge's body was found in the back alley on the other side of the street, a few buildings down from the saloon where he worked. Emmett Brown said he always walked back to his boarding house that way."

"Who found him?"

"Doc Spaulding and Tom Nunnley. They both heard Pudge screaming and went to see what was going on."

"Did they see the bear itself?"

"No, it was gone by the time they got there, but it left plenty of evidence behind. Nothing else could've torn Pudge apart like that."

Smoke thought about what he had just learned and deduced something else from it.

"That's why so many of the men are back in Big Rock instead of out hunting the bear," he said. "Now that it's killed right here in town, they're afraid to leave their families unprotected."

"That's right. Come sundown, the streets clear out in a hurry. Everybody goes home, hunkers down to wait for morning, and hopes the bear doesn't come prowling around."

"The bear didn't come back last night?"

Monte shook his head. "Nobody saw or heard it, but that doesn't mean it won't be back tonight."

Smoke had been standing at the foot of the bed while he talked to Monte. Now, he took hold of the ladderback chair that sat against the wall, turned it around, and straddled it. He thumbed his hat back on his head and frowned in thought.

"It's unusual for a bear or any other wild animal to wander into a settlement. Usually they steer clear of people as much as possible."

"I've heard about bears showing up in towns and rummaging around in folks' trash, and we've had wolves and mountain lions right here in Big Rock."

"That only happened during bad winters when game was scarce," Smoke said.

"That's true, I suppose, but I don't know how a bear's brain works. Especially one that's gotten a taste for human flesh."

"Yes, but this one doesn't eat its victims, just rips them up," Smoke pointed out.

"That's even worse. It's not starving. It just kills for the thrill of killing."

Smoke nodded slowly. He wasn't going to argue with Monte, but something seemed off about this whole terrible business, and the longer it went on . . . the more victims the bear claimed . . . the more Smoke felt like they were missing something.

He would ponder on it later, though, he decided. For now, he had been away from home for a couple of days and he wanted to make sure everything was all right at the Sugarloaf.

"I'm going to head out to the ranch if there's nothing else you need me to do," he said as he got to his feet.

"Can't think of anything," Monte said. "Unless you want to come back and stay in town tonight, in case that bear shows up again."

"I'll think about it, but I reckon I'd rather spend that time with my wife."

Monte chuckled and said, "Can't say as I blame you there."

Smoke nodded to him and went out. He paused in the front room to speak to Dr. Spaulding, who was standing there wiping his hands on a rag.

"How's that fella who got shot in the arm doing?" Smoke asked.

"The wound's not too serious," Spaulding replied. "Whoever tended to it did a good job. The arm will be stiff and sore for a good while, but barring complications, I expect the fellow will make a full recovery. The friends who brought him in are seeing to it that he gets home, and I'll look in on him a couple of times a day."

"What about Monte?" Smoke kept his voice low so the sheriff wouldn't overhear the question.

"Oh, he's healing superbly. He can start to get up and around in another few days. He has an iron constitution."

"Monte was always a pretty tough hombre," Smoke said with a smile. He grew more serious as he went on, "He told me you were the one who found Pudge's body."

"Well, Tom Nunnley and I did. We just happened to arrive on the scene first. The poor man's screams must have woken half the town."

"I reckon the area's been pretty well trampled by now."

Spaulding raised an eyebrow. "You're thinking about tracks? Yes, there were some around the body, but you're right, so many people have been back there in that alley that they've been obliterated. But I did see them, and while I'm certainly no expert on such things, they looked like bear tracks to me. Tom agreed."

"A lot of tracks or just a few?"

Spaulding frowned and said, "Just a few. The ground is packed fairly hard back there, so there aren't a lot of spots where tracks would be visible."

"That's where you saw them, though."

"Yes. Of course, you have to remember, it was night, all we had to see by was lantern light, and it was a very upsetting experience." A little shudder went through the doctor's frame. "Even for a medical man, that was a terrible thing to see."

"I'm sure it was. Well, I'll leave you to your work, Doctor."

Smoke stepped out onto the porch and paused there to tug his hat down. As he did, a man rode up and reined his horse to a stop in front of the doctor's house. He was trailing a couple of pack horses behind him.

The man was a stranger, wearing a black suit that had a layer of trail dust on it, as did the flat-crowned black hat he wore. The white shirt and black string tie under the black coat made him look a little like a preacher.

Smoke didn't think he'd ever seen a preacher with eyes so cold they looked like chips of ice, though. That was the gaze this man turned on him. The stranger had a narrow, deeply tanned face with a hawk nose arched over a dark mustache.

"You don't look like any sawbones I've ever seen," the man said, "but that sign says this is Dr. Colton Spaulding's house and medical practice."

"That's right," Smoke said. He pointed over his left shoulder with his thumb. "The doctor's inside. Are you in need of medical attention?"

He hadn't noticed any sign that the stranger was injured or sick.

"No." The man's curt answer made it pretty plain that he didn't care to impart any more information on the subject of his health. Or anything else, for that matter.

He dismounted and looped his horse's reins around the hitch rail in front of the doctor's house. The two pack animals were tied to the horse's saddle mount. The man went up the walk to the porch steps and gave Smoke a look clearly calculated to make him step aside.

The stranger didn't know he was aiming that menacing look at Smoke Jensen, though. Smoke stayed where he was and asked, "What's your business with Dr. Spaulding?"

The man paused at the bottom of the steps. "Funny. You don't look like his nurse, either."

Smoke was tired and in no mood to exchange banter with

this cold-eyed stranger. He said, "I'm not, but I am a friend of his, and I don't want anybody causing him trouble."

"What makes you think that's what I intend to do?"

Smoke nodded toward the ivory-handled revolver riding in a black holster on the man's hip. The coat was pushed back on that side so he could reach it easily.

"You mean because I'm carrying a gun? You're here, and you're packing iron," the man pointed out.

"The doctor and I are old friends. I never laid eyes on you before, mister, and I doubt if he has, either."

A tiny sound came from the man. It took Smoke a second to realize it was a chuckle.

"Is everybody in this town as friendly and welcoming as you?" The stranger shook his head. "Never mind. We seem to have gotten off on the wrong foot, and I'd like to rectify that. My name is Major Mordecai Daylight, and it's not actually Dr. Spaulding I want to see. I was told that the local sheriff is here, recuperating from a bullet wound. He's the one I need to talk to."

"Sheriff Carson's a friend of mine, too." The easiest way to get to the bottom of this would be to let the man in, Smoke reasoned, and honestly, he didn't have any right to keep anybody out of the doctor's office. Nobody had appointed him to guard the place. He moved a step to the side, inclined his head toward the front door, and said, "Go on in."

"Thanks," Major Mordecai Daylight said in a dry tone that rankled Smoke.

He controlled that reaction and said, "I'm coming in, too, though."

"Certainly. I have no objection to that."

Smoke followed Daylight into the house. That was an odd name, he mused. Maybe it was the name the stranger had been born with, or maybe he had given it to himself at some point in his life.

A lot of men had headed west to make a new start after the war. Some of them had taken new names to go with it. That was their own business, and it wasn't considered polite to ask too many questions about a man's background, including his name.

This man was old enough to have been in the war, and the fact that he used a military rank even though he wasn't in uniform tended to confirm that. Quite a few men who had been officers during the conflict continued to refer to themselves by their rank.

Dr. Spaulding was still in the front room, sitting at his desk now and writing some notes. He set the pen aside and got to his feet when Daylight came in, followed by Smoke.

"Can I help you, sir?"

Daylight lifted a finger to the brim of his black hat and said, "You're Dr. Spaulding?"

"That's right."

"I'd like to speak to a patient of yours, if that's all right."

"The only patient who's staying here at the moment is Sheriff Carson."

"Just the man I need to see," Daylight said.

Spaulding looked past the stranger at Smoke, who shrugged. He didn't know what this was about, either, but he wanted to find out. His thumbs were hooked casually in his gun belt. He could reach the Colt in less than the blink of an eye if he needed to.

"I believe the sheriff is awake," Spaulding said as he stepped out from behind the desk. He extended a hand toward the hallway leading to the back of the house. "If you'd come right this way . . ."

The doctor went down the hall first, with Daylight following him and Smoke bringing up the rear. The door of Monte's room was open. Spaulding paused in it and asked, "Do you feel up to another visitor, Sheriff?"

Smoke heard Monte reply, "Sure. Who is it this time?"

Spaulding moved aside. The tall, lean stranger stepped into the doorway and introduced himself. "My name is Major Mordecai Daylight, Sheriff. I'm pleased to make your acquaintance."

"Pleased to meet you, too, I suppose, Major. What can I do for you?"

Daylight took off his hat as he came into the room, revealing thinning, dark brown hair streaked with gray. Smoke stopped in the doorway and propped his left shoulder against the jamb on that side.

Monte didn't miss that—or Smoke's vigilant air. He would have noticed the chill in Daylight's eyes by now, too, Smoke knew. Monte had lived as long as he had by noticing things.

Daylight glanced back over his shoulder at Smoke and said, "I'm here on official business, Sheriff, and I'd rather discuss it privately with you. Unless this man is one of your deputies . . . ?"

"Well, he's actually been serving as the acting sheriff for the past few days, but he's not a full-time lawman. He's one of my oldest friends, though, and anything you can say to me, you can say in front of him. This is Smoke Jensen."

Surprise showed in Daylight's eyes. Only for a brief instant, but it was there and Smoke saw it.

"Smoke Jensen," Daylight murmured. "Yes, I've heard of you."

"Can't say as I can return the favor," Smoke drawled. It was a little petty of him, maybe, but this so-called major rubbed him the wrong way.

"Daylight . . ." Monte said. "Wait a minute. I think I've heard of you, Major. You're a hunter."

Daylight nodded. "That's right. I make my living as a tracker and hunter. I've worked for cattlemen all over the frontier, eliminating wolves, mountain lions, or anything else that threatens their stock. If it has four legs, I can track it. And if I can track it, I can find it and kill it."

"So when you say you're here on official business . . . ?"

"That's right," Daylight said. "I've come to offer my services to the town of Big Rock and the people of this valley. I'll find the bear that's been causing so much trouble around here and kill it . . . for the right price, of course."

Chapter 21

Major Daylight's audacious words hung in the air for a moment as Smoke and Monte exchanged a look.

Then Monte said, "The businessmen here in town have gotten together and put up a reward of a thousand dollars for whoever kills that bear."

Daylight clucked his tongue and shook his head. "I'm afraid that's not enough, Sheriff. I'm going to require a payment of two thousand dollars."

"That's a small fortune!" Monte burst out. "Most folks would have to work three or four years to make that much money."

"Most *folks* can't do what I can do," Daylight said in a smug tone that didn't do anything to improve Smoke's opinion of the man.

Smoke straightened from his casual pose in the doorway and moved around so that he was facing Daylight, too. He said, "You must be mighty sure of yourself, mister."

"Major," Daylight corrected him. "And aren't you confident in your own abilities, Jensen?"

"Smoke's demonstrated what he can do, time and time again," Monte said.

"So have I. And I'm not just talking about the hunting jobs I've taken on."

Daylight reached in the pocket of the white shirt he wore and brought out an item that he displayed on his palm. It was a military medal of some sort, Smoke saw, attached to a short, dark green ribbon.

The medal itself took the shape of a square cross with a wreath and two crossed rifles overlaid on it. Writing embossed onto the metal circled around the interior.

"This is the Berdan Sharpshooters Medal," Daylight explained. "I served in Colonel Hiram Berdan's First United States Sharpshooters regiment and fought in every significant Eastern engagement with the enemy, from the Second Battle of Bull Run to the Battle of Cold Harbor. I received the Medal of Honor for my actions at Gettysburg, where I personally killed eight Confederate officers at distances of more than five hundred yards. The Berdan Medal is more meaningful to me, however, because it commemorates the fellowship of the men of the regiment."

Daylight tucked the medal back in his pocket and continued. "So you see, gentlemen, I don't have to get close to that bear in order to kill it. All I have to do is be able to see it."

"I figured the same thing," Smoke said, "but I haven't laid eyes on it yet."

Daylight smirked and said, "I intend to be more successful at the effort than you've been."

Monte said, "Mister . . . I mean, Major . . . you may have heard of Smoke, but you don't know what he's capable of. I'm not saying you're not a good shot, but I reckon Smoke can match up with you, round for round."

"Perhaps we could settle that with a competition . . ." Daylight began. Smoke was about to give in to impulse and take him up on that when Daylight continued. "If I cared the least bit about such a thing, which I don't. I'm here to kill a bloodthirsty predator and collect an appropriate fee, and that's all. I have no interest in any . . . shooting match."

From the corner of his eye, Smoke saw Monte's face flush with anger. The sheriff started to sit up straighter in bed. Smoke knew he was about to tell Daylight to go to hell.

Getting all worked probably wouldn't be good for Monte while he was still recuperating, so Smoke changed the subject by asking, "What kind of rifle do you use, Major?"

"I have a Sharps that I carried during the war, and since then I've acquired a Whitworth .451, the English rifle used by the damned Rebel marksmen." Daylight's narrow shoulders rose and fell slightly. "The Rebs may have been filthy traitors, but they knew a fine rifle when they found one. The Whitworth is perhaps the most accurate weapon I've ever fired."

Smoke bristled a little inside at Daylight's reference to the Confederates as filthy traitors. The Jensen family came from the Missouri Ozarks and had supported the Confederacy during the war. Smoke's father, Emmett, and brother, Luke, had both fought on the Southern side.

In an indirect way, the war had been responsible for Emmett Jensen's death, and Luke had come very close to giving his life for the Southern cause. For quite a few years, in fact, Smoke had believed that his older brother had perished during the final days of the war.

But that terrible conflict was a decade and a half in the past now. As far as Smoke was concerned, it was best forgotten. He had befriended and fought alongside many men during his time on the frontier. Some had supported one side, some the other.

It just didn't matter anymore, or at least it shouldn't.

Major Daylight, though, clearly still carried some

animosity toward the Confederates. That was his affair and none of Smoke's, so Smoke reined in the irritation he felt.

"The Sharps is a mighty good rifle, no doubt about that," he said. "I have one myself and took it with me when I was out hunting that bear. I don't recall if I've ever fired a Whitworth, but I've heard of them."

Daylight ignored that comment and said to Monte, "What about it, Sheriff? Do you agree to my terms?"

"How in blazes am I supposed to do that?" Monte said. "I don't speak for the town."

"Who does? Your mayor, I suppose?"

"Him and the town council." With obvious reluctance, Monte went on. "Or you could talk to Emmett Brown. He's the one who got the group together to put up a reward. I don't know if they'd be willing to increase the amount."

"I don't care where the money comes from, whether it's the town's responsibility or from private funds, as long as I get paid. Where will I find this Emmett Brown?"

"He runs the Brown Dirt Cowboy Saloon. Smoke, do you mind showing the major where that is?"

"That won't be necessary," Daylight said before Smoke could answer. "I'm sure that in a town this size, I won't have any trouble finding it."

Big Rock was actually a decent-sized frontier settlement, but Daylight was right: a man could see all of it in less than an hour.

"How many men has this bear killed so far?" Daylight continued.

"Four," Monte replied, "and the last one was just a couple of nights ago, right here in town."

Daylight raised his eyebrows. "I suppose it's too much to hope that any tracks it left behind were preserved?"

"They're all gone, trampled over," Smoke said. "I was out of town myself, but I already asked about that."

"Serving as acting sheriff?"

"That's right. I led a posse after some bank robbers who thought it would be a good time for a raid, since so many fellas were out hunting for the bear instead of being here in town."

"Was your mission a successful one?"

"It was," Smoke said.

"I'm sure the town is grateful to you. Just as they'll be grateful to me when I eliminate the threat of that rogue grizzly." Daylight put his hat on. "I'll go speak to this Emmett Brown. Who's the mayor here?"

"That would be Mayor Goldstein," Monte said. "He was just elected to the position a few months ago. You'll find him over at the mercantile he owns."

Daylight nodded and started to turn away, then paused.

"One more thing, Sheriff. Jensen mentioned that some of your citizens have been hunting the bear?"

"That's right."

"You need to order them to stop. I don't want a bunch of men who don't know what they're doing barging around, cluttering up the landscape and generally getting in my way while I'm trying to do my job. Do we understand each other?"

"I can enforce a curfew here in town," Monte said. "Not that I need to, because from what I hear, folks have been sticking pretty close to home since the last attack, but I can't control what everybody out in the valley does. The army would have to come in and declare martial law to accomplish that."

"I'm not sure even the army would be enough," Smoke said.

"Fine," Daylight said curtly, "but I won't be responsible for the safety of anyone who interferes with me. Spread the word that I'm to be left alone. You can do that much, anyway."

With that, he stalked out. Smoke and Monte heard his footsteps leaving the doctor's house. Daylight didn't pause to say anything else to Dr. Spaulding.

After a moment, Monte said, "That fella didn't go out of his way to be likable, did he?"

"I reckon not," Smoke said. "He rubbed me the wrong way, that's for sure. But if he can do what he says he can, putting up with him might be worth it."

"He can't be any better at hunting and tracking than you are!"

"I wouldn't say that. There's always someone who's better, no matter what you're talking about."

Monte just shook his head as if he couldn't believe that. Then he said, "Do you think he can talk Brown and the others into upping the reward?"

"Maybe. And if he can't, there's a chance the town council might be willing to put up a thousand to go with the other reward. They're probably even more anxious for somebody to eliminate the threat now that the bear has struck right here in town."

"More than likely," Monte said, nodding.

"But that's out of our hands," Smoke went on. "Right now I want to get home and see my wife."

"Yeah, you kind of got sidetracked from that when you tried to leave before, didn't you? Did you run into the major right outside?"

"Yep."

"You knew he might be trouble the second you laid eyes on him, I expect."

"That, too," Smoke agreed, "but if he's as good as he says he is, maybe he can do us some good."

Monte laughed. "Isn't there a part of you that wants to

find out just how the two of you would stack up against each other in a shooting match?"

"As reluctant as I am to agree with that hombre about anything, I reckon I have to on that score," Smoke said. "For a second there, I was annoyed enough that I would have gone along with the idea, but I don't really care."

As always when he had been gone, even for a fairly short spell, Smoke and Sally were glad to see each other. When he got back to the Sugarloaf, she was waiting for him on the front porch. He swung down from the saddle, handed the bay's reins to the ranch hand who came up to take the horse, then went up the steps to the porch and pulled her into his arms.

A passionate hug and kiss later, Smoke kept his arms around her waist and smiled down into her beautiful face.

"How did you know I was going to be riding in?"

"Haven't you realized by now that we have a connection, Smoke? It's mysterious, almost supernatural. I could just feel that you were getting closer, feel it in every ounce of my being."

She gazed up at him for a moment and then laughed.

"That, and one of the hands happened to be in town when you and the posse rode in, and he rattled his hocks back out here to let me know that you'd be coming home soon. I've been listening for the sound of your horse ever since."

With a smile, she went on. "There's fresh lemonade, and I just took an apple pie out of the oven."

"That sounds mighty good," Smoke said, "but won't that pie need to cool for a while?"

"I think we can come up with something to do to pass the time while it does," Sally said.

* * *

Later, while they were sitting in the parlor with Pearlie and Cal, Smoke told them about how the posse had caught up with the bank robbers over east a ways.

"Sounds like you did a good job of dealin' with those varmints," Pearlie said. "Of course, if I'd been along, it probably would've been even easier."

"How do you figure that?" Cal wanted to know. "He had Mr. Longmont with him. Are you saying you're better with a gun than Louis Longmont?"

"I don't like to brag—"

"Since when?"

"Just watch what you're sayin', youngster."

"I wouldn't want to bet my life on the difference in gun-handling skills between those two," Smoke said. "Here's something you don't know about yet. The posse and I weren't the only ones who rode into Big Rock today. A fella showed up who claims he can get rid of the bear . . . for a price."

"You mean a professional hunter, like in Africa?" Sally asked.

"What's this about Africa?" Pearlie said.

"There are professional hunters over there who go out and shoot lions and elephants and things like that. Most of them are Englishmen. My father was introduced to one while he was in London."

"This man hunts wolves and mountain lions and bears now, but he used to be a sharpshooter during the war," Smoke said. He explained about Major Mordecai Daylight, including the man's name. "I didn't care much for him, but he claims he can do the job. I reckon we'll see, if the town can meet his price."

"How much is that?"

"Two thousand dollars."

Pearlie and Cal both whistled, impressed by the amount.

"That's a dang fortune!" Cal exclaimed.

"It's a lot of money," Smoke agreed, "but if he can do what he says, it might be worth it."

"That beast has killed four men so far," Sally pointed out. "I think any man's life is worth more than five hundred dollars."

Smoke wasn't sure she was right about that—he had run into plenty of bad hombres he wouldn't have given a plugged nickel for—but he understood what she meant.

"We can afford to contribute to the reward fund if we need to," Sally went on.

Pearlie snorted. "Pay some fella to do what Smoke can do? That don't sound right to me."

"I haven't found that bear yet," Smoke reminded him.

"Well, you got distracted by huntin' down that bunch of no-good bank robbers, so you got a good excuse."

Cal said, "Are you going to go out hunting again, Smoke?"

"Major Daylight made it plain he didn't want anybody interfering with him. I suppose we should at least give him a chance and see what he can do."

"Well, I hope he's successful," Sally said. "It's time to put an end to this threat. Too many people have been hurt already, and everyone in the valley can't go on living in a state of fear all the time."

She was right about that, Smoke thought. Whether he liked Major Mordecai Daylight or not—and he didn't—Smoke wished him good luck in his quest.

CHAPTER 22

Now that he was home, Smoke concentrated on working around the ranch for the next couple of days.

As he rode across the range, he was struck, not for the first time, by how well the Sugarloaf was run.

Smoke didn't give himself any of the credit for that. For a man who had spent a significant part of his adult life as a hired gun, Pearlie had turned into a top hand and an excellent foreman. Cal and the rest of the crew did fine work, too.

Even though Smoke kept busy and somewhat distracted, he couldn't help but wonder how things were going with Major Daylight's bear hunt. Assuming, of course, that the major had come to an agreement with the town on his price.

If he hadn't, he might have ridden on and left the valley to the doubtful mercy of that rogue grizzly. If that was the case, Smoke needed to take up the hunt again. He decided to ride into Big Rock on the third day after his return with the posse, just to find out what was going on and if he needed to step in again.

He didn't need that excuse to satisfy his curiosity, because early that morning a rider from Big Rock arrived at the Sugarloaf, carrying a message for Smoke from Monte.

Smoke recognized the horseman as Billy Bragg, a young deputy.

Smoke read the brief message scrawled on the folded piece of paper the youngster handed him, which was a request for Smoke to meet Monte at his office that morning, if possible.

"The sheriff's not staying at Dr. Spaulding's house anymore, Billy?"

The deputy shook his head. "Nope, he moved back home yesterday afternoon. He says he's able to get around just fine with a cane. You know how stubborn Sheriff Carson can be."

"Yeah, I've seen plenty of evidence of it over the years," Smoke said with a smile. "Do you know what this is about?"

"No, sir, I don't have any idea. Not sure Sheriff Carson would want me to say, even if I did."

"I was planning to go into town anyway. I'll throw a saddle on a horse and ride back with you, Billy."

"I'm obliged to you, Mr. Jensen. When the sheriff gives me a job, I don't like to let him down."

They were standing in front of the ranch house. Smoke nodded toward the front door and told the young man, "Go on inside and get a cup of coffee from Mrs. Jensen. There are some biscuits left over from breakfast, too. Grab one for yourself and put some honey on it while I saddle up."

"Yes, sir!" Bragg said with an eager grin.

Smoke ran into Pearlie in the barn when he went in to get his saddle from the tack room. He told the foreman about being summoned to town by the sheriff.

"What do you reckon it's about?" Pearlie asked.

"Young Bragg claims he doesn't know, and I believe him."

"Yeah, that kid's too wet behind the ears to lie about

anything. From what I've seen, though, he's got the makin's of a good deputy . . . if he lives long enough. That ain't hardly guaranteed when you pack a badge for a livin'."

"You could have stopped when you said it wasn't guaranteed," Smoke pointed out.

"Yeah, like the Good Book says, the sun goes down and comes up again, but it don't say nothin' about whether or not we'll be there to see it!"

By the time Smoke led his saddled horse from the corral to the house, Billy Bragg was back on the porch, talking to Sally, who had followed him outside.

The deputy was saying, "I'm mighty obliged to you for the coffee and that little snack, Miz Jensen. I reckon that was just about the best biscuit I ever did eat!"

"I appreciate you saying that, Billy, whether it's true or not," Sally told him.

"Oh, it's true, ma'am. I wouldn't lie about such a thing to a fine lady like you." Bragg turned to Smoke. "You ready to ride, Mr. Jensen?"

"Let's get going, Deputy," Smoke said.

The Sugarloaf was located approximately seven miles west of Big Rock. Smoke and Deputy Bragg moved at a smooth, efficient pace and covered the distance in an hour and a half. It had been a little more than three hours since Bragg had left the settlement, which put the hour in late morning. Even though it was possible Monte wasn't still at the sheriff's office, Smoke knew that was the logical place to start looking for him.

When he and Bragg reined to a stop in front of the office, Smoke frowned as he looked at the wagon parked there. Its team of four sturdy mules was tied at the hitch rail.

The enclosed, brightly painted vehicle immediately reminded Smoke of Doc Endicott's wagon. This was no peddler's cart, however. This was a full-blown medicine show wagon.

Arching across the top of the side walls were the words:

DOCTOR JASPER T. ROCKLIN.
MEDICAL RESEARCHER AND INNOVATOR.
MIRACLE ELIXIR—CURES ALL ILLS—
RESTORES VITALITY.

Below those words, stretching from front to back, was a pastoral scene depicting a beautiful blue lake surrounded by wooded banks. Several Indian tepees were on one bank. On the other side of the lake, the figure of a bear stood on its hind legs, its forepaws in the air, but somehow the creature lacked a menacing air and looked more like it was waving a friendly hello to the Indians on the other side of the lake.

Underneath that painted scene were more words:

SECRETS OF THE CHIPPEWA—
NATURAL GOODNESS IN A BOTTLE!

Smoke nodded toward the wagon and asked Bragg, "Was that here when you left to fetch me, Deputy?"

"Yes, sir. It rolled in bright and early this morning."

Smoke figured the medicine show wagon had something to do with why Monte wanted to see him. No other explanation really made sense.

Also, that painted bear had caught his attention immediately. He recalled how the rogue grizzly had appeared suddenly in Fred Jackson's cornfield, standing up on its hind legs and waving its paws in the air.

Nelse Anderson had described the creature in the same way. To see a bear in that pose painted on this wagon was a mighty big coincidence to swallow, Smoke thought as he swung down from the saddle and tied his horse, keeping it a good distance from the mule team. Mules liked to cause trouble sometimes.

Billy Bragg dismounted, too, and hurried to open the office door for Smoke. As they went in, the deputy said, "Howdy, Sheriff. Here's Mr. Jensen, just like you sent me to fetch."

Monte was behind the desk, turned sideways in his swivel chair so he could prop his wounded leg in another chair that had been pulled up close by. A cane lay across the desk.

A visitor who no doubt went with the garish wagon outside was seated in front of the desk. He twisted around in his chair to look over his shoulder at the newcomers, then stood up and turned to face them.

"Don't get up, Monte," Smoke said.

"Don't worry, I don't intend to," the lawman replied. "Doc Spaulding is already irritated enough with me because I went back to my own house to finish my recuperation. He told me to rest this leg as much as possible and said that if I messed it up, he'd fix it so I couldn't go gallivanting around anymore." Monte shook his head. "I'm not sure what he meant by that, but it sounded pretty threatening."

"You should always follow your doctor's advice, Sheriff," the stranger said. "He's only trying to help you."

"I don't doubt that," Monte said, "but I've got a responsibility to the town and the rest of the valley. Smoke, this is Dr. Jasper Rocklin."

"I guessed as much from the wagon outside," Smoke said as he stepped forward and extended his hand.

Rocklin chuckled as he grasped Smoke's hand. "Eye-catching, isn't it?"

"You could say that," Smoke agreed. He could have also said that the wagon was garish and gaudy, but he didn't see any point in that.

As he shook Rocklin's hand, he studied the man. Rocklin

was of short stature and definitely on the stocky side. He wore a brown tweed suit with a gold-brocaded vest under the coat. A showy jeweled stickpin glittered in his silk cravat. Several gleaming rings were on each pudgy-fingered hand. A brown derby of a darker shade sat on the corner of Monte's desk.

Rocklin had a rounded head topped with thin white hair. Bright blue eyes were set in pits of gristle. His nose was large, and its reddish hue, along with the thin strands of red on the man's cheeks, told Smoke that he was a drinker.

At the moment, however, Rocklin seemed stone cold sober, and those blue eyes shone with intelligence. Despite his overall appearance, there was nothing soft about his grip as he clasped Smoke's hand.

"What brings you to Big Rock, Doctor?" Smoke asked.

"Before we get into that," Monte said, "Billy, you should make the midday rounds."

"Are you sure, Sheriff?" the young deputy asked. Clearly, he wanted to stay and hear what the men were going to say.

"I'm not in the habit of giving orders I'm not sure about." Monte's voice rose a little as he spoke. "Now get on about your duties, Deputy."

"Yes, sir!"

With an obviously reluctant glance over his shoulder, Bragg left the office and closed the door behind him.

Monte settled back in his chair and went on. "I think it would be best if the three of us keep this to ourselves for the time being."

Now Smoke was more intrigued than ever. He pulled up the remaining ladderback chair in the office, turned it around, and straddled it as Rocklin resumed his seat, too. Smoke waited with an expectant look on his face.

"The sheriff assures me that you are, ah, trustworthy,

Mr. Jensen." Rocklin's accent told him that the man was no Westerner but was more likely from back East somewhere.

Smoke nodded and said, "I like to think I am."

"I'm here because I read newspaper reports about the so-called killer grizzly bear that's been terrorizing this vicinity in recent weeks."

"Are you here to make an offer to kill the bear for a price, too?" Smoke asked bluntly.

Rocklin leaned back in his chair as his eyes widened in alarm.

"Good heavens, no, sir!" he exclaimed. "The last thing in the world I want is for that bear to be killed!"

Smoke frowned slightly, cocked his head to the side, and said, "You're going to have to explain that, Doctor. That bear's gone rogue and has killed four men."

Rocklin shook his head emphatically. "I don't believe that, not for one second! Barnaby would never harm a soul."

"Barnaby?"

"That's his name. You see, Mr. Jensen, Barnaby is a tame bear. An attraction, so to speak. He's part of my show."

Smoke glanced at Monte, whose shoulders rose and fell in a shrug.

"I figured you ought to hear it for yourself, Smoke," the sheriff said. "I know I never heard anything like it."

Rocklin leaned forward and went on. "I've had Barnaby for years, and he's never given me the least bit of trouble. He's friendly and gentle as a lamb. Oh, he can act terribly fierce, mind you, but that's all it is . . . an act. I've taught him how to stand up on his rear legs and wave his paws in the air and roar at the top of his lungs, as if he's about to attack. But it's all a performance. After he's done that and convinced the audience that he's going to break his chain and come after them, I approach him."

A smile wreathed Rocklin's face, making him look even more cherubic.

"You should hear the spectators cry out in horror," he went on. "They believe Barnaby is going to tear me to bits, but then I give him a bottle of my elixir to drink."

"Isn't that stuff mostly whiskey?" Monte asked. "Most snake oil . . . I mean, medicine show elixir . . . is, isn't it? No offense meant, Doctor."

Rocklin chuckled. "Oh, none taken, Sheriff, I assure you. Indeed, most of the elixirs, potions, and nostrums sold by men in my profession are composed primarily of alcoholic spirits. I'll admit to you that my famous Chippewa Elixir contains a small amount of the finest whiskey, but it also contains pure spring water and many healthful herbs." He waved a hand, the rings glinting in the light. "However, that's not what I give Barnaby, even though it's in one of my elixir bottles. I use a mixture of water and honey. After he drinks it, he gets down on all fours again and rubs against me as I pet him. I tell the customers that if my elixir can tame such a savage beast, surely it can cure what ails them!"

Monte leaned forward, clasped his hands together on the desk, and said, "Uh, Doctor, you do realize you just admitted to a lawman that you're a big ol' fraud who cheats people?"

"I merely explained what I've done in the past, Sheriff, and you didn't personally witness any of those activities, did you? You have no real way of knowing if I was telling the truth. Not only that, I have absolutely no intention of carrying on any business dealings here in your town. I came to Big Rock only because I heard about what was happening in this area and want to locate my lost old friend Barnaby."

Smoke said, "I reckon you'd better tell us how he came to be lost."

"I was in Wyoming about six months ago," Rocklin said. "I had visited a settlement and was on my way to another one. Early one morning, a commotion aroused me, and I awoke to find that a large group of men was approaching my camp. They looked and sounded angry, and as they came closer, I recognized some of them as citizens of the last hamlet in which I'd stopped."

"A mob, in other words," Monte said, "mad because they'd figured out that you bilked them."

Rocklin inclined his head in grudging agreement. "I deemed it best to depart posthaste, but then I saw that sometime during the night, Barnaby had gotten loose from the rope with which I'd tied him to a tree."

Smoke said, "You don't have a wagon or something like that to carry him in?"

"Actually, I do have a cage, and he always rode in it while we were traveling, but I'd gotten in the habit of letting him roam a bit while we were camped. Always tied, as I said. I didn't believe that Barnaby would ever stray. He really is a devoted companion." Rocklin swallowed hard. "Was a devoted companion."

"Did he break the chain?" Monte asked.

"Indeed he did. Something must have caught his interest and intrigued him enough to make him want to get loose." Rocklin sighed. "I should have known better."

"You can tame a wild animal," Smoke said, "but a small part of it will always stay wild. Which means you can't always predict what it'll do."

"A lesson I've learned, much to my regret."

"What happened with that mob?" Monte asked.

"I hitched up my wagon, including Barnaby's cage that attaches to the rear of it, and departed the vicinity as quickly as possible."

"Those fellas should have been able to catch up to you," Smoke said.

"I discouraged them by firing a few rifle rounds over their heads. *Well* over their heads," Rocklin added. "I didn't wish to harm anyone. I simply didn't care for the idea of being dragged back to their town and decorated with tar and feathers."

"I don't suppose anybody could blame you for feeling that way," Monte said.

"Under the circumstances, I thought it would be unwise to double back and search for Barnaby right away. I wanted to give those unhappy fellows time to abandon their effort and return to their homes, and sure enough, they did. But when I went back a few days later, I could find no sign of Barnaby." Rocklin scowled. "I believed, or should I say, hoped, that he wouldn't stray far from where we'd parted ways, but unfortunately, that wasn't the case. Since then, the necessity of earning a living has kept me on the move, but I never stopped asking people everywhere I went if there had been any reports of a large bear in the area. I scoured every newspaper I came across for such information, as well."

"You really think this tame bear of yours could have made it this far from where you lost him?"

"I certainly do, Sheriff. Barnaby is extremely intelligent. He could have foraged for food along the way, and bears have been known to range hundreds of miles in their travels."

"Where's his cage?" Smoke asked. "I didn't see it attached to the wagon outside."

"I unhooked it and left it where I camped last night, not far from here," Rocklin explained. "I didn't see any need to bring it into town. I knew I wouldn't find Barnaby here."

Monte said, "That's where you're wrong. He was right here in Big Rock less than a week ago."

"When that bartender you told me about was killed?" Rocklin shook his head emphatically. "I've told you, Sheriff, there's absolutely no way Barnaby could have carried out such a heinous deed. He hasn't killed anyone."

Monte's voice was grim as he said, "We've got four men dead."

"Did anyone actually witness those deaths?"

"No, but what else could have torn up those men like that?"

"Another bear, perhaps, or some other sort of wild animal."

Smoke said, "We can't rule that out, Monte."

"But the bodies had bear tracks around them," the lawman said. "You saw them for yourself, Smoke."

"That's right, and several folks have laid eyes on a bear that acts just like the one you describe, Dr. Rocklin."

"Did the bear harm anyone when he was spotted?" Rocklin asked.

Monte grunted. "You already know the answer to that. He chased one cowboy, but I suppose he could have been chasing the steer that the cowboy was looking for, figuring to make a meal on it. He didn't hurt the hombre."

"And the other times?"

"He just waved his paws in the air and roared."

"Just as I taught him to do."

"And then he wandered off," Smoke mused. "Like he knew the act was over."

"Exactly! I tell you, gentlemen, the bear that's been seen in this area has to be Barnaby, but he's done no harm. He's innocent of those killings."

"And you want us to help you find him?"

"I'd be eternally grateful, Mr. Jensen. If Barnaby and I could be reunited, I swear I'd never allow him to stray again."

"I believe you mean that, Doctor," Monte said, "but the problem is that somebody else is already looking for that bear . . . and if I'm any judge of men, that hombre is a stone-cold killer."

CHAPTER 23

Rocklin's eyes widened in horror.

"What are you talking about, Sheriff?" he asked. "I assumed that Barnaby was in some danger, that he might be the object of a search, but you make the situation sound even more ominous."

"You wouldn't happen to have ever heard of a man called Major Mordecai Daylight, would you?"

Rocklin stared across the desk in blank bafflement for a moment and then shook his head.

"He's a man who makes his living hunting down wild beasts that pose a particular threat," Monte explained. "A few days ago, the town council and some of the local businessmen agreed to pay him a bounty of two thousand dollars if he finds and kills the bear responsible for those deaths."

"But Barnaby didn't harm anyone! I explained all that!"

"Major Daylight doesn't know that," Smoke said. "Even if somebody told him, I'm not sure he'd believe it . . . or care."

"I don't reckon he would," Monte said. "I've got a hunch that hombre doesn't care about much of anything except collecting bounties."

"He has to be stopped. Please, Sheriff—"

Monte's shaking head caused Rocklin to break off his entreaty.

"I'm sorry, Doctor, but I don't have any legal authority to stop the major from hunting a bear. What he's doing isn't against the law."

"But it . . . it's immoral! Barnaby is harmless. He'd never hurt anyone." Rocklin swung his stocky body toward Smoke. "Mr. Jensen, can you help me?"

"What do you want me to do?" Smoke asked. "Go after Major Daylight? I don't have a right to interfere with him any more than Sheriff Carson does."

"But if we could find Barnaby first—"

"We?" Smoke interrupted, cocking an eyebrow.

"I would have to come with you. Barnaby is shy, you see. If you came face to face with him, he'd do his act, just like he has in those other encounters, but then he'd want to go on his way. If you tried to capture him, he might get annoyed."

"And I don't want to annoy even a tame bear."

"It probably wouldn't be wise," Rocklin agreed. "Whereas, if I accompanied you and we located Barnaby together, he would see me and know that no one meant to harm him. I'm certain he would come along with us peacefully."

Monte said, "You figure he actually remembers you after this long?"

"I have no doubt of it, Sheriff. Barnaby and I are friends and will remain so for life."

"You go running up to him, you might find out different."

"I'm willing to risk that. Wouldn't you run a risk for a friend?"

Monte glanced at Smoke and said, "I have, many times, so maybe I understand."

"I do, too," Smoke said. "I'm not really comfortable about taking you along, Doctor, but you've got a point. Barnaby, if it is him, wouldn't cooperate with me. I couldn't bring him back alive. You might have a chance of doing it."

"So you'll help me search for him?" Rocklin asked eagerly.

Smoke nodded. "We'll give it a try. Why don't you come out to my ranch with me, so I can gather up some supplies, and we'll start from there."

"I realize nothing's been said about it, but I'd be willing to pay you—"

Smoke held up a hand to stop him. "Let's leave it with nothing said. I'm doing this to help a man who's lost a friend and wants to find him again."

Smoke rode alongside the medicine show wagon as Rocklin drove back out to the spot where he'd left Barnaby's cage. When they got there, he helped the older man hook it up to the back of the medicine show wagon.

Smoke had seen such wheeled cages before. Traveling circuses used them to transport animals that were part of the show. It was a straw-covered floor with closely spaced iron bars for the sides and a simple flat roof.

Big enough for a bear to stand up and move around a little, the enclosure was small enough that Smoke understood why Rocklin liked to let Barnaby have a bit more freedom while they were camped. It would be hard for any animal to stay cooped up in there all the time.

"You said you chain the bear when you're putting on a show?" Smoke asked.

Rocklin nodded. "That's right. One end of the chain is attached to a shackle around his leg, and the other is attached to the wagon. I make sure the shackle is loose enough that it doesn't cause Barnaby any discomfort, although the customers don't know that, of course. Even so, he's secured quite effectively and can't get loose, even if he wanted to. Which he doesn't."

"He wandered loose when he escaped," Smoke pointed out.

Rocklin winced. "I wish you wouldn't say that he escaped. That makes it sound as if he were mistreated, and I would never do that. It's more like a child that wandered off."

Yeah, a child that weighed a thousand pounds and had razor-sharp teeth and claws, Smoke told himself. That was a disturbing thought.

The campsite was north of Big Rock. They didn't have to go back through the settlement, but rather skirted around it to reach the road that ran to the Sugarloaf. They reached the ranch by midafternoon.

Pearlie came out of the barn as the wagon clattered to a stop. He paused for a moment and stood there with a surprised look on his rugged face. Then he came forward and greeted Smoke by saying, "Looks like you brought in a stray."

"Pearlie, meet Dr. Jasper T. Rocklin. Doctor, this is my foreman, Pearlie Fontaine."

Rocklin tipped his derby and said, "A great pleasure to meet you, Mr. Fontaine."

"Yeah, uh, likewise, I suppose, Doc," Pearlie said. "Smoke, you figure on puttin' on a medicine show?"

Smoke laughed. "Not hardly. Dr. Rocklin is after the same thing a lot of folks are. He wants to find that bear."

"Barnaby is his name," Rocklin reminded him.

"Barnaby?" Pearlie repeated. "That big ol' varmint has a name?"

"It's a long story," Smoke said. "Can you see that the doctor's team gets a drink? Then you can join us at the house."

"Sure, happy to." Clearly, Pearlie was baffled by what

was going on, but he was content to wait for an explanation, at least for now.

"Doctor, that beautiful woman over there who just came out of the house and is waiting for us on the porch is my wife, Sally. Come on and I'll introduce you."

"I never pass up an opportunity to meet a lovely woman," Rocklin said as he hurriedly climbed down from the driver's seat of the gaudy vehicle.

He not only took off his hat but also bowed when Smoke introduced him to Sally. Despite his portly figure, he managed to look graceful while doing so.

"It's my great honor to meet you, madam," he said.

"Welcome to our home, Dr. Rocklin," she replied. She glanced at Smoke. "You didn't tell me you were bringing back company from town."

"When I left here, I didn't know I was," Smoke said, grinning.

"I suppose this has something to do with why Monte wanted you to pay him a visit?"

"That's right. Let's go inside and the doctor and I will tell you all about it."

Smoke motioned for Pearlie to follow them as the foreman approached.

For the next quarter of an hour, Smoke filled Sally and Pearlie in on the situation, aided by Rocklin's explanations. Sally sympathized with the loss of the doctor's friend and companion, and she said, "Smoke, do you think it's possible Dr. Rocklin's bear isn't the one causing all the trouble in the valley?"

They were sitting in the parlor, Smoke and Sally on a heavy leather sofa, Rocklin and Pearlie in armchairs flanking the fireplace. Smoke leaned forward, clasped his hands between his knees, and said, "Almost right from the start, something about this whole business bothered me. It took me a while to figure out what it is. Every time someone's actually seen a bear, it hasn't tried to hurt anybody. It just acted like Dr. Rocklin said, like it was putting on a show."

"That's exactly what Barnaby would do upon encountering humans," Rocklin said.

"And every time somebody saw the bear, it left enough tracks for me to follow it for a ways," Smoke went on. "Sure, eventually I lost the trail, but at least it left a trail, like you'd expect." He shook his head. "That wasn't exactly the case with the killings. There would be a few prints around the body, maybe an occasional track elsewhere in the vicinity, but as far as leaving a trail that could be followed, that wasn't what happened, even in places where tracks like that should have been visible."

"What are you sayin', Smoke?" Pearlie asked. "It almost sounds like you think maybe those poor fellas weren't even killed by a bear."

"That's exactly what I'm starting to wonder."

The eyes of the other three all swung to stare at him. After a few seconds, Sally said, "I thought you were going to say there must be two bears roaming around the valley, Barnaby and a rogue grizzly that killed those men."

"Well, that's the most obvious explanation if you accept Dr. Rocklin's claim that Barnaby wouldn't hurt anybody."

"He wouldn't," Rocklin said. "I'm absolutely certain of it."

"But it couldn't have been a mountain lion or somethin' like that," Pearlie said. "We found bear tracks. They were at the scene of every killin'."

Smoke nodded. "That's right. Because someone wanted us to think that a bear was responsible."

"Well, that's just loco! Who'd do a thing like that?"

"And why?" Sally added to Pearlie's question.

"And how? Them fellas was torn up like a bear or some other wild animal got 'em."

"I don't know those answers," Smoke admitted. "It doesn't make any sense, and there's no evidence that I'm right. It's just an idea that might explain what's been going on, but it's going to take a lot more figuring to know for sure. For now, I think the most important thing is to find Barnaby, if he's really out there, before Major Daylight does."

"I concur," Rocklin said, "and I very much appreciate your help in this, Mr. Jensen."

"Call me Smoke. If we do find Barnaby and get him somewhere safe, maybe then we can concentrate on figuring out the rest of this mystery."

"When are you going to start looking?" Sally asked. "It's too late in the day to start out now, isn't it?"

Rocklin said, "I was hoping we could begin our search immediately, Smoke.

"We can head for the mountains, toward the area where I lost the bear's trail the last time I tried to find him, after he spooked Fred Jackson and his kids. We won't have time to get there today, but we can make a start. We'll need some supplies to take with us."

Sally got to her feet. "I can take care of that." She left the room, headed for the kitchen and pantry.

Pearlie said, "How about me comin' along, Smoke?"

"No, I'd rather you stay here. I never worry about the ranch when you and Cal are around. Also, the fact that none of those men who went after the bear after the reward was posted ever caught sight of it tells me that Barnaby is smart enough to avoid large groups of hunters."

Rocklin said, "Indeed, he's definitely above average in intelligence. I know that from the ease with which I was able to train him. Of course, bears are some of the smartest members of the animal kingdom to begin with."

"So I figure the doctor and I should go after him, just the two of us," Smoke continued. "That way we'll be less likely to spook him and make him hide. You think he'll recognize you if he ever lays eyes on you, Doctor?"

"Without a doubt! Really, all he'll have to do is catch my scent. Bears are very intelligent, but their eyesight isn't all that good, I'm afraid. But if he can smell me and hear my voice, Barnaby will know me. I'm sure of it."

"All right, then. As soon as we can pack those supplies, we'll start out, cover as much ground as we can, then first thing tomorrow morning, we'll head up into the mountains and see if we can pick up Barnaby's trail."

Rocklin smiled. "You sound like you finally believe me, Mr. Jensen . . . Smoke."

"Well, it's still kind of a far-fetched yarn you spin, Doctor, but if you're right, it'll scratch that itch I've been feeling in my brain."

Pearlie said, "But if the doc ain't right, Smoke, you fellas may wind up with a thousand pounds of killer grizzly in your laps. Not to mention you'd better watch out for that Major Daylight hombre. From what I've heard about him, he might not take it kindly if he thinks you fellas are tryin' to keep him from collectin' that bounty."

Smoke nodded slowly and said, "You and I have always known, Pearlie, that the most dangerous animals are the ones that walk around on two legs."

CHAPTER 24

The next morning found Smoke and Dr. Rocklin several miles from the Sugarloaf, on the north side of the valley heading for the snow-capped peaks in front of them. They had brought along an extra saddle mount tied on a lead rope behind the cage, since eventually the terrain would be too rough for the medicine show wagon.

As he rode alongside the gaudy vehicle, Smoke indulged his curiosity by asking, "How did you ever come by Barnaby in the first place, Doctor? You don't find a tame bear every time you turn around."

"Indeed you don't, Smoke. I was still back in Pennsylvania, putting on shows there, when I happened to visit a town where another attraction was already taking place. A man had set up a wrestling ring and was offering fifty dollars to any challenger who could stay in the ring for two minutes with his champion."

"Wait a minute. Are you saying that Barnaby was a wrestling bear?"

"That's exactly right. And it was quite a spectacle. Man versus bear! Have you ever heard of such a thing?"

"Well, I have an old friend who wrestled a bear one time," Smoke said, thinking about Preacher. "It wasn't a competition or an exhibition, though. It was a fight to death."

A shudder went through Rocklin. "Thank goodness such a fate never befell Barnaby."

"I suppose the fella who had him would charge an admission price to watch the matches?"

"Of course. Plus any man who wanted to pit his strength against Barnaby had to pay a fee to do so. It was all pure profit, since no one was ever able to emerge victorious and the fellow simply kept all the money."

"I'm surprised he found enough challengers to make the whole thing worthwhile."

"Oh, there are always a few men in those small towns who are so confident of their own strength and prowess that they were willing to risk it. Often they've fought each other enough that they're bored and looking for some new excitement." Rocklin chuckled. "And without a doubt, ample helpings of old John Barleycorn were involved, too."

"Most men are braver when they've been drinking," Smoke agreed. "The foolish ones, anyway. Did Barnaby ever hurt any of those fellas who challenged him?"

"Not a single one, as far as I know. He was gentle and well-trained, even then." A scowl replaced Rocklin's amiable expression. "It was the training methods employed that made me determined to get him away from the man who owned him."

"Too hard, was he?"

"Downright cruel is more like it," Rocklin said with genuine anger in his voice. "I'll admit, when I saw Barnaby, my first thoughts were about how I might be able to make use of him in my show, but then I saw the scars and the wounds he had suffered recently, and I knew then and there that I had to get him away. I was prepared to employ any measures necessary to do so."

"Did you steal him?" Smoke asked.

"Certainly not! I'm not a thief. No, I simply inveigled his owner into a poker game with myself and some of the locals. Eventually, they dropped out and it was just Barnaby's owner and myself. The stakes rose until it came to a point where the man had to wager Barnaby in order to see the cards in my hand." Rocklin chuckled again, back in a good mood. "My cards proved to be superior to the ones he held."

"And I've got a hunch you knew that ahead of time, didn't you, Doctor?"

"Are you implying that I cheated him, sir?"

"I'm saying you probably know how to manage a game so that it turns out the way you want."

"Well . . . I suppose there's some truth to that, but as a matter of fact, I didn't have to cheat. I was a superior player, that's all. But I *would* have cheated if I had to, in order to get Barnaby away from that man. I daresay I might have resorted to violence, if it had proven to be necessary. I'm grateful that it didn't."

"So he let the bear go just like that?"

Rocklin shrugged. "I think he'd begun to get the impression that if he continued treating Barnaby the way he did, sooner or later the creature would turn on him. Since he knew no other way to get Barnaby to do what he wanted, eventually the situation would have become dangerous. So in a way, he may have been relieved when he lost. He could always find some other way to gull the unsuspecting masses."

"You and Barnaby hit it off right away?"

"We most certainly did! He responded better to gentle commands than he ever did to harsher treatment. It was like working with a . . . a friend."

"I hope we can find him, Doctor. It sounds like the two of you belong together."

"Indeed we do, Mr. Jensen . . . Smoke. Indeed we do."

When they reached the foothills, their pace slowed as they had to follow routes that Rocklin could travel with his wagon and the attached cage.

"Before the day's over, we'll probably have to find a good place to leave the wagon," Smoke said.

"I'll rely on your judgment on that matter," Rocklin replied. He turned halfway around on the seat to gaze at the vast sweep of the valley that was visible from where they were. "It's difficult to believe we'll ever find him in all this country, but we have to. We simply have to."

"You need to prepare yourself for the chance we might fail, Doctor."

"Do you allow yourself to dwell on such things, Smoke?"

"Well . . . no," Smoke admitted. "I always tackle a problem by thinking that I'm going to beat it."

"I'm approaching this in the same way."

"Fair enough." Smoke pointed up the trail. "About a mile ahead of us is the last place I saw Barnaby's tracks, the last time I was trying to find him."

He had fallen into the habit of referring to the bear by name, he realized, even though they didn't have any proof yet that the creature they sought actually was Barnaby.

Enough time had passed since he'd been there that Smoke didn't expect to find any of the bear sign he had followed before. That proved to be the case. The elements had wiped it out.

However, once landmarks were set in his mind, they stayed there forever, so he had no doubt that he'd led Rocklin to the spot where he had lost the trail.

"All we can do now is cast back and forth," he explained. "It would help if you switched to horseback so we can split up and cover more ground."

"I'm willing to do whatever is necessary to locate my old friend," Rocklin said. "Just tell me where to go and what to do."

Smoke studied the terrain around them. About a mile ahead of them was a knoll covered with brush, including some bushes that might have berries on them at that time of year. He knew bears liked berries and were attracted to them.

To the left of the knoll, the ground fell away fairly gently in a series of terraces dotted with brush and trees but with quite a bit of open ground, too.

A gully curved around the other side of the knoll, and beyond it the slope climbed at a steeper angle. A number of rugged, rocky outcroppings broke the surface. That would be harder for a less experienced rider to navigate, so Smoke pointed to the left of the knoll and said, "You go that way, Doctor. Ride back and forth for a good ways on those terraces, and if you don't find any tracks, drop down to the next one. I'll check the slope above the knoll for sign."

"You think Barnaby may have foraged among those bushes for berries, is that it?"

"Seems like a possibility," Smoke said.

"I agree. We might even be lucky enough to find him still dozing among the vegetation."

"That doesn't seem very likely. He's probably moved on long before now, but maybe we can figure out which way he went."

When he was there before, Smoke had covered a wide circle of ground looking for the bear's tracks, but he hadn't made it as far as the knoll. He had no way of knowing if Barnaby actually had gone there, but the chance seemed worth a look around.

Rocklin set the brake on his wagon, climbed down from the seat, and went to the saddle mount tied to the back of the cage. As he loosened the reins, he said, "You're certain this animal is gentle natured, Smoke?"

"She's one of Sally's favorite mounts."

Smoke didn't mention that Sally was an excellent rider and could stick to a hull better than a lot of men. She had ridden the range with him many times when they were just building the Sugarloaf, back in the early days of their marriage. If she'd put her mind to it, she could have been a top hand, but she had so many other interests and abilities that she'd never tried.

The chestnut mare Smoke had picked out for Rocklin to ride really was a good-natured, easy-gaited mount, though, as well as being calm and not easy to spook. That was important with a relatively inexperienced rider.

Rocklin grasped the horn, got his left foot in the stirrup, and grunted with effort as he swung up onto the mare's back. She never budged as he settled himself in the saddle.

"What do I do if I find anything?" he asked.

"You've got a Winchester there in the saddle boot," Smoke said. "I reckon you know how to use one since you said you discouraged the mob that was after you by firing rifle shots over their heads."

"I'm familiar with the weapon's operation, yes."

"If you find bear tracks or if you run into any trouble, fire three shots in the air. I'll come a-runnin'."

"Very well." Rocklin swallowed and lifted the reins. He nudged the mare's flanks with his heels and said, "Get along there."

Smoke tried not to smile at the man's visible nervousness. Rocklin would get used to being on horseback and settle down. Smoke heeled his mount into a trot that carried him at an angle away from the medicine show man.

When he reached the gully north of the knoll a short time later, he paid particular attention to its bed. Earlier in the year, with rain and snowmelt, water must have run through here, but the weather had been dry enough in recent weeks that the ground was all sand and rock now. The sand would take prints. Smoke rode along the gully for at least half a mile, looking for them.

He didn't spot anything out of the ordinary. He found some tracks, but smaller animals had made them. Nothing anywhere near big enough to have been left by a bear. Nor did he find any tufts of hair hung on the brush or on rough tree bark.

That didn't mean the bear hadn't come in that direction. A hard wind might have blown away any tracks left in the past few days. Or maybe the bear was smart enough that it had stayed on the rocks and hadn't left any prints. By this point, Smoke wouldn't put much of anything past the critter.

He moved out of the gully and up the slope, riding back and forth. When he glanced back to the south, he couldn't see Rocklin, but it was possible the knoll was between him and the medicine show man. He hadn't heard any shots, shouts, or anything else from Rocklin.

In a careful, methodical manner, Smoke worked his way upward. Most of the time he watched the ground for tracks, but he kept an eye on the landscape around him, too. Getting too focused on one thing could be dangerous out on the frontier.

Trouble could come from any direction, with little or no warning. That was a lesson Smoke had learned at an early age, and his experiences since coming west had only reinforced it.

He reined in and leaned forward in the saddle as he spotted some broken branches on a bush. His eyes narrowed.

The breaks appeared to have been made in the past couple of days. He reached out and pulled one of the branches closer so he could study the break. Definitely fresh.

Something had pushed past the bush. Might have been the bear, might have been something else. No fur had snagged on the branches. Smoke peered at the gravelly ground and found a smudge. Not really a print, it wasn't distinct enough for that, but he also spotted a short line in the dirt that might have been made by a dragging claw.

It wasn't much, but it was something. He dismounted and started poking through the brush.

After a few more minutes, he had found several other indications that a large animal of some sort had traveled through there in the past couple of days. The sign, faint though it was, led up the slope.

Smoke was about to swing into the saddle and try to follow it when a rifle shot cracked somewhere below him.

He turned his head to peer toward the knoll, waiting for two more shots to follow the first one in an indication that Rocklin had found something, too.

But those shots didn't come, and their lack put a frown of concern on Smoke's face. Rocklin must have been shooting *at* something, rather than as a signal.

Then, abruptly, more shots blasted, but not just two of them. Without thinking about it, Smoke counted as five sharp reports sounded, one right after the other, coming so close together that Rocklin must have been firing as fast as he could work the Winchester's lever and pull the trigger.

Something was wrong, no doubt about it. Smoke practically leaped into the saddle, pulled the horse around, and headed down the slope as fast as he could without risking a bad spill.

The rifle fell silent. That was worrisome. Smoke told himself that Rocklin could be holding his fire on purpose for some reason, though. It didn't mean the medicine show man had been ventilated.

The gully's banks were shallow and gentle enough that Smoke's horse was able to charge into and back out of it without barely slowing down. Then he rounded the knoll and looked down the terraces in the direction Rocklin had gone.

He spotted the chestnut mare moving around skittishly on the third terrace down the slope, but he didn't see any other sign of Rocklin.

Then he saw a thin haze of powder smoke drifting over a spot on the second terrace, near a clump of brush.

Smoke had just started in that direction when he saw the branches jump. A piece of one leaped into the air, then fell back into the brush. At the same time, dirt and gravel kicked up from the ground back to the left.

Those things were enough to tell Smoke that a bullet had just whipped through the clump of vegetation and struck the ground a good distance behind it. That meant a relatively flat trajectory, and the fact that Smoke hadn't heard a shot told him that the round had been fired from quite a way off.

Major Mordecai Daylight. The name burned in Smoke's brain. Daylight had boasted about what a marksman he was at long distances.

But why in the world would he be shooting at Dr. Rocklin, who must have taken cover in the brush?

Smoke hoped the medicine show man wasn't wounded. Rocklin had returned the fire, so that was a good sign. Even so, he wasn't shooting now, and that was a little ominous.

Smoke had reined in as soon as he realized what was going on. He dismounted, pulled his Winchester from its saddle scabbard, and slapped his horse on the rump, sending it trotting back around the knoll, out of the line of fire.

Then he dropped to one knee behind a small tree, levered

a round into the rifle's chamber, and called, "Dr. Rocklin! Can you hear me?"

A reply came instantly from the brush. "Smoke! Yes, I'm here."

"Are you hurt?"

"Only my pride, and perhaps a bruise or two from falling down when I dismounted so hurriedly after that bullet passed by my ear!"

"Did you hear the shot?"

"No, but I've been shot at a few times before. You never really forget what it sounds like when a bullet goes past you at such close proximity."

That humped height was called Camelback Hill, in fact, although Rocklin had no way of knowing that. It was about eight hundred yards away, close to half a mile. At that distance, the bullet fired at Rocklin would have arrived before the actual sound of the shot.

That was true. It was a sound Smoke knew all too well.

"What were you shooting at? Did you see where it came from?"

"Not really. I thought I saw sunlight reflect off something on that hill to the west, the one that somewhat resembles a camel's back."

Rocklin had been wasting ammunition at that range. For a bullet to carry that far required a Sharps or one of those Whitworth rifles Major Daylight had talked about. Smoke was even more convinced now that Daylight was the bushwhacker.

What he couldn't figure out was why Daylight had taken those shots at Rocklin. The two men had never met, as far as he knew. Rocklin had claimed to have never heard of Daylight, and Smoke had no reason to doubt him.

Sheer meanness? Daylight had warned Monte to keep everybody away from him while he was hunting the bear.

Would he actually resort to cold-blooded murder to enforce that edict?

Smoke had a hard time believing that, but at the same time, he knew there were no depths to which some human beings wouldn't sink.

"What are we going to do?" Rocklin called. "This brush was the nearest cover I could find, but it won't stop bullets."

"Maybe whoever's shooting at us is just trying to discourage us," Smoke replied. "Maybe if he thinks we're leaving, he'll let us go. Can you crawl backward out of there, Doctor?"

"I suppose. I've already abandoned any pretense of dignity."

Smoke whistled. Down below, the chestnut mare lifted her head and looked toward him. Smoke whistled again. The mare began to lope in his direction.

"Shinny out of the brush and grab that horse when it comes by," Smoke told Rocklin. "Try to keep her between you and the bushwhacker. It's a risk, but you can't stay where you are. He'll just keep shooting into the brush until he hits you."

"I understand." Rocklin sounded scared, but he didn't argue.

Smoke stood up, still pressing himself against the tree trunk. He didn't bother aiming at the distant height. He knew he couldn't reach it with the Winchester.

Rocklin backed into the open, squirming on his ample belly like a doodlebug. As the mare came closer, he leaped to his feet, moving slowly and more awkwardly than was ideal. As he hurried to grab the horse's dangling reins, more dirt and gravel erupted from the ground near his feet.

Major Daylight must not be the marksman he thinks he is, Smoke mused. The man had taken at least three shots at

Rocklin and had missed with all of them. Of course, those shots had been near-impossible ones . . .

Rocklin got hold of the reins and the saddle horn and hopped around frantically as he brought the mare under control. He wedged his left foot in the stirrup and hauled himself up with such haste that he almost spilled off on the other side before he settled his weight in the saddle.

Then, leaning forward, he kicked the mare into a run that carried him away from the brush where he had sought shelter.

Smoke leaped into the open, waved an arm, and shouted, "Around the knoll!" He broke into a run and headed in that direction himself.

His muscles were tensed. He halfway expected to feel the shock of a bullet striking him at any second. But he and Rocklin both made it to the far side of the knoll, where Smoke's horse was cropping contentedly at some grass on the bank of the gully.

Smoke threw a glance over his shoulder. He couldn't see Camelback Hill anymore. The knoll was in the way. That meant the bushwhacker couldn't see him and Rocklin. He lifted his hand and motioned for the medicine show man to stop.

"We're safe back here for now," he said, "but we need to head back east so that rifleman can see us going. He'll think he scared us off, so I don't expect him to follow us."

"But we can't abandon the search for Barnaby!"

Smoke slid his rifle back into the saddle boot on his mount and said, "We're not giving up, Doctor. We'll just let him think we are, but now we have two objectives for our search. We're going to find Barnaby . . . and we're going to find that son of a gun who just tried to kill you and have a nice long talk with him!"

CHAPTER 25

That same morning, Sally realized she needed flour, sugar, coffee, and other supplies for the pantry, so she went out to the corral, where Pearlie was watching Cal work some of the roughness out of a proddy gray horse.

"I'm going to Big Rock, Pearlie," she told the Sugarloaf foreman. "Is there anything you need?"

"No, ma'am, you ain't."

Sally raised an eyebrow in surprise at being spoken to that way.

"What I mean is," Pearlie went on, not thrown by her reaction, "that Smoke likely wouldn't want you headin' into town by yourself these days. He usually goes with you himself or asks one of us to go along, and that's when there ain't no killer grizzly roamin' around the valley."

"I can take care of myself, you know."

"Anybody who's been around you more'n a minute knows that, but I still say Smoke'd want somebody to go with you."

A sudden yell from the corral made both of them look around. Cal was flying through the air, having just been bucked off the horse he was riding. The young puncher was agile enough to roll when he landed, taking away some of the impact, but he still wound up sprawled in a cloud of dust, shaking his head groggily.

Pearlie slapped his thigh and hooted with laughter.

"Let your guard down when he stopped buckin', didn't you?" he called to Cal. "And as soon as he felt you relax, he throwed you right off! How many times are you gonna let him pull that same trick on you?"

The horse stood off a ways, on the other side of the enclosure, and tossed its head up and down as if it were laughing, too.

Cal climbed slowly to his feet, picked up his hat, and swatted at his clothes with it to get some of the dust off.

"All right, if the two of you think it's so danged funny, why don't you get in here and climb on his back, Pearlie?"

"Because I got more sense than the both o' you put together, that's why. Come on outta there, kid. You can dance with that horse some other time. Right now I got a job for you."

Cal clapped his hat back on his head. "Fine. What is it?"

"Go hitch up a team to the buckboard and throw a saddle on one of your strings. You and Miz Sally are goin' into Big Rock."

Cal frowned for a second, as if he wanted to argue, just on general principles, then he shrugged and climbed out of the corral. As the young cowboy walked off toward the barn, Pearlie watched him go and said quietly, "He's a good hand and I'd trust him with my life. But don't you go tellin' him that, Miz Sally."

She laughed and said, "I understand." Emotions just weren't something these rough men were comfortable with.

A short time later, she and Cal set out for Big Rock. Sally brought along the Winchester carbine she carried on her saddle when she was riding. It lay on the floorboards at her feet. Cal was armed with a Winchester and a holstered Colt.

"What do you reckon the chances are we'll run into that bear?" he asked as he jogged alongside the buckboard on horseback.

"Rather slim," Sally replied. "I hope we don't."

"Me, too," Cal said fervently. "Pearlie told me there's a chance it's really a tame bear and that it didn't kill those fellas. Do you think that's true?"

"Dr. Rocklin insisted that's the case. He seemed so sincere. I hope he's right, for his sake, and I hope Smoke can find Barnaby and reunite them."

"Barnaby," Cal said, shaking his head. "What a name for a bear."

"What would you name him?" Sally asked.

"I don't know, but I don't reckon I'd come up with Barnaby in a million years." Cal shrugged. "It kinds of fits, though."

They rode along in silence for a few minutes before Cal went on, "I saw the bear sign where some of those fellas were killed. It sure looked real to me."

"Smoke seems to think someone may have put those tracks there to make everyone think a bear killed those poor men."

"How would you even go about doing that? You'd have to have a bear's paw . . ."

His voice trailed off, and when Sally looked over at him, she saw that a frown had put deep creases on his forehead.

"Could you do that?" she asked. "If you had a bear's paw that was preserved somehow, could you use it to leave tracks like the ones you and Smoke found?"

"Well . . . I don't see why not. If you just had one paw, you couldn't make it look like the bear walked around or anything like that, but you could put a print here and there.

That's the way you find bear sign sometimes, just one track and not all four together."

"That makes sense," Sally said, nodding, "but it doesn't explain why anyone would want to do such a thing."

"You've got me there, ma'am. I don't have a clue."

The conversation had started wheels turning over in Sally's mind, though, and they continued to revolve just like the buckboard wheels for the rest of the journey into Big Rock. It was possible the bear tracks could be faked, but how would anyone carry out such grisly killings . . . and why? A person who would do such a thing would have to have a really compelling reason. As far as Sally knew, no connection existed between the four men who had been killed . . .

When they reached the settlement, she went into the mercantile and gave Mr. Goldstein the list of the supplies she needed. Cal headed to Longmont's for some coffee and would meet her later.

When Sally came out of the store, she paused in thought for a moment, then turned toward Monte's office.

Monte was seated behind his desk with his wounded leg propped up. When Sally came in, he lowered the newspaper he'd been reading and said, "Well, howdy. Good to see you, as always, Sally."

He folded the newspaper, tossed it on the desk, and started to get up, but Sally motioned for him to stay in his chair.

"Hello, Monte. How's your leg?"

He slapped his thigh lightly. "A little better every day. It won't be long before I'm running around as spry as I ever was. What brings you to town? I reckon Smoke's still out looking for that bear with the medicine show fella?"

"Yes, they left on their search yesterday afternoon, and I haven't heard anything from them. I came in to pick up some supplies. Cal rode with me, and on the way into town he and I started talking about everything that's been going on."

"The bear and the killings, you mean."

"Exactly. I decided I might try to do a little detective work."

Monte frowned and repeated her words. "Detective work? How do you mean?"

Sally sat in one of the chairs in front of the desk and folded her hands in her lap. She asked, "Did Smoke tell you his theory about how someone could have planted those tracks to make it look like a bear was the killer?"

"He never came right out and said it, but I knew something was bothering him. Reckon that could've been it."

"Cal and I discussed how someone could have done that if they had a bear's paw."

"Yeah, but it sounds like a loco thing to do," Monte said. "And it had to be a bear that killed them, the way they were torn up."

"Perhaps not." Sally had been thinking about it as she walked to the sheriff's office. "If you had an implement of some kind . . . a tool . . . with claw-like blades attached to it . . . and if you incapacitated the victim somehow, say by knocking him unconscious so that he couldn't fight back or even cutting his throat with a knife . . . you could do an incredible amount of damage with something like that."

Monte leaned back in his chair, frowned, and shook his head.

"You don't think so?" Sally asked.

"Oh, that's not what I'm shaking my head at. What you're saying sounds mighty far-fetched, but there could be some truth to it, I suppose. I'm just a little surprised that a, uh, lady would come with such a gruesome theory . . ."

Sally laughed. "I'm no shrinking violet, Monte. You

know that. I don't get the vapors and swoon at the thought of such things."

"No, ma'am, I do know that. But even admitting that such a thing would be possible . . . maybe . . . who in the world would do something so vicious, and why?"

"I don't know, but I'm going to try to figure it out. And I want to start by asking you about the four men who were killed. What can you tell me about them?"

Monte clasped his hands together over his stomach and frowned in thought.

"Chuck Haskell was a wrangler, an old bachelor who used to be a cowboy until he got too stove up. Roy Ford was a rancher, had a nice spread and a family. Then there was Doc Endicott, the peddler, and finally Pudge, who tended bar at the Brown Dirt Cowboy."

"What did they have in common?"

"I don't have any idea," Monte said. "I reckon they were all about the same age, but that doesn't mean anything. There are dozens of other men in the valley who are around that age."

"Did they know each other?"

"I wouldn't be surprised if they did. All of them except Doc Endicott lived in these parts, and he passed through fairly often."

"What about their backgrounds? What did they do before they came to Big Rock?"

Monte looked like he was about to shake his head and deny any knowledge of that subject, but then he said, "Wait a minute. Now that I think about it, I recall Haskell talking about how he was a sergeant in the Union army during the war. He was right proud of that."

Sally leaned forward. "What about the other men? Were they in the war, too?"

"Most men that age were, if they lived back East. I

was already out here on the frontier, or I probably would've gotten drawn into it. I never asked them about it . . . You know how no man pries too much into another fella's life . . ."

"Of course," Sally said.

"But I think I remember Pudge talking about being in the army, and I know Doc Endicott was. That's how he picked up that nickname. He was a field surgeon." Monte shook his head again. "He saw so many terrible things he swore he'd never practice medicine again. That's why he became a peddler."

"What about . . . What was the other man's name? Roy Ford?"

"I don't have any idea," Monte said. "I don't think I ever heard him say anything about where he was from or what he did in the past. He was never a talkative sort."

"But still, a connection exists between the other three."

"That they were all in the army during the war?" Monte shook his head again. "It's not really a connection when you've got it in common with thousands of other men. I could find several dozen other men here in the valley who served in the Union army, and almost that many who were Confederate soldiers. I can't see how it means anything."

"Maybe not yet," Sally said, "but it's a start."

Sally had a feeling that Monte believed her attempt at detective work was a waste of time, but she didn't allow that to stop her. When she was convinced she had gotten all the information out of him that she could, she left the sheriff's office and headed for a squarish building constructed of red brick. The sign on the awning above its porch read U.S. POST OFFICE.

When Big Rock had been founded to replace the outlaw

town of Fontana, the first post office had been located inside one of the stores. As the settlement had grown, more space was needed for the mail service, and eventually, an actual post office had been built.

The postmaster was a jovial, fair-haired man named Morrow. From behind the window at the counter in the front of the room, he greeted Sally with a smile and said, "Morning, Mrs. Jensen. Come to pick up the Sugarloaf's mail?"

"I'll do that while I'm here, of course, but actually I'd like to ask you a few questions, Mr. Morrow."

"Sure. If there's anything I can help you with, I'd be glad to."

She debated how much to tell him. She was confident that he was trustworthy. Otherwise, he wouldn't have been appointed postmaster.

After that brief pause, she said, "I'm trying to find out as much as I can about those four men who were killed by the bear."

A sympathetic look came over Morrow's face.

"Wasn't that just the most terrible thing?" he said. "I don't know what I could tell you about any of them, though."

"Well . . . you probably knew Pudge's real name, if he ever got any mail."

"Yeah, I do. His name was Horace Ward."

Sally thought back to the few times she had seen the man and commented, "He didn't really look like a Horace ."

Morrow chuckled. "That's because everybody knew him as Pudge, and the name suited him so well. He told me once . . . he'd talk your ear off, you know, if you ever gave him the chance, and when he'd come in to pick up his mail, I was sort of a, what do you call it, captive audience. Anyway, he told me once that when he was in the war, some of the men in his outfit tried to nickname him Slim, but it just wouldn't stick."

"Did he tell you which side he fought on?"

"He wore the blue. He was in some infantry unit that had a lot of marksmen in it."

Sally felt a surge of excitement. That was some information she hadn't known.

"What about the other three men? Did they ever talk to you about being in the army?"

"Doc Endicott didn't. I heard rumors from other fellas that he'd been a surgeon during the war, but I never heard that directly from him." Morrow rubbed his chin and frowned in thought. "I'm pretty sure Chuck Haskell fought for the North, too. He never talked about it much."

"What about Roy Ford?"

"Roy wasn't the friendliest sort. We never talked much, about that or anything else." The postmaster's eyes widened, as if something had just occurred to him. "But you know, he and Chuck Haskell were friends, so they might have gotten to know each other in the army."

"They were friends?" Sally said. Nobody had said anything about that until now, either.

"Well, I suppose they were. They wrote to each other before Roy moved here with his family. Not a lot of correspondence, mind you, just a few letters, but I definitely remember handling them. Seems like Ford lived over in Kansas back then."

"I wonder what the chances are that they were all in the same company or regiment or whatever you call it."

"I don't know how you'd ever find out, since they're not around to ask about it anymore."

"No, they're not," Sally said slowly.

But even though three of the four victims had been bachelors, the fourth man—Roy Ford—had had a family.

And she wondered just how much they might know.

* * *

"You're going where?" Cal asked as they were riding back out to the Sugarloaf a short time later.

"Across the valley to the RF Connected," Sally repeated.

"That's the Ford spread."

"I know. I want to talk to Mrs. Ford. She and her children have moved back out to the ranch, haven't they?"

"As far as I know, they have," Cal replied. "Smoke had some of us going over there to keep up with the chores and make sure the cattle were tended to, but the widow and young'uns came back from town after a few days. That oldest boy, Edgar is his name, I think, has a proud streak in him. He insisted he could take care of running the ranch." Cal shrugged. "We figured he deserved the chance."

"As soon as I get these supplies put up, I'm going to saddle a horse and ride over there."

"Let me saddle the horse," Cal suggested, "since I'll be going along with you. Pearlie's not gonna let you traipse across the valley by yourself."

"Pearlie's gotten kind of handy about giving orders," Sally commented.

"You're not telling me anything I didn't already know, ma'am. He's always been bossy!"

At least Cal hadn't tried to talk her out of making the trip. She was grateful for that. Not that it would have stopped her if he had, but it was nice not to have to argue about it.

She could tell that Cal was very curious, but she didn't want to reveal just yet the nebulous theory that was taking shape in her mind. It would be better to wait until she knew more and could be more sure of what she was thinking.

When they got back to the Sugarloaf, Sally didn't waste any time putting away the supplies and changing into a riding skirt. Cal had one of her regular mounts saddled for her by the time she reached the barn, carrying her carbine.

"Let's get started before Pearlie comes along and tries to horn in on this," Cal said as he handed her the reins. "He'd probably say for me to get back to work, and he'd go with you to the RF Connected."

"I appreciate the way both of you look after me."

Cal shrugged. "Just doing what Smoke would want us to do."

Sally knew it was more than that. Both Cal and Pearlie were devoted to her, would lay down their lives for her. She knew that, and it made a feeling of humble gratitude well up in her.

She could tell that Cal was intensely curious, but he didn't press her for explanations as they rode across the valley toward the Ford ranch. It was a beautiful day, and she hoped nothing ruined it, like running into a giant killer grizzly bear.

She was becoming more and more convinced that the bear roaming in the valley might be big, but it was no killer.

They reached the RF Connected a few hours later, although they didn't know for sure they were on the Ford range until a young man on horseback hailed them and rode up to them.

"Hello," Sally said as they all reined in. "You're Edgar Ford, aren't you?"

"Yes, ma'am," the youngster said as he touched a finger to his hat brim. "And I know you. You're Miz Jensen. Smoke's wife." A grin flashed across his face. "Everybody knows Smoke."

That her husband was so well-liked made a warm feeling go through Sally. She said, "Would it be all right if I rode on to your ranch house and talked to your mother?"

"Why, sure. I'll show you the way." A sudden frown

replaced the boy's amiable expression. "Unless you've come to talk to her about buyin' the place. We're not selling the ranch. We're gonna keep it going. That's what my pa would've wanted."

"I know that. I just want to ask your mother some questions about another matter."

"Come ahead, then, and welcome."

When they reached the house, the two teenage girls were washing clothes in a tub while their mother hung the wet garments on a line to dry. They all stopped what they were doing to watch the three riders come in.

Marie Ford's face showed the strain of the past few weeks, Sally thought, but she was still a handsome middle-aged woman. She pushed back some strands of graying brown hair that had gotten loose from the bun on her head and said, "Hello, Mrs. Jensen. What brings you all the way over here on this side of the valley?"

"I'd like to talk to you, Mrs. Ford."

"She's not here about buying the ranch," Edgar put in.

"Good," Mrs. Ford said, "because it's not for sale."

"I'd like to ask you a few questions about your husband if you don't mind. I know it might be painful . . ."

Mrs. Ford shook her head and said, "Life's always painful in one way or another. If not now, a body's fortunate, because it will be tomorrow. No sense in worrying about it. Come on inside. There's coffee in the pot." She turned to her daughters. "Girls, finish up with this washing. Edgar, go give your brother a hand with his chores in the barn."

"Whatever this is about, I'm old enough to hear it, Ma," Edgar said.

She thought about it for a moment, then said, "All right, I suppose you are. Come on in." She added, "Just don't get in the habit of arguing when I tell you what to do."

CHAPTER 26

"Roy had a freight business over in Kansas," Mrs. Ford explained a few minutes later as she and Sally sat opposite each other at the kitchen table with cups of coffee in front of them. Edgar sat at the end of the table, and Cal propped a hip against the counter. The two young men had coffee cups, too.

Mrs. Ford went on, "The line was pretty successful. Roy had plenty of contracts to haul goods and several men working for him. He'd been a teamster during the war, you know, but he'd always had a dream of owning a ranch. So when Chuck Haskell wrote to him and told him what a fine valley this is, Roy decided to sell the line and start a spread like he'd always wanted to. Chuck helped him find a place he could buy."

"It's actually the war I wanted to ask you about," Sally said. "Your husband and Mr. Haskell served together?"

"That's right. Chuck was a sergeant and Roy was a corporal. They were in charge of transporting the cases of ammunition the sharpshooters used."

"Sharpshooters?"

"Berdan's Sharpshooters. That was the name of the outfit they belonged to." Mrs. Ford smiled at the memory. "I mean, neither of them were great shots, mind you, but no matter how good you are, you have to have somebody to haul all your ammunition from one battle to the next!"

"That's not the sort of thing that most people think about when it comes to war, but I suppose it's true," Sally said. The next question was what Smoke might call a shot in the dark, but she asked it anyway. "Do you know if your husband served with a couple of men named Cleveland Endicott and Horace Ward?"

Mrs. Ford frowned for a moment as she considered the question. Then she shook her head and said, "Neither of those names sound familiar . . . Wait a minute. Are you talking about Doc Endicott, the peddler?"

"That's right."

"I don't guess I ever heard his real name. Roy just always called him Doc."

Sally leaned forward in her chair. "So they did know each other?"

"They weren't close friends or anything like that, but Doc stopped by here sometimes to sharpen knives for us when he passed through the valley. He and Roy might mention the war in passing, but they didn't talk about it much. I got the feeling that it wasn't a pleasant subject for Doc."

"No, I don't imagine it would be," Sally said. "I was told he was a field surgeon, so he would have seen some terrible things and had terrible memories of those days."

"Roy always said there was nothing glorious or adventurous about war, no matter how many stirring songs were written about it. He just said it was hard, ugly, unpleasant work."

Sally nodded, then said, "But the name Horace Ward doesn't mean anything to you?"

"No, I'm afraid not."

"What about Pudge?"

A look of understanding dawned on Mrs. Ford's face.

"Oh, Pudge!" she said. "Was that his real name? My, I never would have guessed that."

"So you knew him? Your husband knew him?"

"Of course. He was in the same outfit, Berdan's Sharpshooters. He was a teamster, as well."

Sally tried to contain her excitement. She had established that a connection existed between the four men who had fallen victim—supposedly—to the bear roaming the valley. That was more than anyone else had been able to do.

Her next question was more difficult. She said, "Mrs. Ford, I hate to ask this . . . but do you know of any reason why someone might want to hurt your husband?"

"You mean, besides that awful bear?"

"I'm not convinced your husband was attacked by a bear."

"That's loco!" Edgar burst out. "I saw Pa's body! I saw what the bear did to him! How can you say it was something else?"

"Edgar!" Mrs. Ford's voice was sharp. "You mind your tongue, boy. You'll speak respectfully to your elders, and to our guests, or you won't speak at all. Now apologize to Mrs. Jensen."

With a sullen look on his face, Edgar said, "I'm sorry, Mrs. Jensen. I didn't mean to speak out of turn."

"That's all right," Sally told him. "I understand why you're upset. I'm just trying to find out what really happened to your father and those other men."

"It's not like they were close friends," Mrs. Ford said. "I suppose Roy and Chuck were the closest of the four. Doc Endicott didn't want anything to do with reminiscing about the war. And Pudge . . . Well, Pudge would talk about anything, any time, but Roy didn't see him very often. Just occasionally, when he had some reason to go into town. They didn't get together or anything like that."

Sally nodded. She had run out of questions, and Mrs. Ford seemed to have run out of answers. They chatted for a few minutes longer, but Sally seemed to have uncovered all the information she was going to get at the RF Connected.

"I should be getting home now," Sally said as she got to her feet. "I'm very sorry for your loss."

Edgar stood up hurriedly when Sally rose. He said, "Do you think somebody . . . some man . . . killed my pa and those other fellas, Mrs. Jensen?"

"I think it's possible," Sally admitted, "but I don't have any idea why."

"If you find out, will you tell me? Because I'll find the lowdown skunk and kill him!"

"Edgar! You'll do no such thing," Mrs. Ford scolded him.

"If I can find out, I'm going to tell Smoke," Sally said. "If there's a cold-blooded killer out there, Edgar, I think you can rest assured that Smoke will deal with him."

Smoke let himself and Jasper Rocklin be sky-lined atop a ridge within view of Camelback Hill as they rode east, but they were far enough away to be out of reach of even a fancy Whitworth rifle.

Major Daylight would be able to see them through a tel-escopic sight, though, and might believe he had scared them off, even if he hadn't killed them.

That was what Smoke hoped Daylight would think.

As soon as he figured they had gone far enough, he led Rocklin on a course that circled back higher into the mountains. The more rugged terrain meant that they couldn't travel as fast, especially since Rocklin wasn't the most experienced rider in the world.

For the time being, though, it was more important that they stay out of Daylight's sight and let him assume he had chased them off.

Because of the caution Smoke exercised, it was late afternoon by the time he and Rocklin warily approached Camelback Hill. He left Rocklin screened behind some rocks and trees and rode toward the hill alone. He held his Winchester across the saddle in front of him, ready for instant use with a round already in the chamber.

After a diligent search, Smoke found a spot where a horse had been tied earlier that day. Droppings and some freshly cropped grass told him that much.

He explored the hillside facing the area where Rocklin had been when the shooting started, looking for shell casings, but he didn't find any. Not surprisingly, Daylight appeared to be the sort of hombre who picked up his brass.

"We know he was here," Smoke said. "Let's see if we can pick up his trail."

"I still can't fathom why this man, this Major Daylight, would try to kill us. That seems like an extreme reaction to the possibility that we might interfere with him hunting for Barnaby."

"Unless he's really determined to kill that bear and claim the reward."

"If he kills Barnaby—" Rocklin's voice choked off as emotion overcame him and made it impossible for him to speak.

"If he kills Barnaby," Smoke continued for him, "then we'll never have any way of proving that Barnaby didn't kill those four hombres. Of course, I reckon it would be hard to prove that, anyway, but if we find Barnaby first and you can show everybody that he's tame, that'll cast a lot more doubt over what happened."

A frown creased Smoke's forehead as he paused beside his horse, not mounting up yet. As he stood there, he tugged on his right earlobe and then ran his thumbnail down his jawline, two signs that he was deep in thought.

Finally, he said, "If Daylight had something to do with

those killings, then eliminating Barnaby would leave him in the clear. Barnaby would get all the blame, and nobody would ever believe otherwise except you."

"That makes sense, although it's quite a leap of reasoning," Rocklin said. "But why would Major Daylight want to harm those men? He didn't come to Big Rock until after the killings."

"He didn't, as far as we know," Smoke pointed out. "He could have been around in the area before anybody was aware of it."

"Ah, yes, I see. But such a theory requires Daylight to have both a diabolical mind and a strong motive."

"Having met the man, I can believe the part about the diabolical mind," Smoke said. "The motive's a mystery, though. Maybe what we should do is find him and ask him."

Smoke found the tracks Daylight's horse had left when the marksman rode off. They followed the trail to a spot where the tracks of a second horse joined the first. That would be Daylight's pack animal, Smoke knew. The major had left it tied up while he carried out his ambush.

The sign led them northwest. They kept climbing higher into the mountains. The light was fading, and although Smoke didn't want to stop, he knew they would have to. He began looking for a good place to camp.

He found one at the base of a boulder-littered slope where a tiny spring emerged from the rock and formed a pool. The horses would have grass and water, and there was level ground where the men could spread their bedrolls.

"We'll have to make a cold camp," Smoke explained to Rocklin. "We don't want to announce to Daylight that we're still following him."

The medicine show man sighed. "Some hot coffee would be nice," he said, "especially flavored with some of my, ah, potion, but you're right, of course. We'll do without tonight in order to have a better chance of achieving our goals tomorrow. I don't mind the hardship if it helps us find Barnaby. Have you seen any sign of him?"

Smoke shook his head. "No, I'm afraid not. It could be that by following Daylight, that'll put us closer to Barnaby, as well. He claimed to be a mighty good tracker. Who knows, maybe he's right."

"I swear, I don't even know what to hope for anymore."

"Too much of the time, life's like that," Smoke said.

He picketed and unsaddled the horses, then got some jerky from their supplies and shared it with Rocklin. The older man chewed determinedly on the stuff, then commented, "This might go down easier with some elixir."

"If you brought some with you, Doctor, I won't stop you from drinking it. But if you're faced with what may be a hard job, it's generally easier to do it with a clear head."

Rocklin sighed. "You're correct, of course. I'll be all right."

Smoke hoped that was true. He had a hunch that there hadn't been many nights in recent years when Rocklin was completely sober, and now this was the second one in a row. That had to be hard on him.

Night dropped a curtain of darkness over the mountainside. Smoke told Rocklin to turn in whenever he was ready.

"I'll stand watch for a while," he added.

"I don't mind taking a turn. Wake me whenever you like."

"I might take you up on that," Smoke said, even though he actually had no intention of doing so.

Rocklin rolled up in his blankets. At this elevation, even hot days were followed by chilly nights. Smoke sat with his back propped against a tree trunk. He didn't doze off, but he drifted into a state where his senses were all still keenly alert while his mind was at rest.

It didn't stay that way for long, though. His brain began

to consider the question of why Major Mordecai Daylight would want to kill a horse wrangler, a man who owned a small ranch, an itinerant peddler, and a bartender. Besides being casual acquaintances, what did those four victims have in common with one another that made them targets of a cunning killer? Smoke couldn't think of a thing.

Which meant maybe the motive lay somewhere in the past, in the time before Chuck Haskell, Roy Ford, and Pudge moved to this valley. Smoke had never talked to any of those men except to exchange brief pleasantries, so he knew very little about their backgrounds.

Doc Endicott had been in the war. The other men were of an age that they could have served in the army, as well. Maybe that was the connection.

That was pure speculation on his part, though, he told himself. He had no evidence of it.

Had they all served in the same unit as Major Daylight? That was something he could check out when they got back to Big Rock, Smoke told himself . . . assuming that he and Rocklin didn't already have answers to all the questions by then.

The more he thought about it, though, the more his instincts told him that the solution to the mystery did indeed lie in those days more than a decade and a half earlier when war had split the nation in two and threatened to destroy it.

When he had reached that conclusion, his mind slipped back into a more tranquil state. If anything happened, it would rouse him back into complete alertness in less than the blink of an eye.

That was exactly what happened as a low, rumbling sound came from somewhere above them.

Smoke was on his feet instantly, twisting to peer up in the direction of the rumble. He had heard similar sounds before and knew right away what they meant.

That realization formed a cold ball of fear in the pit of his stomach.

Because of his reputation and the adventures he'd had, folks thought of Smoke Jensen as fearless. The scribblers who penned dime novels about him certainly considered him such. They wrote about his courage often enough in their purple prose.

But what so many people failed to understand was that true courage meant being scared . . . but saddling up to do the job anyway. Feeling the fear of facing overwhelming odds but knowing it was the right thing to do. Taking action, even though that cold ball was rolling around in your stomach, making you sick.

So Smoke felt that split second of fear, sure enough, and then got moving.

"Doctor!" he called as a long step carried him to Rocklin's side. He reached down and grasped the arm of the medicine show man. "Doctor, get up!"

Smoke hauled the heavyset older man to his feet almost as effortlessly as if Rocklin were a child's toy.

"What . . . what . . . Jumping Jehoshaphat! Smoke, what—"

The rumbling noise was louder now.

"Hear that?" Smoke asked. "Somebody just started a rockslide coming our way!"

"Good Lord! We'd better grab the horses and head downhill—"

"You can't outrun an avalanche," Smoke interrupted him. "We need to ride across the slope, and there's no time to saddle. You'll have to ride bareback, Doctor. Let me give you a hand."

Rocklin didn't argue. He put his foot in the makeshift stirrup Smoke made out of his hands. Smoke lifted him onto the back of the chestnut mare, then quickly put the headstall, bit, and reins on the horse.

Smoke had been listening to the ominous rumble, which was now more of a roar, as he worked, trying to estimate its likely course. He pointed and told Rocklin, "Head that way! It'll give you the best chance of getting out of the path!"

"But you—"

"I'll be right behind you," Smoke said. "Hang on!"

He slapped the mare's rump to get the animal moving. The horse leaped away and vanished into the shadows, along with its rider.

Smoke bent and pulled both rifles from their scabbards where the saddles lay on the ground. He thought fleetingly about trying to get some of the supplies but decided the Winchesters might be more important. He and Rocklin wouldn't starve to death in the time it would take them to get back to the nearest ranch, assuming, of course, that they survived the rockslide coming toward them.

He had learned to ride bareback on the farm in the Missouri Ozarks, all those years ago, so that wasn't a problem. The last thing he noted before he left the ground was that it had started to shake under his feet.

Hatless, he leaped onto his mount and headed the same way Rocklin had gone.

The roar was so loud it seemed to engulf Smoke as he dashed across the slope and urged his horse on to greater speed. The avalanche wasn't far away now. Within moments, it would sweep down over where he was, and all he could hope to do was get out of its way. Clouds of dust were already billowing out ahead of the slide, stinging his eyes and threatening to choke him.

He hoped Rocklin had gotten clear. Smoke was certain Major Daylight had realized they were following him and had doubled back to try again to dispose of them. This time he might actually succeed.

A rock half the size of a man flew in front of Smoke, barely visible in the darkness and the dust-clogged air. But he saw it and knew the leading edge of the avalanche was right on top of him. Most of the rumble came from behind him now. He wasn't that far from the edge of the massive rockslide, but he had to clear it completely or be swept away.

The fact that he hadn't seen Rocklin told him the medicine show man must have gotten out of the avalanche's path. Smoke was glad of that, anyway.

An instant after that thought crossed Smoke's mind, a tumbling rock smashed into his mount and knocked the poor animal off its hooves. It screamed as it went down.

Smoke flew free into the air, not encumbered by saddle or stirrups. He lost one of the Winchesters but hung on to the other one. He hit the ground hard enough to knock the air out of his lungs, but he ignored that as he let his momentum carry him over and up again. He was running as soon as he was on his feet again, gasping for breath as his mad dash turned into more of an out-of-control stumble.

Rockslides usually thinned out along the edges. Up ahead, Smoke spotted several trees growing closely together. They *might* form enough of a screen to protect him if no boulder big enough came along and flattened them. He ran harder, trying to reach them in time. Falling rocks bounced and sailed all around him. Almost there . . .

He launched himself in a long dive that he hoped would carry him to safety, but as he did, something crashed into his head.

Smoke had made his jump . . . but he landed in oblivion.

CHAPTER 27

Smoke had been knocked out a number of times in the past, often enough to make Dr. Spaulding worry about the long-term effects on his brain.

Smoke had reassured the physician that his skull was nice and thick and that the impacts had done no lasting damage.

Only time would tell which one of them was right, Smoke supposed.

His head certainly ached when he crawled back up from the black pit of unconsciousness this time. He lay motionless as some diabolical imp from Hades played a booming tune on a big bass drum inside his skull.

After a few moments, he realized that imp was his own heartbeat.

One advantage of being able to hear his pulse like that was knowing his heart was beating at a strong, steady rhythm. He knew he must have been hit by one of those flying rocks, but maybe it had just struck him a glancing blow, enough to knock him out momentarily but not doing any real damage.

As the scattered impressions in his mind coalesced into coherent thought, he realized he didn't hear the avalanche's roar anymore. It was over . . . and he was still alive.

A strong scent of pine filled his nostrils. The last thing

he remembered, he'd been trying to jump for cover behind several trees growing tightly together. Maybe he was smelling those trees.

He tasted dirt in his mouth, too. His face was pressed against the ground. He forced his head up, spat out some of the grit, and pried his eyes open. Even though it made the booming inside his skull worse, he turned his head and looked above him.

Enough light filtered down from the moon and stars to reveal the pine boughs, thick with needles, that loomed over him. He had made it to the trees, which still stood tall and straight. They had withstood the pummeling at the edge of the rockslide.

Smoke got his hands underneath him, pushed up onto his knees, then grasped the nearest tree trunk and held on to it for support as he pulled himself to his feet. He stood there for a moment as the world seemed to spin crazily in the wrong direction around him.

Then things settled down into the correct perspective. He dragged in a deep breath through his nose and both felt and heard his racing pulse slow slightly. A couple more of those breaths and, other than a dull ache in his head, he felt mostly human again.

Somewhere not far away, a man yelled and a gunshot sounded, hard on the heels of the shout.

Smoke winced as his head jerked instinctively toward the sounds. Then he told himself to ignore the pain and checked to see if his Colt was still in its holster on his hip. It was, so he looked around for the Winchester he'd been holding when he made his desperate leap for safety.

Starlight reflected on the rifle where it lay on the ground a few feet away. Smoke picked it up, checked the barrel for fouling, and found it clear.

No more shots or yells had disturbed what was now

a quiet night. Smoke had already fixed in his mind the direction of what he'd heard, so he started angling across the mountainside toward it.

The avalanche had cut a wide swath through the trees and brush behind him, but it hadn't caused a great deal of destruction in the direction he was going. The ground was littered with rocks, some the size of a man's head, some just fist-sized or smaller gravel.

Here and there, a large boulder had come to rest. Smoke knew he was lucky one of them hadn't knocked down those trees and crushed him along with them.

He stopped short as he heard something again. This time it was a horse—no, two horses, he corrected himself—moving up the slope away from him.

One of those mounts probably belonged to Major Mordecai Daylight, Smoke thought. The other might be the chestnut mare that Dr. Jasper T. Rocklin had used to flee the avalanche.

Smoke felt a moment of regret for his own horse, which had been swept away by the tumbling rocks.

He followed the horses up the slope. He hoped there were two riders as well as two horses, but he remembered that ominous single gunshot. Daylight might have already killed Rocklin. If that turned out to be the case, Smoke swore he would settle the score for the medicine show man.

In this rugged terrain, a man on foot could move almost as fast as a man on horseback, so Smoke wasn't worried about losing the trail. He stayed within earshot of his quarry and only slowed down when the hoofbeats stopped. He didn't know what that meant, but he intended to find out.

A few minutes later, as he continued his careful way up the mountainside, he smelled woodsmoke.

Daylight had built a campfire. Smoke drew that conclusion, and from it he also deduced that the sharpshooter believed he was dead, a victim of the avalanche. Otherwise, Daylight wouldn't have been so nonchalant about giving away his position.

The major was going to learn soon that he had made a mistake, but not until the time was right.

Smoke followed the campfire smell and continued his cautious approach. A few minutes later, he climbed a rocky outcropping and stretched out at the top, where he overlooked some level ground that backed up to another bluff on the far side.

That was where Daylight had made camp. Flames danced and crackled merrily from the blaze, which was surrounded by a ring of stones. A coffeepot sat at the edge of the fire, heating up to a boil.

Three horses were picketed where they could graze on the grass at the base of the other bluff: Daylight's saddle mount, his pack horse, and the chestnut mare, which appeared to be none the worse for its frantic flight from the avalanche.

The same couldn't be said of Rocklin. He sat on the ground with his back propped against a log. A streak of blood showed starkly against his wildly askew white hair. As far as Smoke could tell, Rocklin wasn't seriously injured, but the way his arms were pulled uncomfortably behind him, his hands had to be tied together back there.

Daylight sat on a slab of rock on the other side of the fire, smoking a pipe as black as the clothes he wore. He studied Rocklin with an expression of mild curiosity.

For a few moments, neither man spoke, then Rocklin asked in a sullen voice, "Why did you drag me up here? Why didn't you just finish me off?"

Daylight kept his teeth clamped on the pipestem for a couple of heartbeats before he took it out of his mouth and said, "Because I'm curious. How do you keep surviving?

I had you dead to rights the first time I took a shot at you, and then later that avalanche should have gotten you, like it did Jensen. To make things even more puzzling, I thought I'd killed you with that shot a little while ago. And yet here you are, creased but still alive. How do you manage it? Are you just the most phenomenally lucky man on the face of the earth?"

"Clean living, I suppose," Rocklin answered.

A bark of harsh laughter came from Daylight. "Hardly. One look at that face of yours is enough to tell me you put away plenty of whiskey. I saw officers in the war who looked like you. They never went into battle sober."

"I admit that from time to time, I partake of the elixir I sell—"

"Elixir!" Daylight interrupted. "Snake oil, you mean. Whiskey mixed with opium and who knows what else. That just makes you a drunk. It doesn't explain why I haven't been able to kill you."

"Perhaps you're no longer the crack shot you believe yourself to be."

Daylight drew in a sharp breath and glared. He put the pipe back in his mouth and puffed on it furiously for a moment. Then he took it out and said, "It doesn't matter. You'll die this time, as soon as I'm good and ready. But first, since you're still alive, tell me what you and Jensen were doing out here."

Rocklin stared at him. "You mean to say you don't even know, and yet you tried to kill us anyway?"

Daylight shrugged and said, "I knew Jensen was going to interfere with my hunt. He couldn't stand the thought of somebody else getting the acclaim for killing that rogue grizzly."

"Damn you, Barnaby is *not* a rogue!" Rocklin burst out.

Daylight laughed again. "Barnaby?" he repeated. "The

bear has a name?" He threw his head back, slapped his thigh, and let out an actual guffaw. "That means he's a tame bear. He belongs to you!"

"That's right, although I like to think of it as the two of us being friends. He never killed anyone!"

"Oh, I know that," Daylight said. "I know it perfectly well, because I'm the one who killed those four back-stabbing traitors."

That was it, Smoke thought from where he watched and listened. Daylight had just confessed to the murders. Now he hoped the mad major would explain why he had carried out those four killings.

"What are you talking about?" Rocklin asked. "Why did you want those men dead?"

"Because they betrayed me. All I did was carry out my duties as a soldier of the Union, and they turned me in and said I was insane. All because I killed some filthy Rebels, like I was supposed to."

More agitated now, Daylight got to his feet and began to pace back and forth, puffing on the pipe and creating clouds of gray smoke around his head. When he stopped and spoke again, he took the pipe from his mouth and poked the stem at Rocklin to punctuate the words.

"As far as I'm concerned, when you give aid and comfort to the enemy, you're the same as the enemy. Those women fed the Rebs, and the children took care of their horses. They deserved to die! You align yourself with traitors, then you're a traitor, too! Every man, woman, and child in the South deserves to die for betraying our glorious Union! I was just trying to do what was right, and Endicott and the others, they turned me in."

"You killed innocent civilians?" Rocklin asked in a hushed, horrified voice.

"There were no innocent civilians in the Confederacy!

That's what I'm trying to get you to understand. It had to be done. They had to be wiped out like the vermin they were." Daylight trembled from the emotions coursing through him. "I'm just sorry I didn't kill hundreds, even thousands, more!"

Rocklin continued to stare at him for a long moment, then said, "You *are* insane. You can go ahead and kill me, but you're as crazy as a bedbug, and I'm not afraid to say it."

For a moment, Daylight looked furious enough to do it, but he took a deep breath and calmed himself.

"Not yet," he said. "Not until I've found that bear and killed it. You can watch, since you claim that wild animal is your friend."

"But why?" Rocklin asked with a note of misery in his voice. "You've already gotten your revenge. Why is it so important that you kill Barnaby?"

"With him dead, no one will ever think to blame me. I had already tracked down those four craven cowards who betrayed me and would have dealt with them sooner or later, but when I read in the newspaper that what appeared to be a giant rogue grizzly was on the loose in this valley, I recognized it immediately as the perfect opportunity. I could have my revenge, and none would be the wiser, except for the men I killed. Oh, you can rest assured I made certain they knew who was ending their lives, and why. They all died screaming because of what they did to me."

Daylight began pacing again.

"Once I killed the bear, it would get all the blame, and I'd be two thousand dollars richer, to boot. I really am a professional hunter, you know. Everything I told Jensen and the sheriff back in Big Rock was true. My services are in demand by cattlemen and anyone else who has a predator problem."

"Why weren't you ever put on trial for killing those people back in the war?"

"It was a hectic time. The Confederacy was collapsing.

Grant and the other generals weren't interested in any unsubstantiated charges against one of their own. They might have gotten around to dealing with it after the Rebels were completely vanquished . . . but by that time, I was gone."

"You ran away."

"I didn't stay to be persecuted for doing something that needed to be done! I changed my name, came west, and used my skills to establish a new life. But the need for revenge on those who turned against me was always in the back of my mind, and finally justice has been done!"

"Justice," Rocklin repeated. He shook his head. "A far cry from justice, if you ask me."

"No one did, you old fool. Just like no one will care when you disappear—"

Daylight stopped short in his unhinged threat as a loud snuffling sound came from the darkness beyond the campfire. Rocklin's head jerked up. His eyes widened in alarm.

"No!" he cried. "No, Barnaby, no! Don't come any closer! Get away!"

For a split second, Smoke wondered if this was some sort of trick Rocklin had managed to pull.

But no, it was the real thing. The proof of that was one of the largest bears Smoke had ever seen. Barnaby trundled on all fours into the edge of the firelight, then abruptly reared up on his hind legs, waved his front legs in the air, and bellowed to the heavens. It was the same trick Smoke had heard about, and now he was seeing it for himself.

Daylight tossed his pipe aside, reached under his coat, and yanked a revolver from its holster.

"No!" Rocklin cried again. Somehow, even with his hands tied behind his back, the rotund medicine show man was able to surge to his feet. He leaped over and through the campfire and rammed his shoulder into Daylight's back as the major pulled the trigger. The gun boomed and Barnaby roared again, this time apparently in pain.

Smoke bit back an oath. With Rocklin and Daylight tangled up together on the ground, he couldn't risk a shot with the Winchester. He dropped the rifle, put a hand on the rock where he had been lying, and vaulted off of it, dropping lithely to the ground at the edge of the firelight.

Daylight rolled on top of Rocklin, smashed a brutal blow to his face, and had drawn back his arm to strike again when Barnaby loomed behind him and swung a paw in a powerful swipe that caught Daylight in the side. The terrible impact knocked Daylight off the medicine show man and sent him rolling into the fire.

Daylight came up screaming out of the flames. He still held the revolver. As the gun lifted toward Rocklin, Smoke called, "Daylight!"

The major jerked around, saw Smoke, gasped "Jensen!" and triggered a wild shot that whistled past Smoke. Smoke's hand dipped to the Colt on his hip. The gun came out of its holster and leveled faster than the eye could follow. Flame gouted from the muzzle as Smoke fired.

The bullet drove into Daylight's chest and knocked him backward. He tried to keep his feet, but his legs folded up under him. He sprawled on his back, arms and legs splayed to the sides. A final spasm shook him, and then he was still.

Smoke stepped closer, saw the wide-open but lifeless eyes staring at nothing, then turned, well aware that a giant grizzly was nearby.

Barnaby wasn't taking any interest in him, however. The bear, with a bloody gash showing on his left shoulder where Daylight's bullet had ripped through flesh, sat on the ground next to Rocklin. Barnaby made a chuffing noise as he gently prodded Rocklin's shoulder with a massive paw. Smoke noted that the bear was careful not to use his claws when he touched Rocklin.

A groan came from Rocklin's lips. His eyes fluttered open and his head lifted. He looked up at the bear and gasped, "Barnaby! You're alive!"

"So am I," Smoke said, "but Daylight isn't."

Rocklin sat up, struggling to do so with his hands still tied behind him. But he managed, and there was something comical about the little fat man sitting there next to the enormous bear.

"Barnaby, are you all right? I thought that monster killed you!"

For a crazy second, Smoke halfway expected the bear to answer the man, but Barnaby just made another chuffing sound. Rocklin leaned against him.

"Looks to me like Daylight just winged him a little," Smoke said. "Uh, Doctor, are you sure you should be getting that close? I mean, Barnaby is still a bear."

"No, he's my friend, and he would never hurt me."

Smoke wasn't certain of that, but he supposed Rocklin knew what he was doing. He hoped so, anyway.

Now that they had cleared Barnaby of the four killings, he didn't want the bear getting into more trouble.

"I would have liked to have taken Daylight alive," Smoke said a short time later, "so we could have gotten him to confess that he killed those men and why he did it. But we both heard what he said, and I reckon our word will be enough." He hefted the grisly thing he had found in a search of Daylight's gear. "Along with this as evidence."

The firelight flickered on a piece of board about three feet long. One end had been shaped into a handle, and on the other end were four sharp-pointed hooks like ones

used to hang up meat, turned so that the points were down.
Striking flesh with that grisly implement would mimic being
clawed by a bear and would be terribly destructive, as the
dried bloodstains on the hooks and the board testified.

He had also found what looked like a bear's rear paw
that had been preserved somehow. Where Daylight had
gotten such a thing was a mystery that might never be
solved, but Smoke knew he had used it to leave tracks near
the bodies of the murdered men and incriminate Barnaby.

Rocklin had examined the wound on Barnaby's shoulder
and agreed with Smoke that it wasn't serious.

"I have some medicine I can put on it once I get him
back in his cage," Rocklin said. "Actual medicine, not the,
ah, sort of stuff I sell."

"You have something for that crease on your scalp, too?"
Smoke asked.

"The same remedy will do for it, until we get back to
Big Rock."

When Daylight had made camp, he had unloaded the
supplies from his pack animal. Smoke left them where they
were and lashed the major's body over the horse's back in
their place. Then he put Daylight's saddle on the chestnut
mare for Rocklin.

"I can ride his mount bareback," he said. "That won't be
a problem. Having a saddle ought to make the trip easier on
you, though, Doctor."

"I daresay it will, Smoke." Rocklin paused, then went
on, "I can't tell you how much of a debt I owe to you, or
how much I appreciate—"

"Don't worry about it, Doctor," Smoke interrupted with
a smile. "We brought a killer to justice, and the valley can
stop being so scared of that big hairy pard of yours. I'd say
that's a pretty good night's work."

CHAPTER 28

By the middle of the next morning, Smoke, Rocklin, and Barnaby were out of the mountains and on their way down the valley toward Big Rock. After a generous application of the medicinal salve, Barnaby rode placidly in his cage, sitting on the layer of straw and looking around.

The horse with Major Daylight's body on it was tied to the back of the cage, along with the chestnut mare. Rocklin handled the wagon team, having insisted that the wound on his head was nothing serious. Smoke rode alongside on Daylight's horse.

They skirted around the ranches they passed along the way. Smoke knew that once people saw the cage with the giant bear in it, he and Rocklin would have to stop and explain. That would just delay their return to town.

They couldn't avoid the rider Smoke spotted coming toward them, however. Smoke could tell from the way the horseman rode that he was Pearlie.

The Sugarloaf foreman closed the distance quickly. As he reined in, he stared at the cage with wide, awe-filled eyes.

"You caught the dang thing!" Pearlie exclaimed. "He's really tame?"

"Sure is," Smoke said. "In fact, he helped us corral the real killer."

He inclined his head toward the pack horse with its grim, blanket-wrapped burden.

"Who in blazes—" Pearlie began. Then he stopped for a second before continuing, "I'll bet it's got to be that Major Daylight fella, don't it?"

"That's right."

"And he killed those four men because they were all in the same outfit with him durin' the war, and he had a grudge against 'em for some reason. I'm just guessin', mind you, but that makes sense."

"That's right," Smoke said, "but how did you know about them being in the army together?"

Pearlie chuckled. "You can thank Miz Sally for that. She's the one who asked the right folks the right questions and figured it out. Fact of the matter is, that's why I'm out here today. She sent me to find you, so I could tell you about it. Looks like I didn't need to, after all."

"Maybe not, but it sounds like Sally did some real detective work to uncover that information." Smoke grinned. "I just happened to be in the right place at the right time to hear Daylight spout the whole thing."

From the wagon seat, Rocklin put in, "I don't think you can say you just happened to be there, Smoke. You got there through sheer determination and grit."

"With a little luck thrown in."

"Fortune favors the strong and well prepared."

Smoke shrugged, unwilling to devote any more time or energy to the discussion.

"Are you headin' for town?" Pearlie asked.

"That's right. I'd like for Dr. Spaulding to have a look at that wound on Dr. Rocklin's head."

"You're gonna haul that cage with that bear in it down the main street of Big Rock?"

"That's the plan."

"Then I'd best rattle my hocks back to the Sugarloaf," Pearlie said, "because I got a hunch Miz Sally and Cal and all the other boys ain't gonna want to miss that!"

Their entry into Big Rock was every bit the spectacle that Smoke expected it to be. Folks lined the boardwalks to wave and shout greetings. Some of them still looked nervous about being so close to Barnaby, but since the bear was secure in his cage, most were just thrilled to witness such an unusual sight.

Smoke and Rocklin had taken their time about getting there, giving Pearlie chance to carry the word to the Sugarloaf and then on to the settlement. Smoke wanted everybody to know that Barnaby was innocent of any wrongdoing. After everything that had happened, he didn't want anybody getting an itchy trigger finger and taking a shot at the critter.

Clearly, that wasn't going to happen, Smoke thought as he surveyed the crowd. He spotted Sally standing on the boardwalk with Pearlie, Cal, and Monte Carson and motioned for her to join him.

When she reached the horse, Smoke took his foot out of the stirrup so she could use it. She caught hold of his arm, and he swung her easily onto the horse's back in front of him. As they rode along the street with his arm around her waist, he said, "I hear you're like one of those dime novel sleuths now."

She laughed. "Sally Jensen, Lady Detective. I like the sound of that. Maybe some of the authors who write stories about you should make me the heroine of their tales."

"Let's hope not. They just make up a passel of loco lies and call it a yarn."

"And that can't compete with the real thing, can it, Smoke?"

"Nope," he said, smiling as she rested her head against his shoulder. "It sure can't."

TURN THE PAGE FOR AN EXCITING PREVIEW!

SLASH AND PECOS ARE BACK!

**JOHNSTONE COUNTRY.
THE GOOD, THE BAD,
AND THE UTTERLY DEPRAVED**

**Slash and Pecos come face-to-face with the baddest
hombre they've ever known: a kill-crazy madman
who's paving the road to hell—with bloodlust.**

He blew into town like a tornado.
A mysterious stranger with money to burn, time to kill—
and a sadistic streak as wide as the Rio Grande.
He says his name is Benson and he's come to invest
in the town's future. First, he showers the banks
and local businesses with cash.
Then, he hires a pair of drunks to fight and get arrested
so he can check out the local lawmen.
After that, he warms up to a lady of the evening—
with deadly results.

That's just the beginning.

By the time Slash and Pecos return to town after
a quick-and-dirty cargo run, Benson has enlisted half the
outlaws in the territory for his own private army.
With the help of a corrupt colonel, he's sent a veritable
war wagon into the unprepared town—wreaking havoc
and slaughtering innocents, with the brand of carnage one
only sees on the battlefield. The local lawmen are quickly
slaughtered. Even the U.S. marshals are no match for
Benson's military precision. With looters running amock
and killers on every corner, a person would have to be
stupid or crazy to try to take the town back . . .

Luckily, Slash and Pecos are a little of both.
They've been around long enough to see the worst in
men—and they know that the best way to stop
a very bad hombre . . . is to be even badder.

**National Bestselling Authors
William W. Johnstone and J. A. Johnstone**

BAD HOMBRES
A Slash and Pecos Western

On sale November 2023 wherever Pinnacle Books are sold.

Live Free. Read Hard.
www.williamjohnstone.net

Visit us at www.kensingtonbooks.com

CHAPTER 1

Harlan Benson sat astride his horse in the middle of the road, reached into his coat pocket, and pulled out a fancy notebook bound in soft lamb's skin. From another pocket he took a short pencil, hardly more than a stub, pursed his lips, and touched the lead tip to his tongue. Properly lubricated, the pencil slid smoothly across the first blank page in the notebook, recording his initial impression.

He liked what he saw.

Twice, he glanced up at the neatly lettered sign by the roadside proclaiming this to be Paradise. He wanted to be certain he copied the name properly. After he entered the name in a precise, small script at the top of the otherwise blank page, he carefully wrote 532 centered beneath it. The declared population of Paradise was 532. A few more observations about the condition of the road and the likelihood of this being a prosperous town because of the well-maintained sign were added.

He took out a pocket watch and noted the time it had taken him to ride there from the crossroads. All the data were entered in exactly the proper form. Nothing less than such precision would do. The Colonel expected it, and Benson demanded it of himself.

Harl Benson tucked the notebook back into the inside

pocket of his finely tailored, expensive cream-colored coat with beige grosgrain lapels and four colorful campaign ribbons affixed on his left breast. The pencil followed the notebook into the pocket.

"Giddyap," he called to his magnificent coal-black stallion. The horse balked. It knew what lay ahead. He booted it into a canter. He was anxious to see what Paradise had to offer, even if his stallion was not.

After climbing a short incline in the road, he halted at the top of the rise. Paradise awaited him. The town lay in a shallow bowl. A river defined the northern boundary and provided water for the citizens. Straight ahead to the east lay open prairie. The next town over was far beyond the horizon. To the south stretched fields brimming with alfalfa and other grain to feed livestock. That told him more about the commerce in this peaceful Colorado settlement. It was prosperous and enjoyed a good standard of living despite the railroad bypassing it and running fifteen miles to the north.

Giving his horse its head, he eased down the far side of the incline into town. Into Paradise.

Benson's sharp steel-gray eyes caught movement along the main street. He never missed a detail, especially the pretty young woman who stepped out of the grain store to give him the eye. He touched the brim of his tall Stetson, appreciating the attention she bestowed on him.

Benson was a handsome man and he knew it. Handsome, that is, except for the pink knife scar that started in the middle of his forehead and ran down across his eye to his left cheek. He had survived a nasty knife fight, enduring only that single wound. His opponent hadn't survived at all.

Most women thought that thin pink scar gave him a dangerous look. If they only knew.

He was a real Beau Brummell in his dress. The cream

coat decorated with the mysteriously colored ribbons caught their eye, but he wore trousers of the purest black with a formal silk ribbon down the outsides. His boots were polished to a mirror finish, the leather a perfect match to his ornate gun belt. The six-shooters holstered there hardly looked to be the precision instruments of death that they were. Silver filigree adorned the sides of both Colt .44s. He wore them low on his snake hips, the butts forward on both sides.

Most of all, he was proudest of the intricate gold watch hidden away in a vest pocket lined in clinging velvet to prevent it from accidentally slipping out. A ponderous gold chain swung in an arc across his well-muscled belly. A diamond the size of his little fingernail attached to the chain swung to and fro, catching every ray of light daring to come close.

He was quite the dandy and was proud of the look. It was only natural that all the ladies wanted to be seen with him—wanted to be with him.

Benson slowed and then came to a halt. He turned his stallion toward the young lady who was openly admiring him.

"Good afternoon, ma'am," he said. "Do you work at the grain store?"

"If you need to purchase some seed, I'll fetch my pa. He owns the store."

"No, dear lady, that's not true." He enjoyed the startled expression.

"Whatever do you mean? Of course he does. He's Neil Paulson and nobody else in these parts runs a store half as fine."

"You misunderstand me, miss. I meant that *you* own everything within your sight. How can such beauty not dominate everyone who chances to cast his gaze on your female loveliness?"

She blinked and pushed back a strand of mousy brown hair. The surprise turned into a broad smile—a smile that promised Benson anything he wanted. Then she looked discomfited. Quick movements brushed dust off her plain brown gingham dress. Her clothing was no match for his finery, and here he had ridden into town off a long, hot, dusty summer road.

"Do I take it you are *Miss* Paulson?"

The wicked smile returned, and she nodded slowly. She carefully licked her ruby lips and tried to look coy. Eyes batting, she gave him a look designed to melt the steeliest heart.

"Clara," she said. "Clara Paulson."

Harl Benson took his notebook from his coat pocket and made a quick notation in it. He looked up from her to the store and made quick estimates of the store's size and its inventory. As enticing as it would be to have the girl give him a tour of the store and detail its contents, in private, of course, he had so much work to do and time pressed in on him.

"You want to check the grain bins out back?" She sounded just a tad frantic. A quick look over her shoulder explained it all. A man so large his shoulders brushed the sides of the open door glared at Benson.

"That is a mighty neighborly invite for a stranger," he said.

Another quick entry into his notebook completed all the details he needed about Paulson's Grain and Feed Store and its burly owner. Benson caught sight of the shotgun resting against the wall just inside the door. The feed store owner had the look of a man able to tear apart anyone he disliked with his bare hands, but that shotgun? It showed intent.

"I must go, but one parting question, my dear."

"Yes?" Clara Paulson stepped a little closer, leaning on her broom. She looked expectant that he would offer to take

her away from this small town and show her a city where
all the best people dressed like Harl Benson—and she could
show off a fancy ball gown and flashy diamond and gold
jewelry like European royalty. "What is it?"

"Do you have any brothers?"

"What? No, there's only Grant and Franklin working
here, but they're cousins. I had a brother, but he died when
he was only six. He fell into a well. It was two days before
Pa found him."

"Good day," Benson said, again pinching the brim of his
hat. He glanced in her father's direction and evaluated the
man's barrel chest and bulging arms. In a fight, he would
be a formidable opponent. But did he have a box of shells
nearby to feed the shotgun after the first two barrels were
discharged? Benson doubted it.

Benson had faced off with men like Neil Paulson before,
men who toiled moving heavy sacks of grain or bales of
hay. Their vitality often required more than a single bullet
to stop them, even if the first shot was accurately directed
to head or heart.

As he made his way down the middle of Paradise's
main street, he took note of the buildings and their sizes.
How far apart they stood, their construction and position.
Quick estimates of the employees in the businesses were
probably within one or two of actual employment. He was
expert at such evaluations, having done it so many times
before with great success. Not a single man walking the
street or working in the businesses along the main street
slung iron at his side. Perhaps this town really was Paradise
and men didn't have to strut about carrying iron.

Harl Benson made more notes in his precise script.

The horses tethered outside the stores generally had a
rifle thrust into a saddle scabbard. Travelers into town needed
such firepower out on the plains and especially when they

worked their way into the tall Front Range Mountains to the west. Dangerous creatures, both four-legged and two-, prowled those lonely stretches.

He dismounted, checked the horses' brands to find out where the riders had come from, and entered a new notation. All these horses belonged to punchers from a single ranch. Where the Double Circle ran its stock, he didn't know, and it hardly mattered. The hands probably carried sidearms in addition to their rifles and had come to town to hoot and holler. They'd be gone by Monday morning.

Benson entered the saloon. The Fatted Calf Saloon and Drinking Emporium looked exactly like any other to him. Eight cowboys bellied up to the bar, swapping lies and nursing warm beer. That meant they hadn't been paid yet for their month of backbreaking labor. Walking slowly, he counted his paces to determine the size of the saloon.

It stretched more than forty feet deep but was narrow, hardly more than fifteen feet. He settled into a chair with his back to a wall where he had a good view of the traffic outside along the main street.

"Well, mister, you have the look of someone who's been on the trail long enough to build up a real thirst." A hand rested on his shoulder.

Benson turned slightly to dislodge the woman's hand and looked up at one of the pretty waiter girls. She wore a bright red silk dress with a deep scoop neckline. White lace had been sewn along the cleavage because the dress was so old it was coming apart at the seams. If she had let the seams pop just a little more, she would have shown her customers for free what she undoubtedly charged for in private. Benson quickly evaluated everything about her. Her worth matched the cheapness of her dress.

"Rye whiskey," he said. "Don't give me the cheap stuff." He dropped a twenty-dollar gold piece onto the table. The tiny coin spun on its rim and then settled down with a golden ring that brought him unwanted attention from the cowpunchers at the bar.

That gave him a new tidbit to enter into his notebook. Twenty dollars was unusual in Paradise.

"For that, dearie, you can have anything you want," the doxie said. She ran her tongue around her rouged lips in what she thought was a suggestive, lewd manner to inflame his desires. It did the reverse.

"The shot of rye. Then we'll see about something . . . else."

She hurried over to whisper with the bartender. The short, mustached man behind the bar looked more prosperous than the usual barkeep. Benson guessed he owned the Fatted Calf.

He sighed when two of the cowboys sauntered over, thumbs thrust into their gun belts. They stopped a few feet away from him.

"We don't see many strangers in town," the taller of the pair said. The shorter one said something Benson didn't catch. This egged on his taller partner. "You got more of them twenty-dollar pieces?"

"Are you desperate road agents thinking to rob me?" Benson moved a little to flash the twin six-shooters. The dim light caught the silver filigree and made the smoke wagons look even larger than they were.

"Those don't look like they get much use," piped up the short one. "You one of them fellas what brags about how many men you've cut down?"

"I don't brag about it," Benson said. He took the bottle of rye from the floozie and popped the cork with his thumb. He ignored the dirt on the rim of the shot glass she brought with it and drank straight from the bottle. He licked his lips. "That's surprisingly good. Thanks." He pushed the tiny gold coin across the table in the woman's direction. "Why don't you set up a round for everyone at the bar? And keep the rest for yourself."

"Yes, *sir*. And if there's anything more you want, my name's Hannah."

He tipped his head in the direction of the bar in obvious dismissal. Benson looked up at the two cowboys and said, "The drinks are on the bar, not here." He took another pull from the bottle and then placed it carefully on the table with a move so precise there wasn't even a tiny click of glass touching wood.

"You ever killed anybody with them fancy-ass six-guns?" The short one stepped closer. "Or are they just for show?"

Benson didn't answer.

"How many? How many you claim to have gunned down?" The man shoved out his chin belligerently. At the same time, he moved his right hand to his holster, as if he prepared to throw down.

"How many men have I killed? How many men and boys? Well, now, I can't give a good answer about that."

"Why the hell not?" Both men tensed now. Benson had seen his share of gunmen. These two might be good at rounding up cattle, or even rustling them, but they weren't gunslicks. They'd had a beer too many and thought to liven up their visit to town by pestering a tinhorn dude.

"I stopped counting at a hundred."

"A hunnerd? You sayin' you've killed a hunnerd men?"

"Only with these guns. The total's considerably greater if you want a count on the total number I've killed." Benson laughed at their stunned expression.

"Hell and damnation, Petey, he's pullin' our leg." The tall one punched his partner in the arm.

Petey's expression was unreadable. The flash of panic

mixed with disbelief. A sick grin finally twisted his lips, just a little.

"We got drinks waitin' fer us back at the bar," Petey said.

"Yeah, right, thanks, mister. You're a real friend. You got a good sense of humor, too." The tall one punched Petey in the arm again and herded him away. They got to the bar, and the free setup erased any intention of upbraiding the stranger. In a few seconds, they joked and cussed with their partners from the ranch.

Harl Benson added a new notation in his notebook about the quality of the whiskey at the Fatted Calf. He knocked back another shot of the fine rye and started out the swinging doors. A thin, bony hand grabbed his arm. Again, he shifted slightly and pulled away.

"You ready for more fun, mister?" Hannah looked and sounded desperate. "I got a room down the street. It's a real fine place."

"A sporting house?"

"What? Oh, yeah. That's a mighty fancy term. Nobody in these parts calls Madame Jane's that."

He looked over his shoulder toward the rear of the saloon.

"What's in the back room?"

"You wanna do it there? If you cut Jackson in for a dime or even two bits, well, maybe we kin do it there." Hannah looked hesitantly at the bartender. "Better if we go to my place."

"Madame Jane's?"

Hannah bobbed her head.

"Ain't much in the back room 'cept all the whiskey and other stuff. It's crowded right now. Jackson just got in a new shipment."

"Of the rye? How many cases?"

"Hustle the customers on your own time. Get back to work, you scrawny—" the barkeep bellowed. He fell silent when Benson held up his hand.

"'Nuff for a few months. Ten cases, maybe. More?" Hannah looked back at her boss. "Listen, I'll be outta here in another hour. You wait fer me at Madame Jane's. There's a real fine parlor, and she bought a case of that liquor you've taken such a shine to. Fer the payin' customers. Like you."

Benson stepped out onto the boardwalk. A new description in the notebook and he was ready to check on the whorehouse. But first he had one final stop to make.

With Hannah calling after him to enjoy himself until she got to the brothel's parlor, the finest in this part of Colorado, she claimed, he walked directly to the bank down the street. Benson counted the paces and made measurements of the street's width and the location of other stores. When he stepped into the bank, his work was almost completed.

Bustling over when he saw his new customer's fancy clothing, the bank officer beamed from ear to ear. A quick twirl of his long mustaches put the greased tips into points equal to a prickly pear spine.

"Welcome, sir. We haven't seen you before in these here parts. What can we do for you?" The plump bank officer pumped Benson's hand like he could draw deep well water. He released the hand when Benson squeezed down. Hard.

"I'd like to make a deposit."

"A new account. Wonderful, wonderful. How much, sir? Ten? Twenty?"

Benson heard the pride in the man's voice. Those were the big depositors in the Bank of Paradise.

"I was thinking more like five."

The banker's face fell, but he hid the disappointment.

"This way, sir. Our head teller will handle your deposit. Excuse me, but I have other business to—"

"Thousand," Benson said.

This brought the banker up short.

"You want to deposit five *thousand*? That's almost as much as Mister Rawls out on the Double Circle has in our safe."

"You have other deposits of equal size, I take it? I certainly do not want my money placed in a bank without . . . ample assets."

"Five other ranchers, all quite prosperous. Yes, very prosperous. Come this way, sir, let me handle your account personally." The banker snapped his fingers. A man wearing green eye shades and sleeve protectors came from the middle cage.

"You," Benson said sharply to the bank officer. "I want *you* to show me the safe where you'll keep my money. I don't like to deal with underlings."

"I . . . uh . . . underlings? Oh, no, not that. This way." The bank officer ushered Benson to the side of the lobby and through a swinging door set in a low wood railing. "This is our safe. You can see how sturdy it is." The banker slipped his thumbs into the armholes of his vest and reared back, beaming.

"A Mosler with a time lock," Benson said, nodding slowly. His quick eyes took in the details, the model of the safe and how it had been modified. The safe itself wasn't as heavily constructed as many back East, probably due to the cost of freighting such a heavy load into the foothills of the Front Range.

"You know the product, sir?" The banker's eyes widened in surprise. "Then you recognize how sturdy it is and how, excuse the expression, *safe* your deposit will be. Five thousand, you said?"

"That's correct." Benson walked from one side of the safe to the other. It wasn't any different from a half dozen others of its ilk he had seen.

"Let's get the paperwork started," the banker said, rubbing his hands together. He circled a large cherrywood desk and began dipping his pen in the inkwell and filling out forms.

Benson seated himself in the leather chair opposite and made his own notations in the lambskin notebook. He glanced up occasionally as he sketched the safe. While not an artist of great skill, he captured the details quickly and well from long practice.

"Now, sir, your deposit?" The banker looked expectantly at him. A touch of anticipation was dampened by fear that Benson wasn't going to hand over the princely sum. The banker positively beamed as Benson reached into his inner coat pocket and drew out his soft leather wallet. Making a big show of it for both the banker and his head teller, he counted out a stack of greenbacks onto the desk until he reached the agreed upon sum.

Benson almost laughed when the banker visually tallied up how much money remained in that wallet. Only through a great exercise of willpower did he restrain himself from asking Benson to deposit even more.

"Affix your signature to the bottom of the page. Here's a receipt for the full amount. And a bank book. See? The full five thousand dollars is indicated right here with the date and my initials to certify it. Should you wish to withdraw any amount at any time, show the pass book. Or," the banker said, winking slyly, "if you want to add to your savings at any time. That will be entered and officially noted, too."

Benson tucked the deposit book and receipt into the same pocket with his wallet. He stood and held out his hand to shake.

"I look forward to doing more business with your bank soon," he said.

The banker hesitantly shook, remembering the bone-crushing grip. This time Benson made no effort to cripple the man. Sealing the deal with the handshake, Benson turned his back on the man who babbled on about what a fine place Paradise was and how Benson would prosper there as long as the bank was part of his financial plans.

Walking slowly, Benson took in every detail of the buildings and how they were constructed. A few more notations graced his notebook by the time he reached a three-story building that might have been a hotel. He saw immediately this wasn't the case. On the second story balcony, several partially clad women lounged about, idly talking until one spotted him down in the street.

"Hey there, handsome, why don't you come on in? I'll show you a real good time." She leaned far over the railing and shimmied about to show what she offered. "I'll show you a good time if you're man enough to handle a real woman like me, that is!"

The other Cyprians laughed.

Benson started to make a few more notes, but an elegantly dressed blonde stepped into the doorway. She had a come-hither smile that captivated him. Benson had seen his share of beautiful women, but this one ranked easily in the top five. She wore a shiny green metallic-flake dress that caught the sunlight and made it look as if she stood in a desert mirage. The shimmering only accentuated her narrow waist and womanly hips. For a woman in a brothel, she sported an almost sedate décolletage. Only the barest hint of snowy white breasts poked out.

He couldn't help comparing her with the blatant exhibitionism of the whores on the balcony.

She tossed her head back, sending ripples through the

mane of golden hair. Eyes as blue as sapphires judged him as much as his steel-gray ones took her measure. He liked what he saw. A lot. From the tiny upward curl of her lush, full lips, he could see that she shared his opinion.

"You're Jane?"

"I hadn't realized my reputation was that big. A complete stranger to town knows me? I'm flattered." She batted her eyes. Long, dark lashes invited him closer.

"It's my job to know things," Benson said, slowly mounting the steps to the front porch. He stopped a pace away. A tiny puff of breeze carried her perfume to him. His nostrils flared, and he sucked in the gentle fragrance. His heart raced.

"It's French perfume," Jane said. "I buy it from an importer in Boston."

"And I thought it was your natural alluring scent that is so captivating. I am crushed. How could I have been so wrong?" He turned to leave, as if in abject defeat.

"Don't go," Jane said. "Come in. Have a drink and let's talk. You might even persuade me to forgive you your . . . mistake."

"I've already sampled the rye whiskey. There's more that I want to sample, and my time is running out."

"You don't look like the sort of man who . . . hurries."

"Not in all things," Benson said. He stepped up and circled her trim waist with his arm. She leaned slightly into him. Their bodies fit together perfectly.

"I'm not cheap," Jane said.

"Inexpensive," he corrected. "And I never doubted it. I'm willing to pay for the best."

"I can tell that you're a gentleman."

Pressed together they went through the parlor into an expensively decorated bedroom.

"My boudoir," Jane said.

"A fitting place for one so lovely," Benson said.

They worked to undress each other and sank to a feather mattress, locked in each other's embrace. Afterward, Benson sat up in bed.

"I wasn't wrong about you, Harl," she said. Jane made no effort at coyness by pulling up the sheet to hide her voluptuous breasts. "You're a real gentleman and about the best I've ever found."

"This town is well named," Benson said, climbing into his clothes. "It might not be Paradise in all respects, but it certainly is when it comes to . . . you." He turned and put his forefinger under her chin. She tilted her head back for him to lightly kiss her on the lips. "You are both lovely and skilled."

"You come on back any time you want. I don't say that to just everyone." Jane's bright blue eyes watched as he completed dressing.

"Thank you for the fine afternoon. I enjoyed your company so much I am going to give you something special."

"More than my usual?" Jane glanced at the stack of ten-dollar gold pieces on the table beside her four-poster bed.

"More than I usually give because you deserve it," Benson said.

He drew his six-gun and shot her between those bright blue eyes.

Harl Benson settled his clothes, smoothed a few wrinkles, retrieved the fee from the bedside table, and tucked it away in a vest pocket, then walked quickly from the brothel. His work in Paradise had just begun, and he wanted to complete it soon.

CHAPTER 2

"Let me drive," James "Slash" Braddock said peevishly. "I swear, you're hitting every last hole in the road. And them holes got even deeper holes at their bottoms. They might just reach all the way to the center of the Earth, they're so deep."

Melvin "Pecos River Kid" Baker looked out the corner of his eye, then hawked a gob with admirable accuracy so that it missed—barely—his partner's boot braced against the bottom of the driver's box of their Pittsburgh freight wagon.

"If I let you drive, them mules would balk. And rightly so. They don't much like you 'cuz you don't have a lick of sense when it comes to treatin' the lot of them with dignity."

"Dignity!" Slash roared. "They're *mules*. Mules don't have 'dignity.' They're as dumb as . . . as you."

"I wouldn't have to drive so fast if you kept a better lookout." Pecos reared back and sent his long whip snaking out over the heads of his team. The cracker popped as loud as a gunshot. The mules tucked back their long ears, put their heads down, and pulled a little harder.

"What are you goin' on about?" Slash gripped the side of the box and hung on as the wheel nearest him hit a deep rut. If he hadn't braced when he did, he would have been thrown out of the wagon.

Still minding the team, Pecos swept graying blond hair out of his bright blue eyes and then half-turned on the hard wooden seat toward his partner. This freed up the Russian .44 settled down in its brown hand-tooled leather holster. He reached down. His fingers drummed angrily against the ornate shell belt. Arguing with Slash passed the time on a long, dusty trip, but calling his ability into question inched toward fisticuffs. Or worse.

After all, there were limits.

"For two cents I'd whup your scrawny ass," Pecos said.

"You don't have that much, not after you lost everything but your long johns to that card sharp last night at the Thousand Delights."

"He cheated. Anybody could see that. Jay should never have let him set down at a table, not the way he dealt seconds."

"If you knew he was cheatin', why in the blue blazes did you stay in the game? Ain't you ever heard the gamblin' advice, 'Look around the table. If you don't see the sucker, you're it.' And you leave my missus out of this argument." Slash glared at Pecos.

"I think she let him play just to humiliate you. Did you and her have a tiff? That'd explain why you're bein' so disagreeable." Pecos thrust out his chin, as if inviting his partner to take a swing.

"Me and Jay are on the best of terms. Every night's like our honeymoon. And don't you go makin' crude comments 'bout that." Slash felt like posing to show off how much younger than Pecos he looked. His thick, dark-brown hair poked out around his hat. Streaks of gray shot through it, but nothing like that Pecos sported. His temples and sideburns showed the most. To make his point, he crossed his arms across a broad chest and glared back at his partner. His brown eyes never wavered under Pecos's equally flinty look.

"That's why you've been daydreamin' and not payin' a whit of attention to anything around you. You're rememberin' what it's like to have a woman as fine as Jay snuggled up alongside you in bed." Pecos swerved and hit another deep hole. Both men popped up into the air, putting space between their rear ends and the seat for a long second.

"What's stuck in your craw? You're always a mite cantankerous, but this is goin' way too far, even for you."

"You're not payin' attention, that's what," Pecos said. He drew his lips back in a feral snarl. "We got company and you never mentioned it, not once in the last three miles when they started trailin' us."

Slash swung around and leaned out past the flapping canvas covering over the wagon bed. A few seconds passed as he studied the matter, then he returned to his seat beside his partner.

"Your eyes might be gettin' old, but they're still sharp." Slash touched the staghorn grips of the twin Colt .44s he carried butt forward on either hip, then fumbled around behind him in the wagon bed and brought out his Winchester Yellowboy. He drew back the rifle's hammer and took a deep breath to settle his nerves.

"There's three of them. Which one do you want me to take out first?" Slash cracked his knuckles to prepare for the sharpshooting.

"You got an itchy trigger finger all of a sudden? What if they're peaceable travelers and just happen to be headin' in the same direction as we are?"

"You're the one what called my attention to them and bawled me out for inattentiveness." Slash leaned out again to get a better idea what they faced. Still only three riders.

Or was that three road agents? In this part of Colorado, that was as likely as not.

"It don't change a thing if they're on the road to Portrero the same as us, their business bein' in the town and not bein' road agents."

"You have a time decidin' your mind, don't you?" Slash asked. He gripped the rifle and studied the terrain ahead. "Let me drop off at the bend in the road."

"Those rocks make good cover," Pecos said, seeing his partner's plan. "You can knock two out of the saddle before the third twigs to what's what."

"If they're just pilgrims like us, I can save my bullets."

"If they're like us, they're cutthroats."

"That's former cutthroats," said Pecos correcting him. "We've given up ridin' the long coulee."

"I gotta wonder why we gave up such an excitin' life," Slash said, jolted so hard his teeth clacked together when the wagon rumbled over a deep pothole. "Haulin' freight shouldn't be this exasperatin'."

He came to his feet, then launched himself when the freight wagon rounded a sharp bend in the road. Slash hit the ground and rolled. He came to a sitting position, moaning from the impact. Such schemes were better for youngsters full of piss and vinegar, not folks with old knees and aching back like his.

He struggled to his feet and almost fell behind a waist-high boulder alongside the road. It was closer than he liked for an ambush, but he didn't have time to hunt through the rocks for a better vantage point.

Slash knelt, rested his Yellowboy on top of the rock, and took a couple slow breaths to calm himself. Before he sucked in air for a third, the riders rounded the bend.

He hadn't decided what to say to them, but it didn't matter. They were more observant than he had been. All three spotted him right away. The leader held up his hand, made a fist, and brought his two companions to a halt.

"You have reason to point that rifle at us, mister?"

"I ain't fixin' on robbin' you," Slash said, though the thought fluttered through his mind. He and Pecos had given up the owlhoot life and gone straight, as much through threat as desire. They had run afoul of an ornery U.S. Federal Chief Marshal by the name of Luther T. Bledsoe, who promised to stretch their necks unless they did "chores" for him, all of which were outside the law. Chief Marshal "Bleed-'Em-So" Bledsoe used them to go after road agents and rustlers and other miscreants in ways that he could deny, should any other lawman protest the methods.

In return, "Bleed-'Em-So" paid them a decent wage for carrying out his secret orders and let them run a legitimate freight company the rest of the time. And bragged he wouldn't see them doing the midair two-step with nooses around their necks.

But Slash still felt the pangs of giving up the excitement of robbing a bank or sticking up a train or stagecoach. There had always been more than stealing the money. Nothing matched the anticipation after pulling his bandanna up over his nose, drawing his gun, and going after someone else's money. The uncertainty, the promise of danger, even the sheer thrill when they stashed the loot in their saddlebags and raced off seconds ahead of a determined posse made it unlike anything else he'd ever done.

It was always his wits against the world. And he waltzed away with enough gold and scrip to keep him going for months until the next robbery. That had been quite the life.

"I'm married now," he said under his breath. That should have given him all the more reason to close the chapter of his sordid past and move on.

"What's that? You're married?" The lead rider looked at his partners. They shrugged.

"Don't pay that no never mind," Slash said. "Tell me why you're trailin' us. Are you fixin' to hold us up?"

He expected a denial. The leader surprised him.

"That depends on what you're carrying. Gold? Something worth stealing?" The man laughed as if he'd made a joke.

"Truth is, we don't rightly know what's in the crates we're haulin'. They're too light to be loaded with gold and too heavy if they're stuffed with greenbacks."

Slash watched the three cluster together and whisper among themselves. He got a better look at them. If they were road agents, they were prosperous ones. More prosperous than he and Pecos had been except in the best of times. The riders wore beige linen dusters. The leader had his pulled back to show a coat and vest that cost a young fortune. At his hip rode a smoke wagon big enough to bring down a buck. And curiously, on his left coat lapel he wore two colorful ribbons.

A quick look showed the other two also had similar ribbons, though the rider to the left had only one and the third horseman two of different patterns.

"You boys Masons or do you belong to one of them secret societies?" Slash tried to hold down his curiosity about their decorations and failed. He'd never seen anything like them except on Army officers' full-dress uniforms. Never had those officers worn their medals or ribbons on civilian clothing.

The question caused the leader to whirl around. His hand went toward his holstered iron, then he caught himself. The Yellowboy aimed at his heart kept things from getting too hot too fast.

"He's asking about our campaign ribbons, Hutchins,"

the rider with only one decoration said. His tone put Slash on edge. Mentioning those ribbons seemed to be worse than accusing them of being thieves.

"What we wear doesn't concern you," the leader—Hutchins—said sharply. His hand moved closer to his six-shooter.

"We got other things on our mind than your fancy duds," came Pecos' drawl from the far side of the road. He had parked the freight wagon and come back to catch the trio in a crossfire.

Hutchins looked from Slash and half turned in the saddle to find where Pecos had taken cover. The huge man saw the rider's move toward his piece and swung around the sawed-off shotgun he slung across his shoulder and neck from a leather strap. The double barrels carried enough firepower to shred the three men and parts of the horses they rode.

"Whoa, hold on now," Hutchins said. "We're peaceable travelers on our way to Portrero. If you happen to be going there, too, that's purely coincidence."

"Why don't you gents just ride on into town," Slash suggested. "We'd feel easier if you stayed in front of us."

"Damned back shooters, that's what they are," grumbled the rider with the single ribbon.

"We don't have time to discuss the matter," Hutchins said. "The Colonel's waiting for us."

"Trot on along," Slash ordered. He motioned with his rifle. "Sorry to have misconvenienced you," he added insincerely.

Hutchins raised his arm as if he were a cavalry officer at the head of a column. He lowered his arm smartly, pointing ahead. The two with him obediently followed.

Slash and Pecos watched them vanish down the road before leaving their cover.

"Now don't that beat all?" Slash said. "You'd think them

boys was U.S. Army, only they weren't wearin' blue wool coats and brass buttons."

"You're right about that," Pecos said. He lowered the rabbit-ear hammers on his shotgun and tugged it around so it dangled down his back in its usual position. "No officer I ever saw dressed in such finery out of uniform. And none of them wear their combat ribbons. Now, I ain't an expert in such things but I didn't recognize a single one of them ribbons."

Slash nodded.

"Let's deliver our freight and collect our due. I just hope you don't get any ideas about spendin' the money to buy fancy togs like that just to impress your new wife."

"I'll let Jay get all gussied up," Slash said.

"She'd appreciate you takin' a bath more 'n wearin' a frock coat," Pecos said.

Again Slash agreed, then added, "Even one with fancy, colorful ribbons." Slash pondered why the three riders wore those decorations as he hiked all the way back to their freight wagon. He came up empty about a reason.

Visit our website at
KensingtonBooks.com
to sign up for our newsletters, read
more from your favorite authors, see
books by series, view reading group
guides, and more!

BOOK **CLUB**
BETWEEN THE CHAPTERS

Become a Part of Our
Between the Chapters Book Club
Community and Join the Conversation

Betweenthechapters.net